PRAISE FOR
REUNION

One of *Good Housekeeping*'s Best Books of Fall 2014
A *Glamour* "Five Things I'm Loving This Month" selection
A *Chicago Tribune* Editor's Choice
One of *Time Out Chicago*'s Fall Books We Need to Read

"Fast-paced...[Pittard] makes writing short, lively scenes look easy." —*Atlanta Journal-Constitution*

"Hannah Pittard is the writer you won't be able to stop talking about...Her books are the sort that leave you reading the blurbs, scanning the small print, and prolonging the reading experience...She's the kind of writer who gets in your head and makes you evangelize to all of your friends—wide eyes, quick gasp: 'Do you know about Hannah Pittard?' If she's not on your radar yet, she should be...The sibling bond—that complicated and often inexplicable love [is] expertly encapsulated in REUNION." —*Buzzfeed*

"Pittard is working with a fertile premise here—a family's discovery of one another's secrets following the death of its patriarch—that bears some unexpected and affecting fruit. The framework feels reminiscent of Jonathan Tropper's *This Is Where I Leave You*, but the messy blending of Pittard's Pulaski clan gives a familiar construction some very particular complications." —*Shelf Awareness* (starred review)

"Truly unique and insightful."   —*Bookpage*

"Wry, emotionally insightful...REUNION succeeds because Kate is so sharp, and perceptive about everyone—except, of course, herself...Kate's voice resonates and elevates the book beyond a family drama." —Elizabeth Taylor, *Chicago Tribune*

"Kate's narrative voice—raw, comic...is what makes this novel shine."   —*Bustle*

"Emotionally astute...Kate is a winning narrator, whose insights into herself and her family keep the pages turning."
                    —*Publishers Weekly*

"[REUNION] takes a warm and witty look at an unusual dysfunctional family and extols the lasting bonds between siblings. Truly engaging."   —*Booklist*

"That this tale of an epic downward spiral...end[s] on a hopeful note is a testament to the humor and empathy of this very readable family drama."   —*Elle Canada*

"REUNION is uproarious, tender, and riveting, a book about the possibility of family and the value of hope. By the time I finished it I felt like a part of the Pulaski family; I didn't want it to end."
                    —Anton DiSclafani, author of *The Yonahlossee Riding Camp for Girls*

"With REUNION, Hannah Pittard proves herself to be an alchemist of the highest order. In this unique story about the weirdness of family, she mixes pain and humor together to make something magical...REUNION slayed me."

—Kevin Wilson, author of *The Family Fang*

Critical Acclaim for *The Fates Will Find Their Way*

"A stunning novel about making up stories as we go along...[a] mesmerizing debut." —*O, The Oprah Magazine*

"A dreamlike cross between *The Virgin Suicides* and *The Lovely Bones*." —*Time* magazine

"Engaging and vigorously told...I heard all sorts of echoes from other books, from Alice Sebold's *The Lovely Bones* and some of Joyce Carol Oates' stories and novels...[An] excellent first novel." —*Chicago Tribune*

"A wistful novel about how little we know of one another, but how eager we are to tape together a collage of rumors, assumptions and fantasies to answer questions we're too young, too cowardly or too polite to ask...Chilling and touching...harrowingly wise about the melancholy process of growing up." —*Washington Post*

ALSO BY HANNAH PITTARD

The Fates Will Find Their Way

REUNION

A NOVEL

HANNAH PITTARD

GRAND CENTRAL
PUBLISHING

NEW YORK   BOSTON

For Noah and Greta

—

Copyright © 2014 by Hannah Pittard
Reading Group Guide © 2015 by Hannah Pittard and Hachette Book Group, Inc.

Grand Central Publishing
Hachette Book Group
1290 Avenue of the Americas
New York, NY 10104
www.hachettebookgroup.com

Printed in the United States of America

RRD-C

Originally published in hardcover by Hachette Book Group.

First trade edition: September 2015

10 9 8 7 6 5 4 3 2

Grand Central Publishing is a division of Hachette Book Group, Inc.
The Grand Central Publishing name and logo is a trademark of Hachette Book Group, Inc.

The Hachette Speakers Bureau provides a wide range of authors for speaking events. To find out more, go to www.hachettespeakersbureau.com or call (866) 376-6591.

The publisher is not responsible for websites (or their content) that are not owned by the publisher.

Library of Congress Cataloging-in-Publication Data

Pittard, Hannah.
  Reunion : a novel / Hannah Pittard. — First Edition.
    pages cm.
  ISBN 978-1-4555-5361-7 (hardcover) — ISBN 978-1-4555-5360-0 (ebook) 1.
Reunions—Fiction. 2. Reminiscing—Fiction. 3. Suburban life—Fiction. 4.
Psychological fiction. I. Title.
  PS3616.I8845R48 2014
  813'.6—dc23
                                              2013047234

ISBN 978-1-4555-5362-4 (pbk.)

...as soon as I saw him I felt that he was my father, my flesh and blood, my future and my doom. I knew that when I was grown I would be something like him; I would have to plan my campaigns within his limitations.

—JOHN CHEEVER, *Reunion*

1

on the airplane

On June 16, at roughly eight thirty in the morning, I get the phone call that my father is dead. Actually, that's not quite right. At eight thirty in the morning, still on June 16, the plane I'm on takes a detour and lands two hundred miles south of its destination (Chicago) because of a massive storm system that's closed both O'Hare and Midway. We sit on the runway for an hour. As a concession, the flight attendants pass out bottles of water and tell us we can turn on our cell phones until it's time to redepart. I have three messages. They're all from Elliot, my brother, who I talk to a few times a year, which would suggest we're not close, but we are. We don't see each other much, but when we do, it's like everything catches up immediately, like the time between meetings never happened. We are thick as thieves, but we suck at the phone. It's a different thing with my sister. Nell and I talk every day, whether we want to or not. We are addicted to conversation. We are in love with ourselves and our banter and maybe even with each other. That's the family joke, anyway. *The family* now being only me, my brother, and my sister. We do not count our father. Nor do we count the stepmothers and half siblings. There are too many to count.

The first message is Elliot asking me to call him. The second message is Elliot telling me to call him ASAP. The third message is Elliot delivering the news that our father is dead, that he's walked onto the back porch of the condo in Atlanta that he shares with his fifth wife and shot himself in the head.

So I'm on this plane, which is growing increasingly muggy and cramped. The sky outside has become a hostile blue-black. There are multiple babies on board, all of whom have started up with these tiny high squawks, and now my skin is itching. I'm feeling guilty as hell about my contempt for the screaming babies, so I'm practicing this insane smiling technique that my husband (soon-to-be ex-husband, sadly, if he gets his way and I can't convince him otherwise) says is far, far worse than if I would just let my face match up accurately with my true feelings (this, he says, is one of the reasons that he doesn't want to—*can't*—live with me any longer: my true feelings are buried under manure and turds and more manure and turds). But that's not how I was raised. I was raised to smile. I was raised to sit through suffering. I was raised to think that if the yelling got too loud or the humiliation got too painful, you just ignored it. You just ignored it because there was nothing you could do.

And so I am smiling and—if Peter, my husband, is right, which he probably is because he always is, and I mean that seriously and not in any sort of passive-aggressive way—I'm also looking kind of unhinged, and over the PA system, like a bad joke, one of the flight attendants has just announced that the toilets are backed up—both of them—and all I can hear is Elliot saying over and over again, "Dad's dead, Kate. He's dead." And I realize with a start that the people in front of me have turned around to look at me and the old man next to me—Frank from Wisconsin, die-hard Packers fan and, at least according to the past two hours, incredibly decent human being who has loved only one woman in his life and loved her well—is staring at my lap. All this because apparently I've enabled the speaker function of my phone and Elliot really is saying it all over again, only saying it now to an audience of strangers.

Remember that head-scratching final scene in *Four Weddings and a Funeral*—an otherwise decent movie—when Andie MacDowell's character claims not to know it's raining? "Is it still raining? I hadn't noticed." It was universally regarded as a preposterous line—who, after all, has ever stood in the rain and not been aware of the weather?—but what made it even more pitiful was the acting. (They say screenwriters always blame the actors, and it's true. We do.) The point is, whenever I'm embarrassed, I like to think of that scene. I like to think, *Well, this is awkward, but at least I know when it's raining.*

I silence my phone and look at Frank.

Well, this is awkward, I think. "I'm sorry," I say.

The people in front of us reluctantly turn away. I feel like crying.

"Did you just get that news?" asks Frank. He is still staring at my lap, where the phone is stationed like a forgotten extra. "Just now? Just *now*?"

I give a little shrug.

Frank is an old man. He's about my father's age. I'm guessing he knows that. I'm guessing at this very minute he's imagining not my father but himself, lying dead on the back porch of some tawdry condominium in Atlanta.

"Do you need a tissue?" he says. There's a tremor in his hands. My money's on early Parkinson's.

I shake my head. Frank feels worse than I do. I wish I actually *were* crying. He'd feel better about things. We'd both feel better about things. But my hormones have let me down.

The thing is, my hormones are constantly letting me down, and recently, they've been letting Peter down, too. Maybe they've been letting him down all along. I didn't want a baby when we married. I don't want a baby now. But Peter. Poor Peter. Over the last half decade, his hormones have matured, while mine have stayed miraculously immature. We were young when we married, but nobody told us that. Nobody said, "Twenty-six? In ten years—strike that—in *five* years, you'll be a different person. Twenty-six is nothing. Twenty-six is still a kid." Nobody said that. I'm not shirking responsibility, though it would have been nice for someone to have at least *tried* to pass me the note. But then, who would that have been? Not my father, who stopped being an engaged parent the minute he married my first stepmother. Not Elliot, who was and is the poster boy for marriage. Certainly not Nell, who, though she had only just filed for divorce at the time of my engagement to Peter, still believes long-term commitment is the golden ideal.

Frank from Wisconsin has turned away from me. He's writing his obituary in his head. I can practically see him sitting at his desk, lining the paper himself with a ruler and a pencil. He'll write every bit of it down longhand. His life. Letter by letter. Word by word. People are predictable. That's just the way it goes.

I lean back in my seat. The lights in the cabin dim. As if on cue, a voice like God all around us says, "We've been cleared for takeoff." There is a pause, a general murmuring, and then all the other passengers erupt in applause. Frank doesn't look at me while he claps, and I don't look at him. I turn off my phone and close my eyes.

My father is dead. He'll still be dead in forty-five minutes when we land in Chicago.

2

---

there are three of us

There are three of us. Elliot is the oldest and, somehow, the most normal. At least, he's the most outwardly normal. He has a wife, he owns his home, he has three little girls, each with a different color of hair. They all have blue eyes. They don't go to church, but they do go to private school. On the weekends they go climbing together. The five of them. They pack up the Range Rover, gear and everything, and drive from Colorado Springs in the direction of the San Isabel Forest and they climb. The littlest—Ellie, the blonde—is a demon on the mountains. Rita, Elliot's wife, worries that her youngest is going to want to free solo some day. It's almost a guarantee, in my opinion, but I don't tell Rita that. In fact, I think free soloing is the least of their worries. I think they have a base jumper on their hands. But, again, these are opinions I keep to myself, and by keep to myself, I mean share only with Nell, my sister.

So Elliot is oldest and has this adorable nuclear family.

I'm not trying to oversimplify his life by calling it nuclear. I'm just saying that he has the whole package. Are there ups and downs? Of course. He works a hundred hours a week doing something I don't understand. He works from home but he still doesn't see his girls as much as he wants. His wife is lonely. I know this because she's told me so. She's told Nell, too. She has friends. Of course she has friends. But friends aren't a husband. There's this grad student who lives across the street from them. Rita's told me about him. I don't know his name. He leaves tomato plants in coffee cans on the front steps. Sometimes he writes her notes. I've asked, "Is this a problem? Is this boy going to be a problem?" She said, "He's renting. There are two other students. They're renters. They'll be gone in six months. He's not a problem." I called Nell. I said, "Do you know about the tomato plants?" Nell said, "Yeah, right? So suspicious. Apparently he's really good with Joe." Joe—the redhead—is their oldest girl. She's taller than Rita already and, I suspect, will soon be taller than me. She is a complete knockout and I worry constantly both that she'll figure it out too soon and that she won't figure it out soon enough. "Wait," I said to my sister. "This grad student is *really good with Joe*? Nobody's worried?" Nell laughed. "You're so dark," she said. "Not everyone is obsessed with sex. He's never alone with her." It was the first time I'd been accused of being obsessed with sex. I wondered if she had me confused with someone else, but I said nothing. We talked for a few more minutes. Mostly about Rita and the tomatoes and whether we needed to say anything yet about this grad student to our brother.

Nell and Elliot and I don't believe in adultery—not that

we don't think it exists, but we don't condone or excuse it. Our father was a philanderer. After our mother died and he started marrying women like it was going out of fashion, he became an outright expert in infidelity. The word *unfaithful* doesn't even begin to cover it. And so, as a fairly obvious psychological result, my siblings and I are hard-liner opponents. At least in theory. There are things Nell and Elliot don't know. Things I don't want to tell them. They'd call me a hypocrite if they knew certain things and they'd be right, but it's complicated. It always is.

So there's Elliot and his family in Colorado Springs. They're getting by. They're living life. I worry about them in the way that you worry about anyone you love, but mostly I think of them as settled. Mostly I think, *Good for him. Good for them. Proof that it's possible.* Sometimes I get sad when I think about the three of us as little kids. I get this bunched-up feeling in my stomach that reminds me of the last day of summer camp. Does everyone feel this way? I'm not talking about the people who think the best years of their lives were in high school—not at all; I feel *sorry* for people who think that. I'm talking about this other feeling. I'm talking about closing your eyes and seeing yourself as you used to be: not in high school and popular or not popular, but in lower school, in middle school. As a clunky little kid with knees like a giraffe's, wearing her older sister's uniform that's still too big. As a child who carried a Strawberry Shortcake lunch box and whose biggest concern was whether there would be Goldfish or a Fruit Roll-Up packed inside, even while she didn't know which she really wanted, only that whichever one was there wouldn't be the right one. I get sad when I think about those times—when I think about all of us still being young, still having everything ahead of us instead of things behind us. And sometimes I get jealous that we've grown up, that we've moved on, that we've started these other lives that don't revolve around each other. I think maybe I didn't get the instruction book. Other people make it look easy. Elliot makes it look easy. But who knows? Maybe he wakes up at night and goes to the kitchen by himself and wishes, really wishes, that it was still just the three of us—just me, Nell, and him against the world. Maybe.

Next there's Nell. She's in San Francisco. She's a producer, of sorts. She bosses people around. She hires and fires. She approves spreadsheets. She makes money. She wears nice clothes. She invests. She has a fourth-floor condo that you could shoot for a spread in *Dwell* on a last-minute whim and everything would be perfect. There wouldn't be a shoe out of place. When I'm not in Nell's condo—which is most of the time, because I live in Chicago—I am perfectly happy living without the things that she has acquired. But when I *am* in Nell's condo, I feel this ache in my bones to possess things—things I never even knew I wanted that suddenly feel like necessities. For starters: her outdoor furniture. I never knew a person could covet outdoor furniture. But when I'm there, in San Francisco, I do. I *covet* it. I understand the word when I'm there. Understand it in a biblical way. Other things: her espresso machine, her kilim pillows, her antique brass bed. I want these things so badly I get dizzy. I turn wonky. But then I go home. Then I go back to Chicago and, yes, there are things that aren't right in my life—plenty of things, in fact—

but the material longings fade away, and for the most part, I don't even think about them.

Nell is one year younger than Elliot, which means they were friends with all the same people growing up. Nell dated Elliot's friends, Elliot dated Nell's friends. They had parties together, they smoked pot together, they got suspended from school together. Everything you could possibly dream of as a younger sister, those two did together. When it was my turn for high school—four years later—they sat me down and explained that it was up to me to get it right. It was up to me to be the straight one. "Do it for us," they said. I didn't want to disappoint them.

Nell likes to call herself a divorcée. In her twenties she married a ghoul from Spain. The marriage lasted six months. The divorce lasted three years. Immigration was all over them at first. They thought the entire thing was a setup. Nell says sometimes now that it was. But it wasn't. They were in love. For a minute. I think she got swept up by the row house and the ring, then they got to know each other. But this is almost a decade ago now. She hasn't remarried. She says she's okay with being single. She says San Francisco sucks for women nearing forty. She says the worst part is not having someone to hug every once in a while. "Not every night," she's told me. "I don't need it every night. But sometimes, walking through the front door after work, I just wish there'd be someone there. Standing right there. And he wouldn't even need to say a thing. We'd just hug. That's it." Nell can depress the hell out of me sometimes.

Then there's me and Peter. We live on the North Side, on the second floor of a three-floor walk-up. Peter is a therapist;

I'm an assistant professor in screenwriting. My job pays next to nothing—just over thirty grand—but thanks to Peter, we pay our bills on time, and sometimes, late at night, lying in bed, we talk about the possibility of one day buying a cabin somewhere up north. Anyway, we used to.

About two years ago, and out of nowhere, Peter brought home the most adorable little pamphlet. On the front flap was a picture of a baby swaddled in fabric. "Precious," I said. "That baby is eat-up with cute." I put the pamphlet back on the counter and turned away, fully prepared never to think a second thought about that baby. Fully prepared to forget about it the way you forget about the day's most recent kitten meme.

"Kiddo," he said. He touched my waist. I brushed his hand away and slipped on an apron. It was my turn to cook dinner. I kissed him on the cheek. This is my version of events.

"Can we talk about this?" He held the pamphlet toward me again. I looked at the baby, toasty and comfy in its folds of blue cloth. Then I looked down, beneath the baby, and saw the word I'd somehow missed before. *Adoption.*

"Where did you get that?" I said.

"From Dan." Dan is Peter's doctor and also his best friend.

"You talked to Dan about this?"

"He's my doctor."

"Before you talked to me?"

I moved toward the basket of vegetables and grabbed an onion.

"I wanted to know what the possibility was—" He made an awkward circling motion in front of his belly. "Of undoing—" He was talking about his vasectomy, the one he'd had eight years earlier so I could go off birth control and because we knew we didn't want children. He gestured in front of his belly again. He looked ridiculous. I knew exactly what he was talking about, but I wouldn't say the word and neither would he.

"And?" I said. I sliced the onion in half. My hand was shaky. My eyes were starting to water.

"Because of the complications, two percent. Not good."

I nodded and made another slice into the onion. Peter's vas deferens had become infected after the surgery. Dan explained to us when it happened that a reversal probably wouldn't be possible, but we hadn't been troubled. We both agreed that talking about a vasovasostomy while you're still recovering from a vasectomy is a little like planning a prenup and a wedding at the same time. What's the point?

"He said two percent and then he—what? He just handed you that brochure? Voilà?" I gestured toward the pamphlet with my knife. I couldn't look at Peter.

"No." He was beside me again. His hand was on my waist again. "I asked for it."

I rubbed at my eyes with my knuckles. He didn't move away.

"When we got married—" I said. But then I stopped short, realizing I was terribly close to quoting a line from *Two for the Road*:

```
Mark: We agreed before we were mar-
    ried we weren't going to have any
    children.
```

Joanna: And before we were married we
     didn't.

Only, in this scenario, I' was Albert Finney and Peter
was Audrey Hepburn. I wanted us to be better than that. I
wanted *me* to be better than that, and so I did this monumen-
tally dim-witted thing. I lied and said, "Okay."

"Okay?"

I turned to face him.

"We can talk about it," I said.

Understand: Because of Peter, we pay the bills. Because
of Peter, we live quite well.

"We can start talking about it," I said. "Sure."

And we did start talking about it. We included Elliot and
Nell in the conversation. Rita did research. Once a week, she'd
email the names of agencies, with lists of pros and cons. Elliot
called every few nights, which wasn't like him. "I think this
will be good for you," he said. "Man, I think this will be really
good. This is exactly what you two need." Everyone seemed
so happy, and I liked the feeling that gave me. But every time
Peter brought home another stack of paperwork, I felt sick.

It took twelve months of talking and researching and sign-
ing various pieces of paper—until the interviews were just
about to begin—for me to tell him. There wasn't a maternal
instinct in me. That's what I said. He disagreed. At first in
this really loving way, like, "You're amazing, you're so caring,"
et cetera, et cetera. Then, after a few weeks, in this more aggressive way, like, "You don't know what you want. You have
no idea. It's turds. It's manure. Everything you say. Turds and
manure."

Nell called. She was understanding, but I could tell she was disappointed. She'd been fond of the conversations during which she'd list baby names and I'd rule them out one by one. She said Peter would get over it.

Elliot called too. He was less understanding. It broke his heart. That's what he said. Those exact words: "It breaks my heart." He said his girls would grow up without cousins. I said, "Cousins? We didn't have cousins. Who needs cousins?" He said, "You don't get it. And you won't. You can't. Because you don't have kids."

Peter and I stopped having sex.

Strike that: I started going to bed earlier than Peter.

Yes, it was deliberate. And yes, it was that simple. At first I claimed headaches. I'd go out of my way to pop an aspirin or two while he was watching. But it was too sad, how obvious I was being. And so I stopped claiming headaches and joined the gym. I got up at five and was outside the gym by five thirty, just as they were unlocking the doors. At night, after class, I'd look at Peter and say, "I'm beat." And I was. My body was proof. The new muscles and drawn face were evidence.

So we stopped having sex, and the fact of the matter is that it was a relief. I liked falling asleep—though it would only be for an hour or two—without him. I liked not having to worry and wait and see if tonight was one of the nights when he'd want to be quote-unquote intimate, which would always begin with a slow dance of familiar limbs that never tried anything new and end with me in the bathroom alone, wiping between my legs and putting on a fresh pair of underwear.

The thing about cheating—the thing Elliot and Nell may

or may not understand, and this has *nothing* to do with my father, this is just a fact—is that it's easy. It's the easiest thing in the world. My sister says she has a hard time meeting men; she says San Francisco just doesn't cut it for straight women. But she's wrong. All you have to do is put yourself out there. All you have to do is take off your ring and make the decision that you want to have sex. It's a vibe. It's a smell. It's an animal instinct. I never told Peter. But a month ago he found out. Husbands are always finding out.

What Peter said was, "Billy? His name is Billy? You picked a man named Billy?" I didn't say anything. I had already thought the same thing. I had already thought all the same things and worse. The truth, though, is that it felt good to be found out. In fact, it felt great to be found out. That's the other thing no one tells you about cheating: getting caught doesn't have to feel bad. Getting caught can even feel good! Because in that moment, being confronted by Peter like that, I wanted nothing more than to have sex with him. I felt turned on! Maybe I did still love my husband, and maybe I even wanted to help him raise a baby! I believed I wanted to make it work and that I wanted to be an adult, or at least *try* to be an adult and figure out how other adults live. I would tell him everything. All the secrets I tell myself every day, I would tell to him. I had just needed to know he cared. That moment—I swear to God—felt like the beginning of my life. Like the beginning of my life as a grown-up.

"I want a divorce," he said. "You're a fucking liar."

3

---

arriving in Chicago

I'm one of the last ones off the plane. People have all these rules about where they sit on planes—where they're willing to sit. Like Nell's always upgrading to first class, which is a complete waste of money. She says there are fewer germs up there. I love that. Seriously. The idea that wealthy people carry fewer germs or that the germs from economy class know to stay in their place. Then there are people like Elliot and Rita. They're all about bulkhead—"First on, first off," says Elliot. I hear people trying to con the flight attendants all the time: "If I don't get an aisle, I'll get sick. Really. It's bad." I like a good con as much as the next person, but I hate a weak con. I hate a last-minute, poorly thought-out con.

So I'm one of the last ones off the plane, because seating placement isn't something I really care about. If the plane goes down, we're all going down together. Frank from Wisconsin doesn't look at me; it's as if we never talked. It's as if I don't know that his wife's name is Mirabelle, that his dog is his best friend, that he keeps a stash of Elmer T. Lee in the hull of the boat in his basement. My father has ruined everything. I should offer to help Frank with his bag, but he's already grunting and pulling it down all by himself. He thinks, because I spent the last forty-five minutes sleeping and not crying, that there is something wrong with me. He takes it personally. There's a daughter somewhere out there. Or maybe a son. And Frank is scared to death that this daughter or son is one day going to respond to his own passing in such a brutish, callous manner. But here's where Frank's wrong—and I would have been happy to tell him if he'd bothered asking—Frank's a good man, he's no doubt been a good father. No one's ever going to talk about him the way I talk about Stan. The problem isn't me. The problem is my father. But Frank didn't give me the chance to explain.

By the time I'm off the plane and walking toward baggage claim, my cell phone's thumping and I see there are four more messages. I don't bother listening. Two are probably from Elliot. One from Nell. Maybe one from Rita, just to say she's sorry. I delete them all and call Elliot. He answers on the first ring.

"Where have you been?"

"On a plane," I say. "What's the story?"

"Did you know Sasha hasn't been living with Dad for half a year?"

Sasha is our father's fifth wife, and is a year younger than me.

"I did not know that," I say. "No."

"She and Mindy moved out," says Elliot.

Mindy is one of our multiple half siblings. She's the youngest, the fattest, and now, officially, the last.

"Who found him?"

"A neighbor heard the shot," says Elliot. "Called Sasha. Sasha called the building manager. He went over there. Knocked. No answer. Went around back, there he was."

My luggage tips over on its rollers and I forget to speak.

"Hey," says Elliot, suddenly sounding sincere, the business in his voice falling away. "Are you okay?"

"I'm fine." I right my luggage and follow the flow of other arriving passengers.

"Kate," he says. "We'll get through this."

"Right," I say.

"We're a family," he says. "You and me and Nell."

"Of course," I say. I am thinking now of Peter. I am thinking of breaking the news to him. I am thinking that this might earn me some sympathy points. He can't leave now. Of course not. That would be too cruel. He'll have to wait until I've grieved. His friends would disapprove if he didn't. And by the time I'm done grieving, I'll have won him back. I'll have won everything back. And Billy—Billy will be nothing more than an afterthought, nothing more than the dot above an *i*.

"I'm leaving for Atlanta in four hours," says Elliot.

I'm almost to baggage claim, but now I stop short. The person behind me steps on my heel, mutters something, then goes around. I am in the middle of the walkway, standing completely still. If I were seeing me, I'd be annoyed. If I were seeing me, my skin would be itching; I'd be making that insane smile. I'd be thinking about screaming. I am aware of all this, but I can't help it. I can't make myself move.

"What?" I say, though I've heard him perfectly well. It never dawned on me that any of us would have to go down, would want to go down, would be willing to go down. I haven't been back in more than ten years, since before my wedding. It's the same for Elliot. The same for Nell.

"What do you mean you're going to Atlanta?"

"*We're* going to Atlanta," he says.

I'm shaking my head. This is all happening too quickly.

"Nell's already in the air," he says. "She's stopping at the Denver airport and getting on my flight."

"Wait," I say. "I don't understand."

"We're going to Atlanta, Kate."

"Why?"

All around me, people with luggage. All around me, people moving forward. This is O'Hare. This is one of the busiest airports in the world. The odds are good that there is someone else at this airport, maybe not in this terminal, but someone else here whose father has also just died. With people dying and being born every millisecond, it's almost impossible, in fact, that there isn't someone else. But there's no way—no way in the world—that there's someone else whose father has just shot himself in the head but who has no desire whatsoever to find out why.

"Dad's dead," says Elliot.

"And?"

"Jesus, Kate," he says. "Get on a fucking plane."

4

Peter comes to the airport

I hang up on my brother and walk outside. There are people everywhere. It's sheer pandemonium out here. Give us a snowstorm in winter and you couldn't find a more orderly citizenry. We do snowstorms in our sleep. But thunderstorms? Summer rain storms? We have no idea what to do. The storm's passed by now, but you can see the smoky black to the east of the city, threatening Lake Michigan. All the people who were stranded are on the move at once. It's wet and muggy, and I fight my way to the end of the line for a cab. What I should do is go to the front and explain that there's an emergency. I should roll my bag right to the front, not even bothering to look at any of the people I'd be cutting, and say, "My dad's dead. I just found out. I have to get home." I wouldn't even have to cry—thank God—the guy at the front would simply wave me into the first cab. He wouldn't hesitate. He'd get me into the backseat, get my luggage in the trunk with a gentle *thunk*, and he'd see me off. "Go with

God," he might say. Something vague but ultimately inoffensive. And then I'd be off, I'd be headed home, I'd be going in the direction of my husband, of my not-yet-ex-husband, of my new life. Peter would greet me at the curb, pay for my cab, tip extra just because he can. I'd tell him my devastating news and he'd hold me and I'd realize, *Yes, my sister is right. It is everything in the world to be hugged like this. To have someone to hug me like this.* And I would begin at that very moment righting my wrongs. I wouldn't be pushy. I would give him his space. But slowly, he'd remember our life together. He'd remember us at twenty-four, not us at thirty-four, and he'd be unable to resist. Yes, I think. This is what I should do.

And I'm about to do it, too—I'm about to wheel my luggage in a grand Hollywood style to the front of the line when I feel a hand on my shoulder. I turn toward it, ready to shoo it away. But I don't shoo it away, because here is the only hand I have been wanting to feel.

"Peter," I say. He must not have shaved this morning, because his five o'clock shadow is showing, making him look younger, making him look manly and strong. This is my husband. This man is still my husband. "Thank God."

I go to hug him, but instead he takes the handle of my bag.

"Nell called," he says.

I nod. "Right," I say. "Of course."

It is even better than I could have hoped. This is a sign. This is an olive branch. A tiny, tiny olive branch. A twig, really, but it's a twig I'll take.

He turns away from me and walks back into the airport. I follow him, totally confused.

"What are we doing?"

"She said to put you on a plane."

"They're headed to Atlanta," I say.

"I know," he says. "And you're going with them."

In another world, at another time, he would have hated this. He would have said, about Nell's phone call and their travel to Atlanta, that this was typical of their behavior. And what he would have meant by typical is that my father was a despicable man who was equally awful to all three of the "original" siblings. But Elliot and Nell were older than I was. They had a few more good years with him as kids than I did. Which means—if we're being honest—that they got more money from him. They got high school *and* college. I got high school and help with loan applications. By the time it was my turn, there were other, newer, better children to worry about educating. This is not me feeling sorry for myself. This is me recounting the facts. Maybe if Stan had had a sister or a brother—some crazy aunt or uncle to have taken me under a wing and shown me all the zany things to love about him—maybe then I would have felt differently about the man. But there was no one else. There was him and there was us and eventually there was the mounting list of pseudo mothers and half siblings. And even though the three of us agreed—*as a family*—to essentially write him and his horde of additional offspring off the minute I turned eighteen, Nell and Elliot could still be talked into answering his phone calls. They could still be talked into feeling guilty about the state of their relationships. Apparently, a college education meant a modicum of filial responsibility. Especially the older he got. But with me it was different. I felt nothing for him. I felt no guilt because I was a Bill Cunningham devotee: *If you don't take money, they can't tell you what to do, kid.* I remembered none of those alleged good years and so I had nothing to pine for. And so now, of course, with our father finally dead, I am the only one going about her life as usual. I am the only one responding to this suicide—a final act of manipulation—in the proper way. Nell and Elliot are the ones being maudlin, dramatic. Peter, on any other day, would understand all this. You get married exactly for this sort of unspoken understanding. He's been around long enough to know the dynamics of my family, and ordinarily he recognizes all this without me having to explain a single thing.

He wheels my bag to the end of the Delta ticket line and just stands there, looking forward.

"I'm not going," I say. "I have a life. I have things here that are more important."

He says nothing.

"It's so good to be home." I stretch out my hand and touch his arm.

Still he says nothing.

"Besides," I say, "I can't afford a ticket right now. You know that." And he does know that. My semester has just ended. I've one paycheck left before the summer, before I go three months as an unpaid stay-at-home screenwriter.

"Kate," he says.

"Yes?"

"This doesn't change anything."

He puts his finger under my chin and raises it so that I am looking at him.

"I'm sorry about your dad," he says.

"Thank you," I say, blinking.

"But this changes nothing."

For the better part of a decade, Peter has been my best friend. I want him to forgive me. Of course I want him to forgive me. But why—just now—does being so near to him make me want to puke? Why has his finger under my chin turned my insides clammy and cold?

"I know what I want," I say.

"You have no idea." He says this gently, with an air of resignation. "That's the problem."

If my hormones worked, I'd be crying right now. There's a biological imperative that lets every other woman in the world cry at precisely this moment—the moment when her man is standing on a precipice, about to make a life-changing decision. But not me.

"I want *you*," I say. "I'm ready. I am. I promise."

"Ready for what?" The gentleness is gone from his voice. I've seemed needy, panicked. He takes his hand away from my chin and faces the front of the line.

"To get our marriage back," I say. But even to me, my tone registers as flat.

He kicks my bag forward.

"Why did you come here?" I say.

"To the airport?"

"Yes. Why?" I don't want to get angry. I don't want to *sound* angry, because I realize I have no right, but I feel angry. I feel outrageously angry. I feel hurt, and I want him to feel sorry for me. Never have I wanted so badly for someone to feel sorry for me. I want him to feel bad about the way he's acting. "Why did you come here if nothing's changed?"

"Because of Nell," he says.

"What about her?"

"She told me to go to the airport and make sure you got on a plane," he says. He laughs, and it's an ugly, mean laugh, and I think, for half a second, that it is exactly *this* laugh that allowed me to cheat on him in the first place. "And I knew—the minute she told me about Stan—I knew you'd think this would change things."

"I said I was sorry." There's a couple behind us who look annoyed that we're in line at all. We're not being as aggressive with moving ahead as they'd like us to be.

"By 'sorry,'" he says, "what do you mean exactly? I want you to be very clear."

"I mean, I'm sorry that it happened."

The person in front of us moves ahead and Peter rolls my bag forward.

"Do you mean that you wish it hadn't happened?" he says.

"That's not what I said."

"So you'd do it again?"

"No. I would not in the future do it again."

"But if you could go back, you wouldn't undo what you've done?"

I don't say anything.

"So you're *not* sorry."

"I am."

"Then why won't you tell me what I want to hear?" He pauses, and I know what he's going to say next, because it's what he always says when he wants to hurt me. "Pretend we're in a movie," he says. "All you have to do is say the line."

I shake my head. "I'm trying to be honest."

"Honest?" He nudges a shoe into my bag so that it inches away from us. "What do you know about honest?"

"I'm working on it," I say.

"Now she wants to work on it," he says, looking around, addressing an invisible audience. An odious habit. "Now she wants to be honest. Not last week, not last year, but now. *After* the fact." He pauses. "Lucky me."

He's right, of course. I don't know what I want. But it feels impossible to admit this to him. He's backed me into a corner and given me no graceful exit. The couple behind us—the man—coughs. I glance back and make the briefest eye contact with the woman. It's just long enough to see that she feels sorry for me and suddenly—*poof!* out of nowhere!—I'm crippled with shame to be standing in line with my husband, waiting like a child to be manhandled onto a plane.

"Please," I whisper to Peter and try to take the handle of my luggage. "Just leave."

"You won't get on a plane if I leave," he says, pushing my hand away. I don't dare look at the woman. "You're broke, remember?"

Technically, I am not broke. Technically, I am simply in debt.

The man behind us coughs again. It makes me want to gag. Does he think I don't know this is pathetic? Does he think his coughing is teaching us—me—a lesson? Let the man cough all he wants.

"Pretend it didn't happen," I say. "Put yourself in my shoes."

He smiles. "Hold on." Now he nods his head. "Let me give that a try." He nods his head some more. "Your shoes, you say?"

I mimic his nod. *At last*, I think. *Now we are getting somewhere.* This is progress. Progress at last. Why did it never occur to me before to ask him, simply, to consider my side of things?

"Something like this?" he says. His smile is gone. "My wife who loves me and trusts me and supports me—" He pauses. "This wife comes home one day and says, 'Baby love, all I'm asking is that you just think about this *one* thing, that you just *consider* it. I know we didn't want it when we first got together. But we're both reasonable people. We're both adults. And so I know it's within your adult brain's power to just consider the idea of adoption. To just *consider* it.'"

"Stop," I say.

But he doesn't.

"And I, the husband, I say—for some fucked-up, unknowable reason—I say, 'Yes, baby love, let's abso*lute*ly look into that. That sounds like a *beau*tiful idea. Why don't you go do a year's worth of footwork and waste your precious time, while I go out and find a maid to screw?'" He pauses. "Something like that?"

"We don't have a maid."

"Unbelievable," he says.

"You're not trying hard enough," I say. "You didn't even try."

"Know who you remind me of?" says Peter. We are next in

line. We are almost to the front. All I want now is to get this over with. All I want is for Peter to buy my ticket and then disappear. Fuck it. Send me to Atlanta.

"No," I say.

"Your father," says Peter.

It's such a cliché, but my mouth has actually dropped open. I'm tempted to laugh. In all the endlessly exhausting conversations we've had about the affair over the past thirty days, not once has Peter thought to associate me with my father. But today, on the day of his death, he gets the brilliant idea to make the comparison.

"You're going to feel shitty about saying that," I say.

"I won't," he says.

Wrong. Absolutely wrong. He's stooped to my level, and he's already regretting it. I can see it all over his face. Poor Peter: He forgets. He is my husband. I still know him. He can hate me all he wants, but he can't suddenly unknow me. Them's the rules, baby love.

He wheels my bag to the counter and takes out his wallet.

"Atlanta," he says. "One way."

The woman at the kiosk takes his card. I hand her my ID. She doesn't make eye contact with me while she's doing the paperwork. I never wanted to be one of these women. I never wanted to be looked at—or not looked at—by other women with pity.

I am handed my ticket and Peter is handed back his credit card. We walk a few paces away from the kiosk. He turns to me, and I turn to him.

"Do you have any cash on you?" he says. "Any at all?"

"I'm fine," I say. "I'll be fine. They have ATMs at airports."

"How much is in your account?"

I'm looking past Peter, at a trash can outside the women's restrooms. There's a little kid in sweatpants and a sweatshirt. He looks poor. Not dirty—I'm not Nell. Just poor. I wonder what he's doing at the airport. How can poor people afford to fly? I can't even afford to fly. Without Peter, there's no way I'd be able to make this trip, not without asking Nell or Elliot for a loan, which you couldn't pay me to do.

"I have enough," I say at last. I give a little shrug.

Peter reaches toward his back pocket and my neck goes instantly hot. I cross my arms and shove my hands into my armpits. I wish we were invisible. I wish we were in a bubble and no one could see us, because, really, the people who *are* seeing us, what do they think they see? Do they see two awkward strangers? Do they see a shady deal in progress? Or do they see a husband and wife? And if they *do* see a husband and wife, what do they make of the husband taking out his wallet, of the wife staring shamefaced at the floor?

"Kate," he says.

His wallet is poised between us, in the mere inches of ether between his hand and my heart. My breathing is erratic and it occurs to me that if I fainted, if I simply let my body go limp and fall to the ground, he'd have to put away his wallet and tend to me. He'd have to. Facts are facts.

"When you get back," he says, taking out three twenties from the middle sleeve, "we're going to have to figure this out." There are more twenties in there, but he takes out only three.

I don't say anything.

"You know what I'm talking about," he says. "Don't you?"

In fact, I *do* know what he's talking about. He's talking about our financial situation. In part, he's talking about my school debt (close to thirty thousand dollars still). But mostly he's talking about the forty-eight thousand dollars' worth of credit card debt I've been paying off since we married and how he's been covering everything—*everything*—while I cover the monthly installment plan he helped me set up. He's talking about the fact that while it's true that I am employed, it's also true that it's not enough, not nearly enough, to take care of myself *and* continue to make my final year's worth of payments.

"Give me a nod," he says. "Let me know you understand."

"This sucks," I say.

He takes my fist from where it's been tucked into my armpit. We both look down at it, and I think, *How did we get here? How did we get to this exact minute in time?*

He unfurls my fingers one by one, puts the twenties in my palm, then takes his hand away. So many times, on so many occasions, Peter has opened his wallet and handed me a few twenty-dollar bills. Never—not once—has it felt as dirty and loathsome as this. But the fact of the matter is, he's right: my bank account has less than fifty dollars in it and my next paycheck won't deposit until after the weekend, and if he actually decides to cut me off, I'll be without income until the fall semester begins.

I tuck the money into the front pocket of my jeans.

"Peter," I say.

I could tell him what he wants to hear. I could say it now. All I'd have to do is deliver the lines.

"Peter," I say again. Where is my prompt? Where is my whiteboard covered in big block letters?

"Have a nice flight," he says.

And because I can think of nothing less common, I say, "Have a nice life."

And then he's gone.

5

flight to Atlanta

I take my seat in business with a sort of flourish—economy was completely sold out—and order a gin and tonic before we even take off, my second since Peter left the airport. I have forty-five dollars of his pity left. If it's possible, I'll spend every penny of it on booze before I've even reached the baggage claim in Atlanta. My cheeks are flushed and my face is feeling genuinely smiley. I love flying. There's at least that. Every semester, my school foots the bill for me to attend the latest conference on the latest screenwriting techniques, which I am then to bring back to all of my screenwriting students. I'm positively devoted to the flights and the hotels. It's like being a different person. You get to board a plane by yourself and check into a hotel by yourself and you could be anybody. You could be a woman with a husband, for instance, or you could be a woman without one. Take your pick.

I check my phone. Two new messages. They're both from Nell. I push play and cradle the phone to my ear, careful this time not to engage the speaker function. I lean against the window and close my eyes.

"Kiddo," says Nell's recording. "I'm in Colorado. Elliot's here. Rita brought the girls. I had time to go through security and meet them at the drop-off. Joe's gorgeous. It's gross." Elliot says something in the background. Nell muffles something back to him. There's a pause, maybe a sniffle. "We can't wait to see you." Then she's gone. The next message is just static.

By my calculation, the plane I'm on will land about an hour before Nell and Elliot's—just enough time to negotiate the airport, order a few drinks, and be waiting at their gate as a sort of surprise. I can spend forty-five dollars in an hour. I can spend it in a heartbeat. Just watch me.

On a different night, under different circumstances, I'd be thinking about Nell and Elliot. I'd be jealous that they're on a flight together, catching up without me—me, eternally the little sister. But tonight. Tonight I am thinking, reluctantly, of my father. "Toughen up," he used to say when he'd catch me crying in a corner. "What's the matter with you?" Sometimes he'd hold up his hands, turn his palms outward, and say, "Hit me. Come on. Hit me. You'll feel better." This started when I was five, just after our mother died. It continued until I left for college. Thirteen years of seeing those palms, of being asked to hit them, of being told feeling better was as simple as following through. But if I did hit him, it was never hard enough, which meant I wasn't committed. And if I didn't hit him, it was because my personality was milquetoast. That was his word. *Milquetoast.* And now Peter's gone and said I'm just like him. Daddy issues? Absolutely not.

The one time I was brazen enough to suggest to Nell and Elliot that their commitment to our father was predicated on his having purchased their college educations, they shot me down. Elliot had just turned thirty. He was already pulling in close to two hundred thousand dollars a year. Nell was only a production manager then, but she was in the high five figures and poised to move into the realm of the sixes any minute.

What Elliot said was, "Horseshit. That's total horseshit. If he'd offered you tuition, you'd have taken it. You're pretending we should put you on some sort of pedestal because you turned his money down."

"But he didn't even offer you money," said Nell. "It's our fault? We should have said no? We should have guessed that he wasn't going to give you any?"

I told them they were missing my point. I tried to explain to them that I could care less about the money—a lie, since tuition was only a taste of the massive debt I was already in the process of acquiring—it was the fact that the money had blinded them to certain realities about his character. "There were no good years—never," I said. "That's a lie you tell yourselves to make it okay that you took money from the Nazis."

"Is she comparing Dad to Hitler?" said Elliot. "I think she's comparing our father to the Fuehrer."

"She'd have taken his money," said Nell. "She'd have taken it in the blink of an eye if he'd offered it to her."

I was standing right in front of them. We were in the same room. We were also drunk. All three of us.

"Are we supposed to feel sorry for you?" said Elliot. "Is that what you want?"

"I think she wants her share," said Nell. "I think she wants us to pay her back or something."

"I don't feel sorry for her," said Elliot. "Not even a little."

The reason they didn't feel sorry for me was that the year before—my first year out of college—I'd sold a screenplay. I'd gotten twenty thousand dollars up front. I quit my job as a waitress and moved to Berkeley. The money was gone in four months. I hadn't paid a cent toward taxes. But everything was okay. Or it seemed like it was okay, because I had applied for and been granted this amazing little thing called a credit card. Of course, Elliot and Nell knew nothing about this. They only knew that I'd sold a screenplay and appeared, on the surface at least, to be their successful artist sister.

Of course, the film never got made. But that's not the point. The point is that the one time I tried to illustrate to Nell and Elliot that their perception of our father might be *slightly* skewed because of his financial contributions to their educational development, they shot me down so quickly and so cruelly that I never again broached the subject. At least not with them. With Peter, yes.

By the time I met Peter, my debt—not even counting school loans—was in the low thirties. By the time we married, it was in the low forties. Wait, you say. Hold on there just one minute. Tell us about these amazing things you were purchasing with all this credit. Tell us, please, that those cash advances were to help the hungry family of four who lived below you or to support yourself while you toiled away endless hours at the shelter, or if not the shelter, then surely some do-gooder nonprofit, and if not a nonprofit, then while you advanced your burgeoning artistic career with dozens of new screenplays. But the answer is no. None of that. The answer is that I spent it on clothes. Clothes and shoes and booze and food. Debt? It's as easy as infidelity. It's easier.

At first it's just a thousand dollars. And you lie awake thinking, *How did I let it get to be so much? That was so stupid. Just pay it off and be done.* But instead of paying it off, you only pay it down. And just when it feels almost manageable, they send an offer: Take a month off from payments, they say. Just one month! We'll increase your APR, but you'll have thirty days—thirty whole days!—during which you won't once lie awake thinking about how to repay it all. So you say, *Yes.* You say, *Bring it on.* And then one thousand turns to two and then two turns to four and then four turns to twelve, and then you realize there's no way out. There's no way out, that is, until this lovely human being asks you to marry him and it dawns on you that in order to say yes, you're going to have to come clean. And so you do. Mostly.

THE FLIGHT ATTENDANT brings my gin and tonic. The man next to me orders tomato juice. I consider making small talk—perhaps offer to buy a mini bottle of vodka to go with his juice—but then I remember Frank from Wisconsin and decide against it.

Instead I dial Rita. She answers on the first ring. Goddamn I love this woman sometimes. I mean, I always love her. But sometimes I just want to swallow her whole and carry her around in my belly.

"Hi, you," she says.

"Hi," I say. Every once in a while, I think about telling Rita the truth. I think maybe she's the only one out of everyone who might possibly understand. In the movie version of our lives, she's played by a young Diane Keaton or maybe a young Katharine Hepburn. It's the mother in her, maybe, but I truly believe that I could tell her about the affair, about Peter's talk of divorce, about the debt and how it's almost over, about all the million secrets I tell myself every single night as I'm falling asleep, and she wouldn't judge me. She'd just smile and nod, refill my glass of juice. Maybe.

"How's your brain?" she says.

"Wishing it were on drugs."

I squeeze the dried-up lime wedge into my glass and then drop it in so that it's floating there on top of the ice cubes.

"Where are you?"

"On a plane," I say. "About to leave Chicago."

"Is Peter going with you?"

I shake my head and take a sip of my drink, but then remember Rita can't see me.

"No," I say. "He can't miss work." There are a few people I don't like lying to, and Rita's one of them.

"That's good," she says. Rita can spin just about anything but her own life into something positive. "More time for you and Nell and Elliot. You guys need this. This will be good for you."

When I told Rita about calling off the adoption—this was almost a year ago exactly—she didn't even blink. All she said was "Listen to your heart," an expression whose cheesiness and overuse normally make me grimace, but which, given the circumstances, sounded like the wisest advice I'd ever heard.

"How are the girls?" I say, happy for the moment not to be

constructing a compare/contrast chart of me and my father in my head.

"Getting ready for camp this weekend. Pigpie wants to back out." Pigpie is Ellie, the blond demon and their youngest. "But she also wants a dwarf pig for her birthday, so what does she know?"

"Are you going to let her?"

"Get a dwarf pig? Uh, no."

"Skip camp," I say.

Rita laughs. "Right. Well. We'll play it by ear. The mom in me knows she needs this experience. But the little girl in me thinks we'd have a blast just the two of us with Joe and Mimi gone."

"I wish you were coming to Atlanta," I say, and I think I mean this. Because she has a point about the three of us—Nell, Elliot, and me—getting to be alone together. It's been too long. But, again, there's something soothing about Rita that I wouldn't mind taking advantage of right now.

"I might," she says. "Once the girls are off, depending on how long you're down there. I might just come."

We get off the phone and I realize that I haven't even considered the return flight. Peter bought me a one-way ticket. He was probably hoping I wouldn't be able to afford to come back. As of right this minute, there's nothing pressing me to get back, other than my finances. I'm off for the summer. Classes don't begin again until September, so I'm technically free for the next two and a half months. My accountant would like me to sell another screenplay. He thinks we could bring the back taxes current and pay off the last of my debt if I make one solid sale.

My school would also like me to sell a screenplay. They haven't come right out and said it, but they'd like it if, for once, the screenplay wasn't just optioned, but actually brought to life. When they hired me, I had four active scripts on the burner. I had AMC and HBO flying me to location shoots on a regular basis. Nothing ever materialized. But Hollywood is like a puppy on drugs. It's got ADD. I was only interesting as long as there wasn't a dirty tennis ball bouncing across the floor.

If Peter doesn't cut me off completely, if he's willing to help me out for a little while, I could go back to San Francisco with Nell when this is over and renew some old film school friendships. Or do a stop in Colorado for a few weeks with the girls, check out the documentary world, and then head west to my sister's for August. I haven't had time to myself like this without having to consider anyone else in years, in close to a decade. The feeling is unfamiliar. Not exactly unwanted, but not exactly longed for, either. And anyway, things with Peter might still turn around. He gets angry, then he gets over it. That's what happens in a marriage. You say the meanest, most crippling thing possible to the person you ostensibly love more than anyone else in the world, and then you sit back and wait for it to pass.

When I was little, my dad's form of babysitting was to plunk me down in front of the Turner Network Television channel and then leave the room. If it was a classic, then it was appropriate. That's how his logic went. I remember sitting through the entirety of *Love Story* all by myself one night. The whole house might have been empty. I have no idea. The sex scene was confusing. I was too young to understand what they were doing under those covers, only that he was on top and she was on bottom and I was embarrassed. Then there was that line. That famous line: "Love means never having to say you're sorry." I remember sitting up. I'd heard it before. I'd heard people quoting it and now here it was, in front of me, the source. That night, sitting cross-legged too close to the television, I believed I understood the words of that syrupy-faced girl with the long brown hair. I was eleven and those words belonged to the girl, not to the actress, and I felt sure I understood them as they were meant to be understood. I felt sure my heart was pure, as her heart was surely pure, and from the other side of the screen she was looking at *me* and talking to *me*. And what she was telling me was that people in love are incapable of hurting each other; that if you're in love then you can't mess up, even if you want to, because love—which is a mystical, magical force—gets in the way.

Now, twenty-some years later, a full-fledged adult, I know I was wrong. In fact, it's just the opposite. Being in love means you can hurt the other person all you want. Being in love means having a personal punching bag. That's why you do it. That's why you fall in love in the first place—to be the worst you can be and get away with it. Otherwise, what's the point?

6

asleep on the plane

I fall asleep before takeoff and have one of those dreams where you know you're dreaming and you're kind of enjoying it, but it's also beyond your control. Like there's this feeling of *Ah, yes, I am asleep and wonderfully asleep and isn't it funny how I feel different and even better and am somehow allowing myself to derive satisfaction from this fantasy life even as I know that at some point in the very near future I will wake up and the entire fantasy will be ripped away from me and perhaps I will even feel worse but who cares?* In my dream I am directing a movie starring Matt Damon, who is, strangely, playing himself. He is playing himself and in the movie he has given up acting and is now pursuing a career as a comedian. He is failing miserably in that he isn't funny, but he's packing the house every night because people are mesmerized by this superstar-turned-not-funny comic. His agent is livid but likes the money. His wife, who loves him and whom he loves, is confused, especially since his now-famous punch line to every joke is to raise his voice and, apropos of nothing, shout, "And I *hate* my wife!" There's one joke that has me laughing so hard— even though it's not funny—that even as I sleep I am afraid that I am laughing out loud, on the plane, and that people are perhaps looking at me. But I'm not so afraid that I actually wake up. There's this moment where I'm aware of giving myself the option—would you like to wake up? Would you like to keep sleeping?—and, oh my God, it isn't even a choice. I stay sleeping because the dream, this kooky movie that I am directing, is so good and so unexpected and so very wonderfully far away from my real life. But this one joke he's telling seems to go on forever. And everyone—the entire auditorium, me, his agent, his wife—we all know the punch line and still we can't wait. He tells the audience that a few years ago he had an affair, and, as though we share one brain, we can all suddenly see the woman. She's wearing a blue dress and she is a goddess and every single person understands the affair just by looking at her and instantly we have forgiven him. All we want is for him to say more. He tells us about a commercial he filmed in Germany. A commercial! Matt Damon in some extended commercial in Germany! The audience is overwhelmed. He says, "And, so, obviously, why all this happened is either because I met someone or because I love Germany or because I *HATE* MY WIFE." The auditorium erupts in laughter. His wife, who is home alone in some kitchen but who I am able to see from where I sit directing, is crying. But me, I am busting a gut. I am loving it. This is my star. Matt Damon is my star. And only I understand.

A hand on my shoulder startles me awake. It is the stewardess from before takeoff.

"Ma'am?" she says. She is smiling, like she is amused with me. Like I've done something embarrassing and therefore charming and even quasi-adorable in my sleep.

I breathe in and sit up straight and try to widen my eyes as a way of answering. Matt Damon is slipping away from me too quickly and I feel that familiar sadness filling up the void he's leaving behind.

"We're here," she says. "We need you to deboard."

I look around and it's true; we are on the tarmac and the plane is empty. Outside my tiny window it is full-on night.

"ATL is waiting for you," she says. And then, almost too sweetly, as if she knows the reason for my flight down here and is sorry for me but also relieved that it is me and not her and so all the kinder as a result—her kindness a thank-you note for taking the sadness from her life and injecting it into my own—she adds, "We'll be clearing out the trash for at least five more minutes. You can take a little bit of time."

Is it wrong, is it so utterly wrong, that this generosity reminds me of everything I hate about the South? And about Atlanta specifically? It's not that I don't think her sweetness is genuine—though, that said, why would it be? It's that it reminds me of all that is fake about the sweetness of the South. It reminds me of my father and his family—the family he came from and the family that he kept growing after his first three children finally left the state.

"Thanks," I say, already standing, already brushing off my slacks and straightening my blouse and returning fully to consciousness.

"You take care," she says.

Yes, I think. *Take care.* But take care of what, exactly?

---

concourse to concourse

The first thing I do is check the monitors. Nell and Elliot's flight is delayed. They're two concourses away from me and so I make my way somewhat wearily down the escalators in the direction of the airport train.

This place, Atlanta, this place where I grew up, it is instantly the same and instantly different. The airport seems both smaller and larger. It is brighter and sharper and louder. It is definitely more crowded. Still, I can't help it; I look around as I wait for the next train and wonder if it was here, or maybe there, or maybe even just beyond, that my mother and father paused, returning home from a trip to Italy, and snapped a photo of me asleep in my narrow stroller, two years old at most, my head bent off to the side, my tiny khaki peacoat buttoned completely up the middle. The thought is so maudlin that it embarrasses me, but I let myself indulge in it anyway. In part because even though it really is a possibility that the stroller was right there more than thirty years ago, it's also a reality that this place is not the same. Too many people have traveled over that stretch of terrazzo—too much wax, too much trash—for it to be the same, for it to be the place of anybody's memories, much less mine.

The train comes. I enter. This hollow feeling inside me, it is not sadness for my father. I do not want to mistake it for what it is not. I do not want anyone to mistake it for what it is not. But what then? Is it Peter? Is this feeling really for Peter? Is it for Atlanta? For my childhood? The uncertainty of my future? Do I really suffer from all the same regrets that every other person on this space-age train is suffering from? I never wanted to be so common. I never wanted to be so obvious. Stan Pulaski would be furious.

My phone buzzes. I didn't turn it on after the flight, which means that I forgot to turn it off before takeoff. Sometimes I really do hate breaking the rules. Other times it's a fleeting moment of proof that the world has gone crazy with regulations. But that sort of confirmation is ultimately flat. Ultimately not that great a reward. *You mean we really have gone too far? Huh. Big surprise.* Maybe it's just this sort of haphazard back-and-forth that got me into trouble with Billy. If I'd just been more casual with my feelings on adultery *before* committing it, then maybe when it presented itself it wouldn't have felt so big, so bad, so fresh and new. If I hadn't adopted my siblings' (*the family's*) hardball theory— you cheat, you die—then maybe I wouldn't have been so tempted. What a strange and unexpected discovery to have made: not that I am disappointed with my life, but that I am disappointed with myself.

I look at my phone. It's Rita, not Peter, and I get this

homesick gush in my belly and I know, with utter certainty that at least for my immediate future, whenever the phone rings I will have to contend with the disappointment of it *not* being Peter. This is beyond my control.

"Rita," I say. "I'm on a train. Can you hear me?"

"I can hear you," she says. In the background, there are the giggly voices of her children, my nieces.

"They haven't landed," I say.

"No," she says. "I know. I was calling to tell you they're delayed."

The train stops at their concourse. I wheel my bag off and head now toward the upward escalators.

"This place is a maze," I say. "I go down to go up to go down."

"Sounds like life," she says. Sometimes I forget that Rita isn't just a mom, that in another world, in another life, before Joe was born and even for a little while after, she was an investment banker with a job and a brain and a checking account all her own. Is it the fate of all mothers—no matter how much they love their children—to look occasionally at their offspring and think, *Why?* It's not a question I plan on asking Rita, but it's a question I think about. It's a question I thought about more than once after that midsummer evening in the kitchen with Peter when he handed me the pamphlet and I said okay.

"Ha," I say. "You said it."

There's static and Rita says something I can't really understand and that I'm not really listening to. I'm looking at the monitors, trying to find the correct arriving flight for Denver.

Now there's a pause. Now silence. Then, "Kate?"

"Yes?"

"Are you okay?"

I find their flight and gate number and realize they'll be getting off right next to the Ruby Tuesday, so I wheel my baggage in the direction of the bar, my phone still shoved between my chin and shoulder.

"I am," I say. "I'm okay. But I don't really know what we're doing here. I don't really know what any of us are doing here."

Rita is more loyal to Elliot than she is to me, and rightfully so: I am not her husband. But because of this she will not flat-out agree that this trip is total BS in the way that, for instance, Peter would once have admitted to me that this trip and all it implies—like, for instance, that we were once a truly happy, committed family, which we were not, at least not since our mother's diagnosis and subsequent premature death—is BS. Rita won't admit it, but deep down she knows it. She is a smart woman. I have seen her glances. I have noticed the twitches in her cheeks when Stan Pulaski, our father, is mentioned. She does not—*did* not!—care for him and had even less to do with him than Elliot did, but she is a loyal wife and therefore she supports this trip (at least in theory) because her husband needs her to and doing so is part of her job as a wife.

She says, "It's the right thing," which I doubt, though I understand how she means it. "If nothing else," she says, "your brother needs you there. Nell needs you there. You're younger, but you're a rock."

"Hmmm," I say. These days, I am more rocky than rock solid.

"You are."

"Do you know what the plan is?" I say. I've wheeled my bag over to the countertop bar of Ruby Tuesday and pulled out a tall, heavy chair. I dig around in my front pocket and pull out two twenties and a five. I put them on the bar in front of me, then mouth the phrase *G and T* to the bartender. She looks too young to be serving alcohol, but what do I know? My students look too young to be let out of the house alone, much less let to live in a city by themselves or pay bills without assistance or, for that matter, receive credit card applications in the mail.

I take my seat and switch the phone to my other ear.

Rita is saying, "To his house, as far as I know."

"Whose house?"

"Your father's," she says.

"Who's going?"

"You are," she says.

"When?"

The bartender slides the gin and tonic in front of me and I tap the lime wedge and mouth the word *More*. She nods, but I can tell she's annoyed—annoyed that I want more lime wedges and annoyed that I'm on the phone. But, listen, I'm also annoyed. I'm annoyed with myself, so there's really nothing to do about it except to continue doing it—continue being me.

"Are you even listening to me?" says Rita. "Kate? Hello?"

"I am, I am," I say. "It's just—I meant, do you know what the plan is for tonight? Do you know what Nell and Elliot have in mind?"

"But that's what I'm saying, Kate. I'm saying that the plan

is to go to your dad's house. Tonight. That *is* the plan. To spend the night."

I have the straw to my lips as she delivers this news. I have the straw to my lips and nearly half the gin and tonic in my mouth. It had never—not once, not for a single moment—occurred to me that my brother and sister, my own reasonably rational flesh and blood, would even think to go to that man's house. At night. With me. To stay. To sleep. I put my hand on top of Peter's cash. My fingers start to shake.

This, I realize, is what it is to be truly speechless.

"Nell talked about you guys staying with Sasha," says Rita. "But Ell thought it made more sense to stay at Stan's. He says you'll have things to go through. Stuff to divide."

"Stuff to divide?"

"Family stuff," she says.

"Family stuff?" I say and I know, I really do, that I am being something of a dim-witted cow with the vaudeville repetition, and even deliberately so, but I can't help myself.

"Photos," she says, and now I hear it, the exasperation. I've pushed her too far; I have behaved like one of her children. Her patience has worn thin. "Photos, jewelry. Your *mother's* jewelry. It's all still there."

"I don't think so," I say, and I don't. Sasha is my father's fifth wife, and even if she's the most decent of them all—which is like calling Brutus the most noble of Caesar's murderers—there's no chance in hell that my mother's jewelry hasn't been divvied out to, or even stolen by, the women who followed in her footsteps and shared my father's bed over the years. All those half siblings, all those daughters, my half sisters, there's no way their mothers didn't convince themselves of their rights to my mother's pearls, to her few diamonds, to her watches and earrings and cuffs. There's just no way. And money? Money to divide? Not a chance. I won't even cross my fingers, that's how little chance there is of an inheritance.

"Listen," Rita is saying, "what do I know? I'm not there. I don't know. I have no idea. I'm just telling you what Ell said. Take it up with him."

On the other end of the line, there is a sharp girl cry that stings my eardrums. Rita says, "I have to go. The girls are going to kill each other. Listen. I'm sorry if I've been snippy. I don't mean it."

"I know," I say. My glass is nothing but ice and lime now. I wave at the bartender, who is trying hard to ignore me, but I catch her eye and point to my glass. I smile. She doesn't like me, but she goes for the gin.

"Rita," I say. "I love you."

"You too, kiddo," she says. "Tell your brother to call me when he lands. Or text." There is another piercing scream in my ear. "Or, you know, we're fine. My hands are full tonight. I'll call tomorrow." I think I hear a doorbell ringing in Rita's background, but the line goes dead before I hear anything more.

8

Nell and Elliot arrive

I am drunk by the time their flight lands. It's close to eleven. Storms have been bullying the entire country. From California to Colorado to Georgia. Our father shot himself in the head this morning and the weather is singing him home. I don't buy it, of course, but it's what he'd say. It's what he'd want any one of us to say at his funeral. The man oozed sentimentality, but he backed it up with nothing. Zilch. Nada. All talk. No substance. And yet here I am.

Actually, *here* I am, slightly drunk, sitting at the far bank of chairs at Gate 39 in Concourse C of the Hartsfield-Jackson Atlanta International Airport under enormous television monitors, trying by sheer force of will to rid myself of hiccups. I'm down to a single five-dollar bill, but I'm trying not to think about that.

Nell and Elliot are among the first to deboard. They probably flew first class. Perhaps Nell was able to intimidate the airline into some sort of bereavement discount. I hadn't even considered such a thing, but it probably does exist. A discount and extra comfort for the bereaved. It is a wacked-out world. Don't let anyone tell you different.

For some reason, when I see them, I do not raise my hand in greeting. In fact, when they turn their backs to me and begin their lugubrious walk toward baggage claim, I do not immediately rise to reveal my presence. Instead, slowly, I kick my bag out in front of me and follow behind them at a fairly healthy lag. From back here, people walking between us, midnight looming, cracks of thunder overhead, water pelting the floor-to-ceiling windows, they look like strangers. Like characters I've dreamed of every night and who finally, supernally, have come to life.

One thing about Nell and Elliot—*Nelliot* if you really want to drive them mad—they're peas from the same pod. At least physically. They are both five ten, which makes them about two and a half inches shorter than me. (Growing up, they called me names—Hateful Kate, Kate with No Date, Too Late Kate, Kate the Fake—but the taunt I truly hated was No-Mate Kate. Of course, now, older, I see that it's clunky and artless and ultimately, I think, unjustified, but at the time I took it as prophetic—and maybe even as a curse— that my unseemly height would keep me forever without a man.) At any rate, they are dark haired and gray eyed and preternaturally prone to muscle and tan. I am bean-y and awkward, and my skin, which gets blotchy when I'm nervous, is a see-through kind of white. Not milky white like a Japanese doll. Not alabaster white like a porcelain plate. A thin, transparent white, as if someone covered my veins with cellophane and forgot to add color. I like to say that our mother had an affair, but I look too much like our father through the face—severe nose, large chin, deep-set green eyes. None of our mother's Cherokee blood shows up in me. Which is not to say I'm unattractive. Not at all. I'm just not *tidy*. Nell and Elliot are tidy.

Ahead of me by a full thirty yards, my brother pulls out his phone. Three seconds later my pocket is buzzing. I don't bother looking. The two of them edge over to the side of the concourse and Nell leaves her bag with Elliot then walks into the women's bathroom. I keep walking, fully expecting Elliot to notice me at any minute and then, at that minute, I'd drop my bag and run into his arms. But he doesn't notice me. Instead, when I'm nearly ten feet from him, he turns away, totally oblivious, and I slip into the women's restroom without him seeing me. I walk the first row of stalls, ducking to look under, but they're all empty. I turn the corner, thinking I'll see Nell in front of the mirror, already washing her hands, but she's not there. So I walk the second row of stalls, still ducking to see under, until I spot my sister's purse and, behind it, her perfectly sized feet in her perfectly sized shoes.

I'm about to say something. I'm about to say, "How about a hug?" but then I hear a mewling, followed by a distinct muffling of tears, followed by a long, wet nose blow, and, I don't know why, it makes me want to pull my hair and howl at the top of my lungs. It makes me want to punch in the stall door and stomp my feet and tear the paper towel dispenser from the wall. Instead, without fully thinking it through, I reach under the stall, grab Nell's purse, turn, and run from the bathroom.

I make eye contact with Elliot as I flee the restroom and

he gives me this *what the fuck* look, but I'm laughing too hard to care. I run until I get to the top of the escalators then double over and grab my side. Nell is beside me in seconds, punching my arm and snatching at her purse.

"What is wrong with you?" she says.

She isn't laughing and her eyes are bloodshot, which bothers me only insomuch as it seems to herald a more somber evening than I'd been hoping for—long, moist-eyed conversations well into the morning about Stan and suicide and what to do next—but I grab her and pick her up so that her feet are a few inches above the ground.

"Tiny baby sister," I say.

"I hate that," she says. She tries to push me away, but I hold her until she gives in and hugs me back.

"You missed me," I say, letting go finally.

Elliot comes up behind her and drops their luggage at his side.

"You get more and more bizarre," he says, then he takes me in his arms and, even though he is shorter, holds me for a long time and very hard and somehow makes me feel small in a surprisingly good way.

I hiccup into his ear. He pulls away and looks at me sideways. "Are you drunk?" he says.

"Are you not?" I say.

"A handful," says Nell to Elliot. "What did I tell you?"

"I talked to Rita," I say, ignoring my sister. The joke is that we are in love with each other. But the love often doesn't transcend the phone. In person, we can drive each other crazy, as she is me right now.

"I think our stewardess was sick," says Nell, blowing her

nose, and I wonder whether she's trying to hide the fact that she's been crying or just being her usual germaphobic self.

"I just tried her," says Elliot. "She's not answering."

"The girls must have pre-camp jitters," I say. "It was bedlam."

He nods and looks away. I wonder if he knows about the grad student, about the tomato plants. I wonder if things have escalated, if there are machinations at work in Elliot's life that Nell and I—or maybe just I—don't know about.

"She says the plan is to go to Stan's?" I say. "To stay at Stan's?"

We begin as a tiny unit, Elliot in the front, down the escalators, toward the trains to baggage claim.

"I wanted to stay at Sasha's," says Nell.

"With the animal child? No way," I say. I want to make her laugh. I want to make her forget about what we're doing here. Even for a minute or two. This whole experience would be less annoying if she would just laugh.

"She's not so bad," says Nell. "She's growing out of it."

"How do you know?"

"She's our sister," says Nell.

"*Half* sister," I say.

Nell puts her hand on my shoulder and squeezes. "Give her a chance, okay? For me?"

"She's the spawn of the devil," I say.

"She's six."

"Girls," says Elliot, stopping suddenly and turning to look at us as a train approaches. He doesn't look amused with our banter. Normally we amuse him. Normally Nell and I— ping-ponging back and forth like this—normally we are the coolest thing since sliced bread to my older brother. "We're going to Dad's," he says. "We're staying there, and we'll go through whatever we have to, and we'll do it as a family."

I bite my lips together. Nell says nothing. The train is stopping; the doors are about to open.

"Can we get on the train and get out of here?" Nell says at last.

"Can you two behave?"

I shrug. I feel suddenly tired, suddenly unwilling to respond, unable to articulate. The train doors slide open and I walk through. Nell and Elliot follow. We stand three abreast, not talking, looking out the thick glass windows as we roar past the underbelly of the airport—its wires and pipes and steel. It's late. There are only a few other people on the train and they too are quiet, stunned into silence by the awkwardness of the hour. Everything slows down at night. Even the airport. There's a reason people are scared of the dark.

9

---

taxi to Dad's place

Our cab hurtles its way through this city, this big, sprawling city. These overpasses. These underpasses. Red lights blurring through rain into pink blurring into lavender. The old Peachtree sign high above the intersection of I-75 and I-85. Spaghetti Junction all around us. A two-seater convertible on the side of the highway, a man straddling the windshield and the backseat, presumably trying to release a malfunctioning top. The smell. The smell of humidity. The smell of trash. The smell of roaches and wet concrete and banana peels and money and, yes, I'll go this far, childhood, even.

This cabbie drives the city like he was born here. Like he woke up as a baby one morning and there was his mother and there was a car and the car never stopped. Just him and his mom and this city and its streets. He darts and weaves and moves effortlessly to the left when 75 splits west, and before I know it, we are on Northside Drive and there is Bobby Jones Golf Course and, dear God, there is Piedmont Hospital, where all three of us were born, and there is Benihana, where we went on our birthdays whether we wanted to or not because our father thought we should like the knife work. He thought children who were interesting and were worth a damn—*his* children—should like a place like Benihana, should grow up exposed to other cultures, more interesting cultures than ours. No McDonald's for us. No Red Lobster. No Piccadilly or Morrison's like our friends on their birthdays. We were different. Whether we wanted to be or not. "Your mother's dead, goddamn it," he said to me once. "Start acting like it." What he meant, I still don't know. Only what he didn't mean. Only that what I was and how I was wasn't right, wasn't interesting or compelling. "Do something," he sometimes said to me. "Have an opinion at least."

We take Collier to Peachtree and I wonder if this is as strange and foreign but also familiar a drive for my siblings as it is for me. I wonder if they're thinking the same thoughts, the very same thoughts. Are they looking at Piedmont Hospital and thinking of our mother? And if they are, are they thinking of her as a new mother or as a mother on her way out? As a mother covered and withered in the back of one of the hospital's ambulances?

An ambulance wouldn't have taken our father away this morning. What would it have been? A van? A police van? A coroner's van? A van belonging to the city? Or a private van? The funeral home's van? I know the answers to none of these questions. Until this moment, I hadn't even thought to ask.

We pass the duck pond and next the dueling cathedrals. To our left is Habersham Road, where the parents of my first boyfriend lived. The Rutherglens. They were good people.

They were nice, normal, wealthy people. They let me spend the night whenever I wanted. They put me in their daughter's bedroom—Gretchen, who was off at Hotchkiss playing field hockey or something—and never once worried that Tucker and I would cross the line. They walked me through Stan's divorce from his second wife and his marriage to his third. They drove me to the hospital when my first half siblings— the twins—were born. They never made me feel like a pariah for having a dead mom and an oversexed father. They just wanted me to feel safe. They just wanted me to be happy. Until I started going with Tucker's best friend. They stopped letting me spend the night after that. God, maybe Nell is right. Maybe I am obsessed with sex.

Behind Habersham is Woodward, where we lived until our mother died. First we moved to Howell Mill. Then to Tanglewood. Then, when Nell and Elliot left for college, my father and I moved into the high-rise and then into the house of his third wife. It wasn't the same. Nothing is ever the same. He moved a few more times after I finally left for college. The last place being the two-story condo in a tiny, tasteless gated neighborhood on Pharr Road, which we are now too quickly approaching.

The cab slows and I hear the *click clock* of the turn signal. We turn left and then slow even more.

"Up there," says Nell. "I have the code."

The cabbie turns where instructed and stops so that Nell's window is in front of a squat brick structure with a keypad hidden at just the right height. She rolls down her window and plugs in a series of numbers. She does not, that I see, consult a piece of paper.

"Been here before?" I say.

"Have you?" she says, rolling up her window.

The gates in front of us open slowly. The cabbie pulls through at a turtle's pace.

It occurs to me that I'm going to have to tell Elliot and Nell about the affair. And I'm probably going to have to do it this weekend. It's not like I was planning on keeping it a secret forever, but this sudden reunion certainly makes the revelation seem more imminent. I assumed that at some point—some point in the distant, blurry, fuzzy future—I would tell them. But I imagined us gray and wizened by then. I imagined that one day we would wake up old and that decades would be behind us and they would be versed. The knowledge would have seeped into their minds and they would know and they would understand and they would have—years earlier, somehow, in the way magic works—already forgiven me.

The neighborhood—lower middle class: lower if you're old, middle if you're young—is really just a large cul-de-sac around which pods of four attached row houses have been placed. There are four pods in all, sixteen condos total. Our father's is the first condo in the second pod—the only one with the front light still illuminated. It's a blue shingled affair, like all the rest. In front is a short manicured lawn that looks blue in the moonlight and leads up to a quick flight of a stairs, which in turn lead up to a modest front porch. Really, the front porch is shared with the other three connected condos, but there are railings to separate them. It's not actually for hanging out. That's clear as day. It's purely decorative. Nobody in their right mind would spend any time on these front porches—you'd have to interact with anybody who came by. You'd have no privacy whatsoever. No, these porches are for the mailman and a hanging plant or two.

We pull up to the curb, and the cabbie pops the trunk. Elliot opens his wallet, and I open the back door. To anyone paying attention, my demeanor should suggest not that I don't *want* to pay, but simply that I've forgotten.

Nell pinches me as I'm setting my bag down on the sidewalk.

"Ouch," I say. Though her pinches, like the porches, are merely for show.

"What's wrong with you?" she says.

"What?" I say. "Are you really mad? I thought you were playing."

"Listen," she says. She is whispering, which instinctively makes me want to whisper. "Get it together."

"What?"

"Elliot's really upset."

"He is?"

"He was a mess on the plane," she says.

"*You* seem like the mess." I have no idea what I'm talking about.

She says, "You have no idea what you're talking about."

Ta-da!

"Are you sure we should be here, then?" I nod my head at the condo. "Are you sure he's ready?"

"It's not just—" She looks at Elliot, who's getting out of the front seat. "I'll tell you later."

Elliot taps the hood of the cab, which performs a careful

U-turn then heads away from us in the direction of the front gates.

Again we find ourselves standing three abreast, not talking, staring straight ahead. Only this time we are looking at our father's home—the last place he lived before he died, a place we've never seen other than the occasional emailed photograph. It feels like a scene from a movie. I wish it were a scene from a movie. I wish I were the camera and I could pull back and watch from a safe distance, somewhere up and away—a tree, maybe, or a power line. Anywhere but here. I have a quick, searing feeling that the entire weekend is going to be a series of still lifes starring me and my siblings standing awkwardly three abreast, each of us waiting for one of the others to make the first move.

Nell, who is standing in the middle, takes my hand. I glance down and see that she's also taken Elliot's. And it's unsettling only because my first thought isn't *Thank God*. My first thought isn't *This is what it is to be in a family*. Instead, my first thought is *What if we're not as close as I think we are? What if everything with everyone has been a series of gestures that suggest one thing but ultimately mean another?*

"Are you ready for this?" says Elliot.

No, I think. *No, I am not.* I have no idea what the status of the back porch will be. The back porch, where Stan Pulaski earlier this morning shot himself. His body is gone. I know that much. Do I know where or how it was removed? No. But I know it isn't here. Like so much of the information floating around in my brain, I can't point to a definite answer, but I can rule out possibilities. What I mean is I have no idea what the back porch will look like. I have no idea if there's blood or police lines. Are there always police lines when a gun is involved? Is there always doubt until a coroner's report? Or are some things certain? Is a sixty-nine-year-old who's found dead with a pistol in his hand and a hole in his forehead an automatically closed case? These are simply more things I don't know the answers to. But I feel as though I should: I once wrote an entire season of *Law & Order: SVU*. They cut the check and everything. (A check I spent on redecorating the condo and upgrading my wardrobe. I could have used it to pay off the debt in one lump sum, but Peter said we were comfortable. He said there was a payment plan in place and we were fine. He said, "Spend it. Be happy.") They filmed the first episode, but nobody liked the arc. What they liked was the witty dialogue. What they didn't like was the number of unsolved cases. Olivia lost her foot in the line of fire. Ice T wound up gay.

Maybe it bespeaks something decent in me somewhere deep down, but my concern with possible blood splatter isn't for me. It's for Elliot. It's for Nell. I don't want them to see it. I don't want them to see it first. For some reason I can't and don't want to understand, this man meant something to them. And even though he meant nothing at all to me, I don't want them to see his mess. I don't want to add that visual aid to whatever their brains are already doing on their own. But the truth is, it's too late. The truth is, it's well past midnight and the man is undeniably dead and here we are already, and whatever is behind that front door and then behind the back porch door is beyond my control. This, all of this, is beyond my control.

"Now or never," says Nell, and the still life advances slowly forward, three against the world.

10

———

inside Dad's place

I should take my time with this. I should go slowly with this next part. It's important I get as many of the details correct as possible:

We approach the front door as a single unit.

At the top step, Nell pulls out a key.

Elliot and I hang back. We watch as she glides the key into place. If there are expectations, I'm not aware of them. If there are pre-images for what I think is waiting on the other side, I'm not privy to them.

Nell pushes the door in, but it opens only halfway. Elliot and I watch as she aligns herself with the doorframe, slips a hand inside the house, and flips a switch.

It is difficult to take it all in at once. That is, once we get the door fully open.

Inside, there are boxes. Boxes and more boxes. Piles. Hills. Mounds. Collections. Mountains. The room—presumably the living room—is completely filled with clutter. Filled shoulder-high with crap. Stan was always a pack rat. Moving to the high-rise with him was a disaster. The doormen said they'd never seen so many boxes. But once we unpacked, the boxes had been flattened. They'd gone to storage just like they were supposed to. The houses I lived in with him, even after Nell and Elliot moved away, were always clean. Crowded— babies, wives, knickknacks—but clean.

I look to Elliot, expecting an explanation. Expecting him to say, "Movers." But I know already this is not from movers. This, right here in front of us, these stacks of starched button-downs and clusters of dying potted plants—this is the stuff of reality TV. My archenemy. This is a hoarder's home. Perhaps merely an entry-level hoarder, but a hoarder all the same. There's no doubt, and yet I had no idea. Oh Stan, you'd better not be trying to make me feel sorry for you.

"Wow," says Nell, shooing away a fly. A fly! I couldn't make that up if I tried. "I had no idea it was this bad."

"This bad? How come I didn't know about it at all?"

Nell pushes a stack of boxes from in front of her and weaves her way to the center of the room.

"Sasha told me about it," says Nell. "But she didn't say it was anything like this. I can't believe she stayed as long as she did."

"Maybe Sasha did the hoarding," I say.

"Sasha did *not* do the hoarding."

"How do you know?" I say. I mean it as a joke, though already I anticipate Nell's unwillingness to see it as one.

"When did you become such an old man?" says Nell. "You're perfect all of a sudden? You can't give anyone else a chance?"

I have no idea what she's talking about. But I do know that Sasha was number five. And that Nell and Elliot weren't around for four years when I had to suffer alone through number three. It's not a terrible thing, I think, for me to be dismissive, joking or not, of the fifth one. She could be a saint, and it would still take another saint—or an angel or something even more divine—to want to spend any time at all with her. Have I met her? Yes, I have. She's my age. *My* age, minus a few months. When I was younger, I overheard stories about my father's "endowment." In fact, number two, Whitney, a botanist, used to tell me about their "lovemaking." "An animal," she'd say, if we ever crossed paths in the hallway in the middle of the night. "He's an absolute animal." Whitney got pregnant in, like, one week. There are plenty of reasons to hate Whitney, who—dear Lord! How many obvious realizations will I have tonight?—it just now occurs to me, I might be seeing in person again after so many years. Will she come to his funeral? She was the wife who dubbed me a "lying, lazy little brat." Who packed my lunches with cans of artichoke hearts. What was he thinking? What was Stan thinking when he brought that woman home? Was he thinking about us at all? Was he thinking about me? It doesn't matter. These questions are moot now. The point is, I've met Sasha and, sure, okay, she isn't as bad as Whitney, but it's insane to think Nell doesn't understand this. It's ludicrous for Nell to want me not to make jokes about this woman.

"Where did he even get this stuff?" says Elliot.

I pick up a seashell that's sitting in an ashtray that's sitting on top of a stack of *New Yorker* magazines.

"Beats me," I say. "The better question is, are we really going to stay here tonight?"

Nell sighs. "You're right."

"I mean, where would we even sleep?" I sweep my hands around dramatically and, as I do, get an even better picture of the squalor and filth in the midst of which our father lived and died. It's enough to make a person feel utterly blue.

"I don't know," says Elliot, who's looking at his phone and not at us. "Let's look around. I need to call Rita."

He walks back outside and I look at Nell, who thankfully seems to be reading my mind. What she's reading is this: *Seriously? You want us to look around? And then you walk outside? What the aphid, dude? Aphid* is the family's stand-in for *fuck*. We adopted it as children in order to feel like we were speaking crassly in the company of adults without getting into trouble.

After Elliot closes the door, I say to Nell, who's still standing sort of dumbstruck in the middle of the room, "You were going to say something before? When we were outside?"

"Things are weird in Colorado," she says.

I push and pull my way through cardboard until I'm standing next to her. We both take seats on boxes near us.

"He said that? He said 'weird'?"

"No," she says. "Not really. But he's different. And he's queer with the phone. Not like he is when it's business. Just watch."

"You think tomatoes?"

"I don't know," she says. "I really don't. But on the plane he was upset in a way that made me think it's about more than just Dad." She pauses. "Not that this isn't also a big deal."

I look around. Overhead is the same chandelier that's been following us from house to house to house. It seems obscene in this condo. Completely out of place. It needs a staircase. It needs a balcony and a foyer and a grand piano. It needs a nuclear family. Mom would have blushed. Or shaken her head. Or merely looked away until she'd found a better talking point. My imagination's version of my mother.

Nell picks up a pair of fingernail clippers and stares at them like they're a foreign object. I put my hand on her knee. "Are you okay?" I say.

She nods, then puts the clippers down and wipes the tips of her fingers on her pant leg. "I'm in shock, probably. I feel sad for him. Not sad for me, but sad for him. Does that make sense?"

"It does," I say. "Yes." I say this not because I necessarily agree, but because I know she needs to hear it.

"But then," she says. "Feeling sad for him sort of makes me feel sad for me also, after all. God."

A mosquito buzzes at my ear.

"This was his life," she says.

I nod.

"This." She gestures to the room around us.

I nod again. I feel faint. Or maybe it's the booze wearing off.

It's not normally so awkward with Nell, but sitting knee to knee with her in this room doesn't feel carefree and easygoing. Instead it feels like a first date. A first date that's going badly.

"Are *you* okay?" she says.

Of course, I could tell her the truth. I could tell her right now while it's just the two of us surrounded by the physical manifestations of our father's mental failings. I could cut the tension with one admission or with every admission. I could tell her about the affair. I could tell her Peter wants a divorce. I could tell her that for the past many years I've been slowly whittling away at nearly fifty thousand dollars' worth of early twenties credit card debt on top of mammoth school loans. But all this would be tantamount to saying, "P.S.: you think you know me, but you don't."

I can't tell her the truth because the truth is that I lie to my sister. I've been lying to her this whole time. Every day. Every phone call. As much as and more than I lie to Peter, I lie to Nell. I feel like I might pass out.

"Don't you think it's strange that Sasha didn't tell anyone?" I say.

"Tell anyone what?"

"About Stan," I say. "About moving out."

She looks down at her lap and picks at an imaginary fiber. "She told me."

"You didn't say anything," I say.

Nell looks older than the last time I saw her, which was over Christmas. Six months and she's already aged. Which is better? To see yourself so often you don't notice the wrinkles? Or to go a year not looking in mirrors, only to be shocked that everything's changed?

She shrugs. "I couldn't have stopped what happened."

I'm about to say something insincere, something like, *It would have been nice to be looped in*, but Nell's right. Being looped in wouldn't have altered anything.

Nell says, "Did Dad have a cat?"

"Why?"

"It smells," she says.

I sit up straighter and sniff the air.

Big Daddy: Didn't you notice it, Brick?
    Didn't you notice a powerful and ob-
    noxious odor of mendacity in this
    room?

Tennessee Williams is not on my side tonight.

"Maybe we're on an episode of some awful show," says Nell. "Maybe we're being filmed. Maybe there's a dead cat under these boxes."

"Maybe," I say. I can ignore the smell for now. "Maybe there's even alcohol in the kitchen."

She looks around at the stacks and mounds and piles of every tiny thing you could possibly think of. "We should probably find out," she says.

11

———

the back porch

It's a screened-in back porch, which I hadn't been imagining. I'd been imagining an open porch, covered, but with a railing, maybe with some plants hung here and there. But this, screened in and closed off from the world, feels more an extension of the house and the clutter of the house than it does a gateway to the outside. If I were on set, I'd say as much to the location scout.

There are coffee cups and coffee cans. There are two small sofas forming an L against the back and side walls. And near the screen door, with ashtrays at its side, is the old white rocking chair that I know for a fact is the one from my bedroom when I was a baby. It was in my sister's bedroom before that. And in my brother's bedroom before that. I remember, as a kid, having a hard time wrapping my head around the idea that it didn't *belong* to me, that I hadn't been the first baby rocked to sleep in it.

On the screen above the rocker, there is a large, dark, circular stain, off center of which is a small circular tear, but that's it. There is no other evidence of anything out here. There is no evidence of a suicide. No evidence of a gunshot.

I look at Nell. She's staring at the stain.

"Here," I say. I hand her the bourbon we found under the sink.

"You think it's safe to drink?" she says.

"Like maybe he poisoned it?"

She smiles but doesn't look at me. She does, though, take the bottle.

"No." She pulls a long swallow. Long and slow enough to make me think there are things—maybe many things—I don't know about my sister as the person she is now. "Safe, as in, I was thinking it might be swill," she says. "But it's good."

"Tasty," I say, which is a callback to a joke about Whitney. I don't remember the specifics, only that it was a word she couldn't stand to hear. *Tasty. Moist. Brainstorming.* There was a whole slew of words that, when used, would throw her into a frenzy.

"I talked to Elliot about this on the plane," she says.

"Irmus," I say.

"What?"

"Irmus," I say. "When you reveal the meaning at the end."

"What are you talking about?"

I take the bottle, steal a quick sip, then hand it back to her. I feel a keen desire to get Nell drunk. "You said, 'I talked to Elliot about this on the plane,' but you haven't yet said what *this* is. Presumably you are now going to define 'this.'"

"Do your students have any idea what you're talking about?"

"No," I say. "Nope. Not a word."

"Are they any good?"

"You mean, can they write?"

"Yes," she says.

I point at the bottom of the bottle and swing my finger upward, indicating that she should drink. She does as directed.

"Yeah," I say. "They can." And it's true. They can. It gives me hope.

"Irmus," she says.

I nod.

"Right, well, what I already talked to Elliot about is the funeral."

"Okay."

"Sasha would like—"

I take a deep breath. I am being deliberately dramatic and she knows it.

"Give me a chance."

"Yes, yes."

The crickets have started. I forgot about crickets. In Chicago there are no crickets. Not where I live. But here in Atlanta, even in the middle of the city, you can't quiet the crickets. I should remember this. The next time someone asks what Atlanta is like, I should say, "It sounds like crickets." It's the kind of statement that wins a person friends. In Hollywood, it's the kind of thing people remember you for. Or maybe I'm giving the sentence too much credit. Regardless. It's true. It sounds like crickets.

"Sasha wants to have an open casket."

"You're kidding."

"No."

I watch her face for some hint that this is a joke, but she holds my gaze and doesn't seem to mind waiting for my brain to wrap itself around this ridiculous idea.

"But his skull." I make a circling figure with my finger at the side of my head.

"I talked to her while we were on the ground in Denver. She's talked to the funeral director and he seems confident that their guy can put it back together."

I don't want to give in, but I feel the repetitions starting again.

"Put it back together?"

She nods slowly, then hands me the bottle. "They make a mold," she says. "They fill in the gaps."

This has happened before. All these things have happened to other people before us. The world has thought of everything. Funeral home directors are prepared for anything. They make a mold. They fill in the gaps. A husband buys his lunatic wife an airplane ticket because she can't afford to buy one for herself and then forces her to get on a plane. My students should be following me around.

"Elliot is okay with this?"

She shrugs. "Listen, he thinks it's unorthodox that Sasha is okay with an open casket, especially since most of Dad's kids are pretty young. I mean, Mindy is six. And that's definitely discomforting to Elliot. I think he'd be less cool with it if his girls were going to be here. But it's what Sasha wants, and she was the last one really in his life, so I guess he wants to give it to her." She pauses. "So do I."

It's probably indicative of a smallness—the fact that I'm so ardently resisting the rationality of this proposal. I wonder if it's something as simple as not wanting to see his face again. But then, why? Do I not want to see him because he means so little to me? Or do I not want to see him because I don't want to see what he's become, to see what old age looks like on him?

"If you guys are okay with it," I say, "then I guess I am, too."

"Okay," says Nell, her head bobbing like I've made a really grown-up decision and she's therefore proud of me, which makes me want to take it back. "This will be good for Sasha. Okay."

Elliot comes up behind us.

"Boo," he says.

I jump a little.

"Bad taste," says Nell. "Too soon."

"You're in a better mood," I say. I hand him the bourbon. He smells it, scowls, then tries to hand it back. I wave it off and he hands it to Nell.

"I talked to Rita," he says. "She sends her love."

Nell and I have been leaning in the doorway, against either side of the doorframe. But Elliot pushes past us and walks over to the screen, to its stain, to its perfect little tear. He traces the outline of the stain with his finger and then, slowly, almost as if he's dared himself, he pushes his finger through the hole.

"Unreal," he says. "Completely unreal."

And I think, *Yes*. I think, *You have no idea*. None of us has any idea. Fewer than twenty hours ago a man, our biological father, walked out onto this porch, sat down in that rocking chair for some unknowable amount of time, then put a gun in his mouth and pulled the trigger. Did he load the gun out here? Did he load it inside and bring it that way onto this porch? Did he give it a second thought? Did he know the night before? What about the night before that? Was there relief? Was there anything at all in that split second after the trigger had been pulled and the bullet released? Was there a dwarf lifting of sadness? A miniscule feeling of joy? These are things we will never know. All we'll know for sure is that this man, this father, walked out here all alone and did what he did and now we are here. Now we are here.

Matt Damon, come back to me.

12

———

going to bed at Dad's place

Bad news," says Nell.

We're in a bedroom—what once must have been Mindy's bedroom, as there are pink images of lamb babies and goat babies and unicorn babies stenciled all over the walls—where we've managed to push the knickknacks and dolls and typewriters out of the way in order to create two pallets made of couch cushions and pillows: a largish one for me and Nell and a small one for Elliot.

"What?" says Elliot.

"Here." She hands a bottle to Elliot and a bottle to me. It's some kind of poison meant specifically for biting mites.

"Oh," I say. "Bedbugs. He has bedbugs."

"Had," says Elliot.

"Not bedbugs," says Nell. "Biting mites."

"Same thing," I say.

"No," she says, "it's not."

"Thou sayest," says Elliot. Then, after a beat: "I'd kill for some pot."

"Or blow," says Nell.

Elliot and I look at her.

"It's big in SF right now," she says. "What?"

"Where did you even find these?" I say, handing the bottles back to Nell.

"The closet."

Who knows? Maybe there was a sale at Sam's Club and he couldn't help buying a couple of bottles. It's no guarantee that there are actually bedbugs in this house. Plenty of people buy bug spray preemptively—bug spray and bandages and sunscreen. Plenty of people.

It's close to three in the morning. We have an appointment at the funeral home at nine. At this point, though I'm dead tired, I have no idea why we're even pretending to try to get some sleep. We should be out looking for a rental car or a moving service or pesticide. But no. Instead we are here. Nell insists that a rental car is unnecessary. She says Sasha wants to drive us around; she wants to catch up. I can tell this annoys even Elliot, but he's gung ho on extended family for some reason and so he's willing to go along with whatever plans and schedules Nell has dreamed up for us.

I crawl under the covers fully clothed. "I feel like a kid," I say. "Like I'm sleeping on the floor at some friend's house. This brings back memories."

Nell gets into bed next to me. Elliot walks over to the light switch.

"Except the friend probably has lice," I say.

Nell fidgets under the sheets. Elliot flips the light.

"And also this friend is a hoarder and also he's just shot himself and for some reason I think it's a good idea to spend the night anyway."

"Shut up already," says Nell.

"We don't say shut up in this house," I say.

"Hey," says Elliot, and I fully expect to be reprimanded yet again. "It's good to see you guys."

I'm quiet. Sincerity has a way of throwing me off sometimes, especially when it's not me who started it. Like, I always feel somewhat caught off guard, somewhat embarrassed for the other person, but also somewhat ashamed for not having thought of it first.

"You guys too," says Nell. "For real. I needed this."

"Yeah," I say. "Ditto." Because it's all I can think to say.

Yellow glow stars slowly come to life on the ceiling overhead. It's been years since I thought of those stars, since I even remembered they existed. I had them in my bedroom on Woodward Way and also in my bedrooms at Tanglewood and Howell Mill. But I gave up on them sometime after that. I can't remember when exactly. And I can't remember why. I'd be a better person, maybe, if I'd had those stars in my life a few more years. I'd be less cynical. My childhood would have lasted a little longer. I should have them in my bedroom now. I should have them in Chicago. I should go first thing on my return to a toy store and buy them out. I should stick them all over the ceiling and all over the walls and I should wait in the dark until Peter comes home, and then I could show him the stars and say, "I'm sorry." That's it. Nothing more. Just "I'm sorry," and see if there's any way that could be enough.

I am so lonely.

Under the covers, Nell reaches over and grabs my hand. Sometimes, I swear, it's like she can read my mind. She gives my palm one squeeze, and I give hers one squeeze back. That's it. That's all there is to it, and then we sleep.

13

---

a bad dream

I dream about a yellow trunk. It's large and heavy—something like what they had on the *Titanic*. Something old and unwieldy and grand. It stands vertically, not horizontally, like you could hang clothes in it if you wanted to. I'm wearing this Polo sweater that my mom used to wear when I was tiny. It's a sweater she was photographed in often. So even if I don't really remember it from my own memories, I remember it from the pictures. The Polo is a dark mustard color and it's too big for me and I keep worrying that it's going to weigh me down. It's too big, it's too big. I fold up the sleeves, but no one is watching me. On my wrist is my mother's gold Rolex, and it's heavy and hard to look at, but I realize—even as I'm dreaming—that I have no idea where the watch is. It's on my arm, yes, but only in the dream. In real life, I have no idea where it is, and this is a strange realization to be grappling with in my sleep. It's here, I keep telling myself. But it's also not here.

That watch was meant to be mine. I remember that. There were so few things appointed to anyone specifically in her will, but I remember that the watch was mine, though I was too small to wear it when she died, and the engagement ring was Elliot's, and the pearls—the black ones—were Nell's. I know Elliot got the ring because Rita wears it every day; I have no idea whether Nell got the pearls. But again, this is all happening in my dream. So I'm confused, but also curious and abnormally certain that these dream facts are also real life facts.

In my dream, I am all alone. Everyone is gone. It's been decades. It's been centuries. And everyone is lost. I look down at my wrists and there is a slow trickle of blood. This isn't how I want to die, but the blood is warm and wet and comforting. I don't fight it. There's no reason to fight it. And then I realize, this is not blood. Then I realize, this is not blood at all. This is urine.

I sit up in bed. My first thought is relief—relief that I've awakened in time. My second thought is that I'm embarrassed by how obvious the dream is—yellow trunk, yellow sweater, yellow watch, yellow urine. I tiptoe out of the room and skirt the junk in the hallway. It's not until I'm in the bathroom, my pants down around my ankles, that I realize I didn't in fact wake up in time. My underwear is wet. Not drenched, not soaked, but wet. My pants are moist too, which means my side of the makeshift bed is also damp. The world thought of everything but not of this.

There's a soft knock on the door.

"Kate?"

It's Nell.

"Yeah?"

"Can I come in?"

I flush the toilet and unlock the door. Her eyes are small and red. Her hair is in an untidy bundle on top of her head. She looks like a little kid with wrinkles.

In her arms is the sheet we were sleeping on.

"Don't worry," she says. "We don't have to talk about this."

I cover my face with my hands.

"I'm so embarrassed," I say.

She stuffs the sheet into the bathroom trash can, which we'd set up before bed, so that now the small bin is almost entirely full.

"Seriously, I'm not going to tell Elliot or anything."

"Thanks," I say.

She puts her hand on my arm tentatively. She looks more troubled than I am.

"Does this happen often?" she says.

I can't help it, I laugh.

"No," I say. "No. Never."

"Kiddo," she says, which is everyone's nickname for me, even Rita's and Peter's. "I think you're more upset by all this than you're letting on."

I put my arm around her and flip the switch in the bathroom. "Maybe," I say. "But also. There's stuff you don't know about."

"What stuff?"

We move into the dark, narrow hallway, made all the darker and narrower by Stan's endless collection of garbage.

"Let's get through the next few days, okay? Let's do that first, then I'll tell you."

We tiptoe one after the other back into Mindy's room. Nell gets under the covers first. Somehow, she's already changed the bottom sheet. She is a natural mother, though there are no real children to prove it. Elliot's every fifth breath comes out a snore. I can feel that Nell is now wide awake next to me.

"It's nothing," I whisper. "I promise. It can wait awhile."

If I borrowed twenty thousand dollars from Nell, I could pay off the last of the credit card debt and come current on the back taxes and have a little left over to lean on during the summer months. There'd still be the school loans, but the monthly payment is so low already—cheaper than most car payments. Of course, all this would involve coming clean. This would involve explaining the debt, explaining the extent of my secrecy. If she said no, then I'd be in the same place I am now, but with the additional discomfort of her judgment. That said, if she agreed and I paid it off, then maybe I could make a fresh start. I could see how my brain feels about Peter when money isn't an issue. But it doesn't matter. I won't ask her.

"Kate," she says, suddenly serious. "Are you sick? Would you tell me?"

I feel for her face and find it. "That's so sweet," I say. "No. I'm not sick." I stroke her cheek once. "Look," I say. "Look at all the glow stars."

I feel her turn away from me, in the direction of the ceiling.

"I'd forgotten those existed," she says.

"Yes," I say. "Exactly."

"Maybe Mindy is more like us than you thought."

I think about this. I think about little Mindy standing on her bed, moving her desk chair around the room, stretching her chubby little arm toward the ceiling, sticking the stars on one by one.

"Maybe," I say. "We'll see."

14

Sasha comes to fetch us

Sasha is outside the apartment at eight on the nose. She doesn't honk and she doesn't come in. She just pulls up in her blue Volvo, steps outside it, leans against the hood, and lights a cigarette. I know all this because I'm watching her from the living room like a reverse peeping Tom. Mindy is not with her, which is a relief. I'm not yet ready for dealing with any of the half siblings, especially the super-young ones.

Here's what I can say about Sasha: she's prettier than I remember. Not many women do that—get prettier over time or out of memory. It's been, what, three years since I last saw her? Which means—can this be right?—it's been that long since I last saw Stan. Mindy was three and had just mastered the phrases "I'm adorable" and "You can hug me if you want." My father had rented a cabin in the Upper Peninsula. They'd flown into Chicago; I'd met them at the airport, gotten a coffee with them, waited while they rented a car. I remember Sasha as having been slightly overweight then, with baby fat still in her cheeks. I remember thinking my father was a fool. I remember him saying, as he got into the driver's seat of the rental, "I love my children," and me saying back to him, "You must. You keep having them." I'd wanted to hurt him. I'd wanted to dismiss his newest wife and newest child. I'd wanted him to feel small and weak and embarrassed by the choices he'd made. Instead he laughed and hit his thigh. "Goddamn," he said. "I like that." Peter had offered to go with me to the airport, but I'd said no. I'd said I didn't want to burden him with my father's aura. But really, if I'm being honest, which I am trying very hard these days to be, maybe I was already feeling bored with our marriage. Maybe he was feeling bored too, which is why he went to Dan and asked about reversing the vasectomy and then, when he found out that wouldn't work, asked about adoption.

Nell comes up behind me. "Ready or not," she says.

"Not," I say.

"Too bad," she says, and then she pinches the back pocket of my jeans.

Outside it's dense and thick and muggy.

Nell is the first to greet Sasha, and I think it's a little weird and maybe even unseemly and definitely unnecessary the way they hold on to each other so long. Sasha whispers something in Nell's ear that I can't hear and the two of them laugh and look my way.

I hold out my hand before Sasha can try to hug me. She obliges by shaking it, and again I feel relief.

"I'm sorry about your father," she says.

I nod. "I'm sorry about your husband."

I'd forgotten about this—the formality of death.

"Well, you know, them's the rules," says Sasha. It throws me a little, to hear her use an expression I associate so closely with Stan. But it makes sense, I suppose. She was married to him.

Sasha's eyes are swollen and sad-looking, but what I suspected from the window of the house is true—she's prettier than before; it's like she's blossomed. She's lost weight, and hiding underneath all along was a beautiful woman. It makes me a little bit jealous.

Elliot is last to the car and shakes Sasha's hand in the same businesslike manner as I did, which makes me glad he's my brother and that he exists and that we're on the same side. He's not going to manufacture some friendship with this wife or any of the exes just because our father is dead. He's here for something else, I'm realizing. He's here for closure, yes, and, sure, okay, maybe because it's the right thing to do, but he's also here for himself as a father. I'm not sure yet. But he's here to figure something out in his own life. I see that now, and I make the decision to be as well behaved and supportive as possible. I can do this for Elliot.

"We've got time for a coffee if anyone wants," says Sasha, and the three of us, nearly in unison, say yes.

NELL TAKES THE FRONT SEAT, and all the way to the funeral home Elliot quizzes Sasha from the backseat about our father's hoarding—when it started, what it was like six months ago, when it got to be the way it is now. She answers his questions patiently, one after the other. A few times her voice cracks and Nell puts a hand on her knee, but mostly she's able to keep it together.

"Why did you leave?" he says.

I hit Elliot's chest with the back of my hand.

"Sorry," he says. "Is that too much?"

"I left because we weren't in love anymore," she says. "Not like we should have been. I wanted to take care of him. He was old, you know." She looks in the rearview mirror when she says this. She looks at me, and I wonder if she's trying to accuse me of something—of not knowing he was old (which I did), or of not caring (which mostly I didn't), or of not being a good daughter (well, yes, she'd be right there too, but the problem started with him being a not-good father). "And I left because one day I came home from work and Mindy was sitting inside a cardboard box with a loaf of bread and an un-cooked chicken in her hands and when I asked your father what he thought he was doing with his daughter, he said, 'Daughter? Daughter? She's not my daughter.' And that was it. That was just it."

Nobody says anything. I'm watching Nell's hand, watching the way it seems to want to reach out and touch Sasha's leg again. I should probably be taking notes.

"That was six months ago," says Sasha. "I checked on him every week. When I left it was just the back porch and half the living room that he was using for storage. I don't even know where he got the things he got. I just know that every week there was more—another television set, a box of key-boards, a box of video games, a box of dish towels."

"I still don't understand why you didn't tell us how bad things were," says Elliot. "I could have helped."

Sasha nods, then shakes her head, then nods again. "I really like you guys," she says. "You know that, right?"

What does her liking or not liking us have to do with anything?

Elliot doesn't say anything and neither does Nell. Perhaps this is a turning point. Perhaps this is—as I would giddily point out to my students—a moment after which nothing will ever be the same.

"To be honest," says Sasha, all business, "I didn't think you'd be of much use. I didn't think you'd do anything differently from what you've ever done." She sighs. I could cut the tension in this car with a knife. "You weren't close."

She's right. At least as far as I'm concerned, and so I look to Elliot, who I hope can put her in her proper place. Whatever that even means. But he's looking out the window at Atlanta limping by.

"Listen," she says. There's not an ounce of apology in her voice. "I'm not pointing fingers or making accusations. But you guys haven't been around."

Now Elliot looks at her. His brow is furrowed. He's all business too. When did he go and get so old? When did he turn so grossly glum? "No," he says, his voice flat. "You're right. You're totally right. I just wish..." He pauses, searching for words, presumably.

"I'm not pointing fingers," Sasha says again. "He wasn't close to anyone but me and Mindy. His devotion was always to what was right in front of him." She's quiet for a minute, but I don't dare look at the rearview mirror; I'm afraid I'll find her staring right at me. "Hindsight is twenty-twenty," she says, and she stops at a red light. She turns in her seat and faces Elliot directly. "I didn't understand how bad it was. Do you know what I mean? I do now. I see it. And it's glaring. It's totally glaring. But I didn't see just how sick he must have been."

The stoplight changes and Nell says, "Green," and Sasha turns forward and once again we're moving.

As teachers, my colleagues and I are constantly being warned about how to deal with problem students: When confronted with a threat or by a violent situation, move immediately to safety. If safety is unavailable, move toward a door. Once through the door, lock it. If the door doesn't lock, secure or barricade it with chairs, desks, tables. If safety or a locked door isn't an option, approach someone for help. If there's no one there who can help, make yourself invisible and then get your story straight and remember as many of the facts and details as you can, because if this kid opens fire, you're going to need to explain how all this shit went down right in front of you. You're going to need to explain why you didn't see the signs before this exact moment when a gun or a knife or a bomb was finally involved.

I know what Sasha means about hindsight, and yet still.

"How did he pay for it all?" I ask, because it's the only way I know to change the subject. "Where was the money coming from?"

Elliot gives me this *what the aphid* look, but I don't care.

"He had a pension," she says. "It didn't amount to much. And I helped where I could."

"Was he depressed?" I ask.

Peter, about a year ago, accused me of being depressed. I accused him of not liking my stance on adoption.

Another red light, and Sasha looks at Nell and then turns to look at me and Elliot.

"Your father was a lot of things, including, I know, a bastard to the three of you. He was good to Mindy, though. Really. The chicken notwithstanding. He was good to her. And he was good to me for a little while." The stoplight turns from red to green, and Sasha steps on the gas slowly. "I don't know what your father was, honestly. He loved you. All three of you. But you don't need to hear that from me."

I wonder if ever he cheated on her. He was old, yes. But he was able to snag Sasha. There's always the chance that she was the first of his wives that he didn't step out on, though that seems unlikely.

Elliot gets out his phone and starts going at it with his thumbs. I lean back in my seat and look out the window at Atlanta. Here again are the dueling cathedrals, their gaudiness on full display in the daylight. And here again is the duck pond and the high-rise I lived in for a short period of time before we moved in with Joyce. My real life is seven hundred miles away from me, fairly convinced he never wants me back and already thinking of ways to cut me off. But here I am in this other place, this giant, hideous city, this place where we were born. And here we are, driving down Peachtree on our way to begin the doleful business of putting our father to rest at last.

15

---

at the funeral home

There's been some sort of confusion at the funeral home. Sasha was under the impression that Stan would be ready today, this morning, this moment. She and Nell are over in the corner now—Sasha gesticulating somewhat manically and Nell rubbing her shoulders periodically. I keep hearing, "It's okay. Really, it's okay." Elliot is out in the hallway with one of the directors. Elliot, I can tell from his mannerisms, is charading as a good old boy. Lots of "womenfolk"-type comments and "They'll be fine." But he's also getting the job done. He's figuring out when Stan *will* be ready for us to see—dressed, poised, restructured in the noggin. It seems as if everybody is at least on the same page that if we're going to do this open casket thing, we should preview the body and make sure it's decent enough for the children. Make sure whatever is going to show up in that box doesn't cause serious scarring.

It's now my job to go through the box of clothes Sasha

dropped off earlier. I'm meant to pick the right shirt and pair of pants, something the funeral director could have done, but since we're here now, it falls to me. How I'm the one who ended up with this chore beats me, but between dealing with the good old boys, dealing with Sasha, and sorting through my dead father's fashions, I guess I'd choose the latter.

These clothes are the clothes of an octogenarian. There's a pair of stonewashed jeans in here with, no fooling, pleats. My father was a good-looking man. He was taller than me, even, and a little bit Alan Alda–looking. He never carried weight and he always dressed to accentuate his height. But these clothes. These clothes belong more to Alan Arkin than to Alan Alda. There's even a pair of white orthopedic sneakers at the bottom that makes me wonder if he didn't recently suffer some sort of crippling fall.

I pick out the only pants that aren't pleated—khakis—and a long-sleeve button-down, white. This seems as good and inoffensive an outfit as any other to spend the next hundred years in. And if anybody has a problem with it, they can go through the box and pick something different. I really don't care.

Too many years of doing a man's laundry—who knows?—but I stick my hand down the back pockets of the khakis. Empty. But in the right front pocket there's a five-dollar bill. I look up. Sasha is still mewling in the corner and Nell is still comforting her.

I hadn't been looking for money. I hadn't been looking for anything. But now here's a five-dollar bill—a five-dollar bill that once belonged to my father. Nobody's watching me and so I take the money and shove it into my own right-hand pocket and discover, of course, the fiver left over from last night. A meaningless coincidence. Do not assign significance where there isn't any.

I slip out of the room with my sartorial decisions and walk past the little snack room where the coffee is made to what I believe is the main office. I knock, but no one answers. At the far end of the hall, Elliot is laughing at something the director has said. Or he's faux laughing. I twist the handle of the door in front of me and open it slightly.

A blast of cold air hits me. I open the door farther and realize too late where I am. I could close the door and turn around, but it wouldn't make a difference. I've already seen what this place is and what's on the tall silver table in front of me. I don't know the name for this room, but it's the place where they're keeping my father, because there he is, ten feet away from me. I feel light-headed. Thankfully he's covered—head to foot—but there's no doubt it's him. They can't get too many near-seven-footers. I'm tempted to step in, to pull back the sheet, to see exactly how much of my father's face they're going to be working with over the next forty-eight hours—how much they'll need to add, how much has already been taken away—but a hand on my lower back stops me.

"Easy there." It's the second funeral director. He's somehow gotten his other hand under my elbow. "I'm sorry you saw that," he says, pulling me back. "Looks like you were about to fall over."

He guides me away from the room and shuts the door, all in a single fluid movement.

"Are these the clothes you've chosen?"

I look down at my hands, at the pair of pants and the simple white shirt. I'd forgotten they were there. I nod.

"Let's get these to Vicky. She'll get them ironed and starched."

I hand the clothes over.

"No tie?" he says.

I shake my head. "He didn't like ties," I say, which isn't exactly true, because in his bedroom closet last night I found a laundry basket filled with bow ties. He must have liked them, or at least liked collecting them, but I'd never seen him actually wear a tie.

"Keeping it simple," he says. "Remembering the man as he was, keeping him comfortable. I like that."

"Thanks," I say.

He is walking me back toward the room where my sister is probably still comforting Sasha. All these rooms have names, I'm sure—grieving room, snack room, deal room, reception room, private grieving room, argumentation room, mediation room, et cetera, et cetera. Maybe one's the money room.

"I knew one family," says the man, "who buried their beloved in his favorite pajamas and a rabbit-fur hunting cap."

"Really?"

"And a pair of wool socks," he says. "He hated to be cold."

"That seems disrespectful."

The man shrugs. We are outside the disappointed-customers room. My brain feels flimsy. Sasha looks under control where they've finally got her seated at the table. Nell and Elliot are on either side of her looking through some sort of large catalog.

"Different strokes," says the man. "I'll leave you with your people."

Your people. Beloved. The South and its terminology.

Sasha looks up at me. "You didn't pick the jeans, did you? I didn't really mean to put them in there."

"No," I say. "Did he ever wear those?"

"He came home in them one day," she says. "He liked how roomy they were."

"I picked a pair of khakis."

"Good," she says. "Thanks." She gives me this small, sad smile, and I think, in another life, I wouldn't have hated her necessarily. In another life, if I'd run into her at a coffee shop or a party, I might not even have minded talking to her for a few minutes.

"What are you guys looking at?" I say. I don't make a move to join them at the table.

"Urns," says Elliot, turning the page in front of him.

"I thought we were burying him."

"He wanted to be cremated," says Nell. "After the viewing, they'll—you know. So we're just looking for something that isn't hideous."

"Is that expensive?" I say.

"Is what expensive?" says Elliot, still not looking up.

"All of it," I say. "If we're not burying him in the coffin, are we still buying it? Is that what's done?"

Sasha still has her eyes on me, which I find more than a little disconcerting. "Don't worry about the money," she says.

Elliot flips a few more pages. "We'll help out," he says. "Kate and Nell and I—we'll help with the costs."

This is news to me. This is absolutely news to me. But here's the thing: Does it piss me off because I can't afford to chip in, or because it demonstrates Elliot's blithe (and there-fore enviable) relationship with money?

"No," says Sasha. "I mean, don't worry about it because it's covered. We planned."

This gets Elliot's attention. Not money. But this. Must be nice.

"You *planned*?" he says. "That doesn't sound like Dad."

"When Mindy was born," she says, her eyes still on me. "He insisted. It was his idea. He didn't want to be a burden."

A novel idea.

"Kate," says Sasha. "What do you think?"

About the fact that my father turned sixty and became a completely different person? The fact that he woke up one day and decided that he no longer wanted to be a burden? The fact that he shot himself and somehow failed to consider the potential *emotional* burden?

"What are you talking about?" I say.

"The urn," she says.

Oh, right: the urn. *Of course.*

"I trust you guys," I say.

"I think we should keep it really simple. Just a wooden box," says Sasha.

"Do they even have that option?" says Nell, still browsing the photographs with Elliot. Their interest in the catalog is gross. Like they're looking for some answer to the human condition in its glossy pages.

"People are odd," says Elliot. "Look at this one."

Nell laughs. "That's so garish."

Someone should point out to them that they're acting like—what's the word?—children. But for some reason I don't think that person should be me. If only the funeral director would tell them how to behave—tell us *all* how to behave— we could go about our day and get on with our lives already.

"Elliot," says Nell, her voice high and excited. She taps a picture in front of her.

"I know," he says. "Jesus."

There's a quiet hysteria lingering on the other side of Sasha's eyeballs. Ten to one, she's medicated in some way, slightly sedated with one or two pink or yellow pills. "They can divide the ashes," she says. "They can do a few tiny boxes if you want." She says this still to me, like I'm the only one in the room worth talking to. (There's an idea.) For some reason she's latched onto me, as if having finally found eye contact, she is afraid to let it go.

I shake my head. "One box," I say. "Wooden sounds nice." The idea of lots of miniature boxes, handed out to all his ex-wives and children, is a little too surreal. It's one thing that we're doing this open casket, it's something else entirely to hand out ashes like they're party favors.

Elliot snaps the catalog closed and stands up. Sasha jumps a little and I think, *Yes, definitely medicated.*

"Let's blow this joint," he says, which seems almost as vulgar as burying some guy in a hunting cap. Rabbit fur or no rabbit fur.

Nell stands and puts a hand on Sasha's shoulder. Finally I am released from the zombie's stare.

"Is there still barbecue around the corner?" says Elliot. "I'm starved."

Maybe, just maybe, I can get my hands on some of Sasha's pills.

a momentary detour: finances explained

Let's get this out of the way. When I married Peter, he helped me enroll in a debt-management program. The payments were obscene the first half year: fifteen hundred dollars a month. Plenty of people say they want to get their finances under control. Few people stick it out. Or rather, few people can. I have the statistics. That's part of the welcoming package.

Also part of the welcoming package is a pamphlet all about food stamps and directions to the Angel Food Ministry warehouse on the South Side of Chicago. When I saw these things, when I opened the brochure and saw the words *Angel Food Ministry*, I went to the bathroom and vomited. Then I went to Peter.

"This is wrong," I said. "You've signed me up for the wrong program."

I held out the food stamp application.

He patted his knee, and I sat on his lap.

"I'm a good person," I said. "I shouldn't have this stuff."

"That's a fairly uninformed comment to make."

"I just mean," I said, "I was raised better than this."

He kissed me on the cheek. "Fortunately," he said, "you have me." He took the pamphlets from my hands. "We don't need these. We're some of the lucky ones." He tapped the pamphlet all about food stamps. "I don't think you'd qualify anyway."

I put my head on his shoulder. We'd been married less than a year. "I don't feel lucky," I said.

"You have no idea," he said.

We stayed like that for a while. He stroked my hair. I closed my eyes and thought about how nice it might feel to be crying. But then I sat up. I looked him square in the face. "Peter," I said. "Peter, you have to promise me one thing."

"Anything," he said. "Name it."

"You can never tell Nell. Or Elliot. They'd disown me."

"They wouldn't," he said.

"They'd be mortified."

"Plenty of people go into debt," he said. "You should be proud of yourself for getting a handle on it."

But I wasn't raised to be plenty of people. I was raised to be a Pulaski.

"Promise me," I said.

"Yes, yes," he said. "Done."

So I JOINED THE PROGRAM and made it through the first six months, paying $750 every two weeks, which was essentially three quarters of my total monthly paycheck. This left me a little less than a hundred dollars a week to spend on gas and the occasional lunch out. Peter covered groceries, the mortgage, the cars, the insurance, the phones, the power, the gas. Everything.

After half a year, the installment was cut back to a thousand a month. But by then my school loans had come due (three hundred dollars a month), plus there were the back taxes (a hundred dollars a month).

Which brings us to where I am now: the balance left on the credit cards is seven thousand. Keep in mind, I once owed forty-eight thousand. Forty-eight to seven! The back taxes are a little higher—eleven grand—but the interest is so much better. Provided I never screw up again and I pay all my future quarterlies on time, the IRS shouldn't inhibit me too much once the credit cards are finally paid off. As far as school debt goes: everyone has school debt. Everyone pays a few hundred toward their education each month. (As long as we're talking turkey, I now pay $186, having talked them down from the original $300.) So it's not like I'm a pariah for that. In fact, I probably owe less than a lot of people.

The conflict—the tangling up or the *noument*, as I would point out to my students—is the next ten months. My last biweekly paycheck before fall semester arrives next week: $1,050. The day after, $500 will automatically be withdrawn from my account. That leaves me two weeks and $550 before the next withdrawal. And in that time, if Peter and I actually split up, I am supposed to move out of my home, put a deposit on a rental, and find a summer job—summer job! What am I? Twenty?—that will cover not just my basic bills (food, board) but also my nonbasic bills (taxes, debt).

What all this boils down to: I've let my upbringing down. Plain and simple. I was raised thinking we had money, comfort. I was raised thinking that same money and comfort would filter naturally into my own bank account. I could blame my father for this—for his bad planning. But how do I account for Elliot and Nell? How do I account for the fact that they were able to make their own money and comfort? They lived up to their private school expectations. I did not.

The truth: In this country, money is everything. It's freedom. It's everywhere. Even when people aren't talking about it, they're talking about it. I'm not saying it's happiness. But I'm also not saying it's not. It's the difference between sleeping at night and not sleeping at night. It's the difference between a spontaneous dinner out and a freaked-out heartbeat because you might not have enough in your account to pay for all the groceries that are moving rapidly down the belt in the direction of the register.

Are you really saying that the person who has to put back a bunch of bananas in front of a line of strangers isn't more likely to be depressed than the dude who pays twelve dollars for a glass of wine without a second thought? That the young woman who has two five-dollar bills in her pocket and fifty dollars in the bank isn't more prone to sleep disorders than the dipshit who nonchalantly offers to help cover unexpected funeral costs?

Fat chance.

picking up Mindy

Somehow Sasha and Nell have talked Elliot into agreeing that the three of us should move our stuff from Dad's place to Sasha's. Given the state of things—boxes of dirty dishes, random collections of ashtrays and television sets, not to mention the powerful smell of misery—it makes sense even to me that we not stay another night on those terrible makeshift pallets.

And so now we're on our way to Holy Innocents' to pick up Mindy from school-slash-daycare before heading back to Sasha's. Whenever the Volvo stops long enough—in a parking lot, outside a store—Elliot hops out and calls Rita. His mood is completely dependent on whether or not she answers. So far, nobody has noticed that I'm not on the phone with Peter every five minutes. So far, nobody's said anything about it at all. When no one was looking, outside the funeral home, I texted him one line: *Can we talk?* It's only been a few hours, but he hasn't written back yet. I'm trying to limit how often I let myself check for a response.

Nell has offered to cook dinner for everyone—like a family, which is how she said it—so we've gone to the Harris Teeter and picked up enough food for a small army. Was it deliberate that I chose to find the restroom just as they were turning the cart toward the checkout? Does it matter?

When we pull up to Holy Innocents', Sasha leaves the car running and I stay by myself in the backseat. Elliot gets out and leans against the trunk and dials Rita, and Nell and Sasha head toward the front entrance together.

"We'll just be a minute," says Sasha over her shoulder. "You sure you don't want to come?"

"I saw too much of this place when I went to school here," I say, and it's true. Just being in the parking lot gives me the heebie-jeebies. I've got that feeling in my stomach like the first time I tried to spend the night away from home at a friend's house and ended up puking the evening away into the toilet. There was nothing wrong with me. Nothing but nerves. Stan—and I do give him credit for this, but it's like giving credit to a hermit for remembering to say hello, because, I mean, congrats, he got *one* tidbit of parenting right, well done there—came to get me at three in the morning and didn't even give me a hard time about it. But then, those were the days of Whitney and he probably welcomed the chance to get away from her. No one liked Whitney, especially not Stan.

My phone buzzes. It's a text from Rita: *Tell Elliot I'm fine. I'll call later. OK? Ell = driving me nuts*. I turn and look outside the rear window of the Volvo. Elliot is looking at his phone like it's disobeyed him. My phone buzzes again. *Don't tell him about nuts. Haha.* I delete the messages and knock on the glass. He comes over to my side of the car and I open the door.

"Rita's fine," I say.

"How do you know?"

"She says she'll call you later."

"You talked to her?"

"No."

"She texted?"

"Yes."

He kicks the rear tire.

"Let me see the text," he says.

I look at my phone.

"I deleted it," I say.

"Why?"

"I don't know," I say and, truly, I don't. It was instinctive. It felt utterly natural at the time. Perhaps I have the instincts of an adulterer. Perhaps they have seeped into me and changed the course of my life for good. Perhaps it's hereditary and there is no going back. Or perhaps I am naturally secretive, I have always been naturally secretive, always looking ahead to the chance that someone might say "Let me see" or "Prove it to me," but I never have to worry because the evidence is already gone. Deleted before it was even considered evidence.

"What's going on with you?" says Elliot. "You're different."

"Dude," I say. "What's going on with *you*? I haven't seen you like this with Rita since you started going out. You're like a little boy with that phone."

"Forget it," he says.

"Fine," I say.

I feel so far away from Elliot, which makes my guts feel gnawed out. There's a piranha swimming around, filling up on my intestines. All I want is for Elliot to hug me again, like he did at the airport, and tell me that this—*life*—is going to be okay. It's all going to be okay. And the thing is, I know that if I were simply to ask him, if I were simply to knock again on the glass and ask for a hug, he'd give it to me in a heartbeat, but for some reason I just can't. I don't want to have to ask. I want it offered. I want someone to read my mind and I want it to be him.

My phone buzzes again. I'm about to hold it out the window—to show the evidence to Elliot and prove both to him and to myself that I don't have to be cagey and guarded if I don't want to—but the text is from my agent, not from Rita.

Call me. I have a crazy idea.

My agent and I are not close. An unnecessary detail, but I'm trying to keep everything as accurate as possible. The point is, this text is out of the ordinary. I didn't even know she was capable of texting. In fact, I can't remember the last time we were in touch.

I lean back against the seat and close my eyes. Peter says I have phobias. He says that waking up in the middle of the night isn't natural. He says the lists I make aren't natural. He said, "Most people don't keep lists of their secrets." I said, "What makes you think there are secrets?" He said, "There's an easier way. You're depressed." I told him I wasn't depressed. I told him, "I'm happy as a clam." He said, "Yes, fine, but there's something wrong." He said, "You're not exactly cool as a cucumber right now." I said, "I'm good. I'm great." He said, "I can feel your heartbeat racing under your sweater." I said, "That's unusual, huh?" He said, "Have you thought of Paxil?" I said, "I spent my teens sleeping under the kitchen table because of Prozac." He said, "I know that." I said, "No, I haven't thought of Paxil, and anyway, I'm not depressed. Don't try to be my therapist." He said, "Stop putting me in that position, then." He says I have a phobia of old age and honesty. He says I have a fear of the dark. I said, "Plenty of people are scared of the dark. It's a reasonable fear. An unreasonable fear? Flying." He said, "Paxil would help you not panic. It would help with your OCD." I said, "OCD? Get out of here." I told him no Paxil. What I should have done was ask for Xanax or Valium, but I get the impression that therapists—even husband therapists—don't like giving out narcotics when you ask for them by name. I get the impression that they like to be the ones to come up with the idea. I wonder if Sasha gets her little pink pills legally. I wonder if she gets them from some doctor she knows socially or from a real therapist. These are things I'm interested in finding out. Also: whether or not she's the type of woman who likes to share.

A bell inside the school goes off loudly enough for us to hear it in the parking lot. It's the same bell from twenty-five years ago. I turn and watch as the littlest children file out in groups. I spot Sasha and a minute later I see Nell. At her side—at my *sister's* side and holding her hand—is Mindy. She's bigger than the last time I saw her. She's thinned out. She's tall and lanky and kind of gray.

Elliot is beside me again, standing at the open door. He punches me in the arm.

"Oh my God," he says.

"I know," I say, rubbing my forearm. "We're not going to be expected to hold her hand, are we?"

"What?" he says. "No, look at her."

I look at the little girl who is hanging on my sister. All I can see is that she is hanging on my sister. All I can think is, *Why is she hanging on my sister?*

"She's the spitting image," Elliot says.

"Of who?"

"Of you," he says. *"Look."*

And I do. I look at her, at this lanky, awkward, gray little thing headed right toward us. She's wearing a cap-sleeved shirt with a Peter Pan collar, and she's got it half tucked in, half tucked out of a blue-checkered Dorothy dress. She's an absolute mess and I can't take my eyes off her.

"So much for being adopted," he says. "You've definitely got Dad's DNA," which is something I'm increasingly aware of.

driving back to Sasha's place

It's a thirty-minute drive back to Sasha's place in Druid Hills. I've had to scoot to the middle so Mindy can sit in her booster seat, which Sasha had been hiding in the trunk. She's different than I remember, this little kid is. She doesn't know why we're in town—Sasha hasn't told her about Stan's "passing"— and it's not really clear if she fully comprehends who we are. Yes, she understands the terms *half sister* and *half brother*, but she seems ultimately unimpressed by the idea, which I don't mind, given that I'm ultimately unimpressed by the idea as well. She also seems curiously attuned to Nell, as in, "Nell, guess what?" and "Nell, did you know . . . ?" and "Nell, ask me a knock-knock joke, but you have to start it." To me she says nothing, just shoots an occasional and skeptical peek. Elliot might as well be in a different country, sitting a full seat away from her.

"Kiddo," says Sasha, looking into the rearview at Mindy, not at me. "These guys are going to stay with us for a few days. I told Nell and Kate they could have your room. How's that sound?"

Mindy pinches at the air in front of her as if there's a delicate spiderweb she's considering dismantling.

"Where do I sleep, then?"

"In my bed."

"When?"

"Tonight."

"*Tomorrow* tonight?"

"*Tonight* tonight." Sasha glances at me and Elliot. She says, "We're struggling with the idea of tomorrow." She doesn't say this to Nell, though. It's like Nell has the skinny on all this already. Like everything that Elliot and I have to be told, Nell already knows. It's just trickled in somehow, instant osmosis.

Elliot nods. "Pigpie has no idea about time," he says, looking at his phone. When parents talk about their children, it's like they're on autopilot. They don't even have to turn on their brains to recount the most recent cuteness. "She cries every night thinking that school is starting in an hour. She can't account for the hours when she's sleeping." It seems like a reasonable enough difficulty to me.

Sasha says to Elliot, "Pigpie. That's Ellie, right?"

"That's right." He puts down his phone finally. Normally Elliot loves all conversations children-related. "First grade."

"No kidding," says Sasha. "We're in second."

"Really?" I feel Elliot squirming next to me. He hates the idea of parents who live through their children's achievements, and likewise he hates the idea of parents who create competitions where there shouldn't be any. In theory at least. "Second, huh?"

"It was a big class last year; they were looking for students to place out."

"And Mindy placed out?"

"People don't believe me, but she was reading at three."

Elliot is silently nodding. He's not pissed. But I can feel him going through the calculations. I can feel him mapping out the six years of Pigpie's life. Maybe they shouldn't have encouraged her to be so physical. Maybe they should have enforced Sunday morning reading time. Of course, I could be wrong. I could be completely making this up, but his rigid arm against mine suggests otherwise.

"So, kiddo," says Sasha, again in the rearview. "What do you think about staying in my bedroom tonight?"

"Fine," she says, still pinching her invisible web. "Bleh. Fine." Pinch, pinch, pinch.

Seriously? This kid placed out of something? Elliot should take a harder look at her. Pigpie wins by twenty. But then, I'd also like for him to take back what he said about Mindy being my spitting image. Was I really that gray as a child? Was I sickly?

Thinking mean thoughts about a child—a stranger's child, a relative's child, my half sister, who happens to *be* a child— always makes me feel kind of small and a little bit guilty. It makes me feel like the bully I never was. I tap Mindy on the knee. This is my silent apology for an offense she isn't even aware of. I am smiling insanely. She looks up at me with wet, wide eyes. I've scared her. Either that, or she's offended that I've touched her without asking. Smart kid.

"My nickname is kiddo, too," I say. "Did you know that?"

"I'm kiddo," she says.

"Right," I say. "But me too."

"How can you be kiddo if I'm kiddo?" She turns and looks out the window. This is an open-and-shut case. To her, the question is rhetorical, not even deserving of a response. But actually, it's not a bad question. How *can* I be kiddo if she's kiddo, too? My answer is, she *shouldn't* be kiddo. My answer is, I'm the original kiddo. It was supposed to stop with me. The same way the rocking chair was supposed to be mine. I was the last kid; it wasn't supposed to keep getting more babies to rock to sleep. But it did. There's a flaw to my logic. There's a piece missing. But I can't see it.

Nell turns from the front seat and squeezes Mindy's wizened knee bone. Mindy squeals with delight and throws her head back.

Nell says, "Want to help me with dinner tonight?"

"Can I cut?"

"Hmm," says Nell. "Maybe not cut, but there's plenty of other dangerous stuff for you to do."

"I like dangerous," says Mindy.

"I bet you do," says Nell. And it's possible I am making this up, it's absolutely possible, but when she turns back toward the front, it looks like Nell's just winked at Sasha and that Sasha, Stan's widow, has winked back. I look at Elliot, who's missed everything. He's tapping on his phone like a schoolboy obsessed. He's worse than my students. Oh man, if Nell and Sasha turn out to be lovers, this weekend might not be a total bust after all. Here's hoping there's a surprise announcement at dinner.

"Two muffins," Mindy is saying to no one in particular, "are baking in an oven. The first muffin turns to the second muffin and says, 'Wooo, it's hot in here.'" She raises her voice in a Southern-sounding singsong. No one says anything. My skin is starting to itch. She continues, "And then the second muffin screams, 'Holy cow! A talking muffin!'" Mindy squeals again. Nell and Sasha chuckle from the front seat. Elliot tap-tap-taps on his cell phone.

What the aphid is going on in this car?

---

the back porch, before dinner

The crickets are up in arms out here. They're rubbing their forewings raw, like there's no tomorrow. It's not just kids who struggle with time, with the idea of tomorrow. It's most of life, I think. The only things that don't struggle to understand the concept are adult *Homo sapiens*. We don't struggle with its idea. No. We struggle with its existence, with its certainty. We know tomorrow will come whether we want it to or not. That's the problem. That's the problem right there.

Miraculously, I have been left alone for the last thirty minutes. And in that time—sitting out here on Sasha's homey back porch—and against my better judgment, I have sent Peter just over a dozen text messages. To my credit—*credit!* Ha!—I've only called him once. I hung up when it went to voice mail.

I have no idea what I'll say to him if he does call me back or if he ever answers. *I'm sorry* isn't seeming to cut it. What he wants, perhaps, is an explanation. What he wants is for me to be honest about what *I* want. But again, I'm struggling here, because I don't really know what I want. I don't know how to prove total transparency because I'm not sure what's hidden or what needs to be revealed. There's a story I read once about a magic hat that you could put on your head, let absorb every single one of your emotions—even the ones there aren't yet words for—then take off, put on someone else's head, and then sit back and watch as the understanding slowly oozes in. But that hat doesn't exist. Not in real life. And besides, it might actually be too late. He might actually have gone through the process of un-loving me. In which case all these text messages and phone calls are completely fruitless. Still, I can't help thinking his level of anger at the airport yesterday is a good sign. In country songs, complacency equals death; struggle, anger, jealousy—these are the telltale signs of enduring love. If only I were living in a country song. A country song or a chick flick.

Instead of texting Peter again, I text my agent.

Crazy how? I write.

Ten seconds later my phone is ringing. It's her. It's Marcy.

"Hi," she says. Marcy has this super-soft voice that refuses analysis, which is to say she is impossible to read.

"What's up?" I say.

"Kate," she says. "First. I'm sorry about your father."

The crickets buzz happily in the yard. *Me too*, they're saying. *We're sorry too. Us too.* But they're crickets, so they can't help saying it with smiles on their faces, which makes them sound disingenuous.

"How do you know about my father?"

"Peter emailed."

Peter emailed? *Peter emailed?* The crickets don't like it, either. Since when does my husband email my agent? *Since when?* the crickets say. *Since when? Since when?*

"He did?" I say.

"Of course he did."

Of course, of course, say the crickets.

"What else did he say?"

"What else *was* there to say? He just wanted me to know, and I'm *so* glad he did."

"Okay," I say. "Thanks."

"Can I ask?" she says. "Don't be mad. But can I ask, was it really suicide?"

What *didn't* Peter tell her?

"Yes," I say.

Yes, yes, yes, yes. These crickets are meddlesome little things.

"And can I ask also—" Her breathiness is getting away from her. Her voice is on the rise. "Was it—? What I mean is, did he—? With a—?"

"He shot himself, Marcy."

The crickets are quiet.

But only for a moment.

"That's what I thought," she says. The breathiness is gone completely now, and I realize—holy shit—this is what excitement sounds like. This is the first time in my life I've heard my agent be excited.

"So listen," she is saying.

Listen, listen, listen, listen. Fickle crickets.

"I have an idea," she says. I wait. "You should write it."

"Write what?"

"Do you think you could?"

"A movie?" I say. "Dead dad? That's been done."

"Not a movie," she says. "A memoir."

Memoir?

"I don't write memoirs."

"Listen," she says. "I pitched it."

"You pitched it?"

"To a friend," she says. "I got Peter's email when I was having lunch with this editor and—"

"Where are you?"

"In New York," she says.

"Why aren't you in L.A.?"

"Will you listen to me, please?" she says. "Memoir is huge right now. Suicide is huger."

"I barely knew my father."

"You could use the trip as research."

"No."

"You could interview family members."

"No."

"Your brother and sister."

"They'd hate me," I say, which isn't necessarily true. They'd probably like to be included.

"You could talk to all his wives," she says.

Wives! Now there's a word the crickets like. *Wives! Wives!*

"Weren't there a million wives?"

Wives! Yes! Wives! Wives! Wives! We love veeeeeees!

I've long suspected that agents keep notes about their clients—that before any phone call with any client, they get out their notes and read the meticulously kept mini biographies.

"I can't talk to you anymore," I say.

Sigh.

"Kate." She's recouped a smidgeon of softness. "Memoir pays," she says. "There's money in memoir. You might not like it, but there's money in suicide."

"That's disgusting."

"Is it?"

Is it? Is it?

"I have to go," I say.

"Just think about it," she says. "You're dead as a screenwriter. I'm not saying that to be manipulative. I'm saying it because we both know it's true."

She stops talking and I let the silence linger long enough to remind her that I'm in control, that she works for me.

And then, out of nowhere, I say, "Peter and I are trying to have a baby."

"But I thought—"

"We're looking into in vitro," I say. "Maybe adoption."

Veeeeetro!

"Wow," she says, and I think for a minute that I've won. That I've stopped her in her tracks and we've nowhere left to go with this conversation. I'm wrong: "But still," she says. "A baby. The money could only help."

Sasha—lifesaver—appears at the screen door. "Knock knock," she whispers.

"Marcy," I say to the phone. "I really have to go."

"Think about it," she says.

I wait for the crickets to mimic her one final time, but they shake their heads. *We're sticking with VEEEtro!*

And so I hang up on my agent.

Sasha's standing on the other side of the screen door, inside her house, knocking to be let out.

"Hey," I say.

She's changed into denim shorts and a T-shirt.

"Am I interrupting?" She pushes the screen door all the way open and walks onto the back porch.

"Nope," I say. "Not at all."

"You want some lemonade?"

"Something stronger maybe?"

"Ha," she says. "That's what Nell said you'd say." She produces a glass from behind her back. "Here." I take the glass. "She also said you don't mind ice in your wine."

"Not when I'm in Georgia, I don't."

I take a sip.

"Mind if I sit?"

I scoot over on the swing in answer and pocket my phone. Sasha says nothing, just pushes us back and forth, and I have this flash of a memory. It's me and Stan. We're on a porch swing just like this, but we're at his mother's house. He's sitting next to me, rocking us back and forth. My feet are too short to touch the concrete floor and so I just sit and let us be rocked. Behind us is the roar of I-85, but before us is an untapped wooded area and a small creek. He's got his hands in the air in front of us, but he's not asking me to hit him. He's making hand animals. "Giraffe," he says, then brings his middle finger and pinkie together with his thumb so that a mouth is formed. His pointer and ring finger aim forward, the animal's horns. "Rooster," he says, then makes a fist of his left hand and presses it against his right, the fingers of which are splayed like a crown. He cocks his left pointer just slightly, and I can see where the eye would be. It's just a flash, but I feel it in my gut before it vanishes.

"Listen to the crickets," I say. Sasha is quiet a minute.

"Nuh-uh," she says. "Those are cicadas."

Now I listen. "For real?"

"Yeah, see, listen. Crickets are high-pitched, more staccato. But the cicadas are louder and they make a longer sound and go slow to fast. Like, *chicka-chicka-chicka-chickachickachicka-chiiiiiii-kah*." Well, that's not *quite* what they're saying, but—

I listen again, and I can hear what she's talking about immediately. "I never thought I'd forget the difference," I say. "I never thought I'd lose the Georgian so thoroughly." I give Atlanta a hard time and I certainly give my father's people a hard time. When it comes right down to it, though, I like being from Georgia. But it requires being somewhere else for me to appreciate how special it is. It's a bad relationship—or maybe the truest kind of relationship. Look. I'm trying to be honest. I like it best when it's not around. Because it lives in my memory, completely malleable, completely disposed to my own fantasies and imaginations. It's a cool thing to be able to say when I'm in Chicago—that I'm a Georgia peach—but when I'm here, the skin isn't so fuzzy.

"So listen," says Sasha.

Of course. This private moment between us is an orchestrated one. Ten to one, she has a favor to ask.

"I have a favor."

Ha.

"I need to tell Mindy about her father—about your father," she says. "If the viewing's in two days, then I need to tell her soon."

I nod. "Completely agree."

"What I'd like…" She leans back against the swing and lifts her legs so she can hold them against her chest. She probably does yoga. "What I'd like is to do it at dinner. Tonight. And I'd like us all to be on the same page."

"I'm listening." Same page? Isn't there only one? The man is dead.

"I'm not religious," she says.

"Me neither." I take a sip of wine and crunch down on a cube of ice. The advantage of sitting side by side like this is that I at least don't have to maintain any kind of manic eye contact with her like I did earlier.

"Right, well, Mindy's different," she says. "She picked up some body-of-Christ, blood-of-heaven stuff at a particular friend's house and at school and she's latched on."

I remember Wednesdays at Holy Innocents'—the cracker, the grape juice. We were allowed to take Communion whether we'd been baptized or not. Although, now that I think of it, it's more likely it was an honor code type of thing. It was probably up to us to self-regulate, which seems like a pretty tall order for a second grader. I wonder if Stan knew what I was up to. I wonder if he sometimes looked down at me and thought, *This one. This one's keeping secrets.*

"Okay," I say.

"So I was thinking I might couch his departure—just for her sake—as, well, just that. A departure."

"Okay."

"And I just wanted to give you a heads up."

"Sounds totally fair."

"And also, you know, if we could not say anything about his involvement in the process, that would also be great."

"You mean his involvement in his death."

"Right."

"You mean the fact that he shot himself."

"Right."

"In the head."

"Right."

"Suicide."

"Exactly," she says, placing her feet back on the floor and steadying the swing. "If we could just avoid that word for the next few days, I'd really appreciate it."

I crunch another cube and answer while I'm chewing: "You got it, chief. Mum's the word."

Tomorrow will come. So will the next day. These things are inevitable. One day Mindy will learn that her father put a gun in his mouth and pulled the trigger. One day she will learn that *the blood of heaven* is just a scary-sounding group of words that's had an uncanny effect on millions of people. One day Peter will call me back, and he'll explain what he meant by emailing my agent behind my back. One day I'll return to Chicago. These things are certain. As certain as tomorrow. The only thing that isn't certain is, which tomorrow?

————

cooking dinner, getting drunk

In the kitchen, Mindy is standing on a stool, watching water boil, and Nell is holding court over a pot of tomatoes. She's stripped down to boxers and a wifebeater, on top of which she's wearing an apron.

"Nice look," I say.

"It's too hot," she says. "I didn't think I'd offend anyone."

"As long as we're the only guests." I open the refrigerator and look around until I've spotted the bottle of wine. "Ta-da," I say, and pour another glass.

"Guests don't arrive until tomorrow," says Nell.

"Where's Elliot?" I say. "Did he talk to Rita yet?"

"They're talking now," she says. "I think. Here." She holds a wooden spoon in front of my mouth. "Try."

"Good," I say. "Really good." I take a sip of wine. Mindy is staring at the water like her life depends on it. I'm tempted to say something, try out an old adage on her, but I like whatever spell the water's working. Let sleeping dogs lie, right?

"Wait," I say. "What guests?"

"It's weird, right?" says Nell, her back to me now, her shoulder blades moving this way and that on either side of the tank top. It's an unusual look for her. In San Francisco, she's always so well put together. Even her pajamas look silky and ready for viewing. This is a fashion statement I've not seen Nell rock before. "The way Rita and Ell are being?"

I'm still puzzling over the boxers and beater, but I'm with it enough to be able to tell her about the texts Rita sent while we were in the parking lot at Holy Innocents'.

"And she didn't say anything else?" says Nell, turning to face me.

"No," I say. "But, seriously, what other guests are we expecting?"

"Ah," says Nell. "I was hoping you weren't paying attention."

Mindy turns on her stool suddenly and looks at me. Like her mother, she picks unexpected moments for intense, direct eye contact. She's like a dog trying desperately to tell me something. Only this dog can speak.

"What's an angel?" she says, apropos—as far as I know—of nothing.

I gulp down some wine.

"Not the right person for that question, Little Bit," I say.

"An angel is a fairy," Mindy says.

Nell winks at me.

"Is that what they teach you in school?" The school wasn't so intense with its religiosity when I was young.

"Fairies can fly," says Mindy, whose cheeks have turned rosy with the heat of the boiling water and who, as a result, looks slightly more alive than when we picked her up. She's a little less gray.

"Fairies can fly and angels can fly?" I say. "Is that the connection?"

Mindy looks at me like I'm the stupidest person she's ever met. Maybe I am. "Angels can't fly," she says. "They aren't real."

I nod. Her logic is even goofier than mine.

"There are real fairies and fake fairies," she says. "Angels are fake."

"Whatever you say." I look to Nell for help out of this conversation, but she's gone back to her tomatoes.

"Like boxes," says Mindy.

I cock my head. Now, maybe, we are getting somewhere.

"Not all boxes are squares," says Mindy, "but all squares are boxes."

"Not quite," I say, "but I like where your brain is headed." And truly, I do. There's something odd at work in this little girl. She's not exactly making foolproof connections, but I'll be damned if there isn't a little mind in there after all, furiously trying to make sense of the world around her. I know what it feels like—that rat wheel on high speed all the time. Nell's right, maybe. I should give this one a chance. It's not her fault—like it's not my fault or Nell's fault or Elliot's—that Stan Pulaski is our biological father. *Was. Was* our biological father.

But Mindy is bored with me and now she picks up a silicone spatula and begins stirring the pot of water slowly. *Witch's brew*, I think. *Bubble bubble, toil and trouble*, but I don't say any of that aloud.

I walk over and stand shoulder to shoulder with Nell. Well, not shoulder to shoulder, but her shoulder to my bicep. "Back to the guests," I say quietly, so as not to distract Mindy on the other side of the stove top.

"Some people are coming over tomorrow," says Nell.

"Like for a keening?" I whisper.

"Ha," she says. "More like a wake."

"For Stan."

"Yes."

I watch as Nell adds spices to her tomatoes and stirs them slowly. There are only so many people who would be interested in attending a wake for Stan Pulaski. They are the same people who would be interested in a funeral. I'm not anxious to see any of them.

"These *people*," I say. "They're coming *here*? To *this* house?"

"Yes."

"A party?"

"Sasha thought it was the right thing to do," she says. "To host something."

"How many people are we talking about?"

"A dozen or so." She's turned away from me now. She's turned to Mindy and is pretending to help her stir the boiling water. *A dozen or so* is how we talk about our father's "extended" family—the wives and children he had after our mother died.

"A dozen or so?" I say. "Seriously? All of them?"

"You thought they wouldn't come?" she says, finally looking at me. "For real, Kate. They're part of the family."

"What family?"

"*Our* family."

I can't even begin to formulate a coherent response to this suggestion—not one that won't end in girl screams and hair pulling. So what I say is "Does Elliot know?" which is almost always my default objection when rational words fail me.

"Yes," says Nell. "Just get on board already."

I go to the fridge, pull the wine out again, and pour the last third of the bottle into my glass, knowing full well Nell is watching and therefore judging. She knows me for the cheap date I am.

Nell nudges Mindy in the side. "Check it out, kiddo," she says.

Mindy turns and looks at me. They are both looking at me now.

"Somebody's throwing a tantrum," says Nell, and the two of them giggle and then go back to their respective pots.

—·—

the ex-wives, explained

If I'm being childish, it's for a reason. And maybe Nell is right, maybe I am throwing a tantrum, but it seems like someone should. It seems like a tantrum regarding our father and all his wives and children is long overdue. The three of us were happy enough simply to slip away—to leave Atlanta, to turn the other cheek. We never got high and mighty, we just saw that Stan had checked out on us and so we did the same. But now the man is gone—irrevocably and selfishly so—and now there are these women circling like sharks, and Nell is going to tell me with a straight face that they're part of the family? *Our* family? When we've never and they've never made any attempts at anything loving or inclusive before? It reeks of turds. The whole thing reeks of manure and turds. I should be making a connection right now. I should be think-ing of Peter and his accusations—that *I* am a phony; that *my* emotions smell of turds. But I'm not there yet. Not in the way I need to be to make it count. Sure, I can *see* the connection, but I can't see it well enough to understand what it means. I can't see it well enough yet to care.

There were five wives total. The first, Mimi, was our mother. If she hadn't gotten sick, if she hadn't been too weak to fight, maybe the others wouldn't have existed in our lives, or maybe they would have. Nell and Elliot say our parents were happy before her diagnosis. But they were kids. They weren't yet ten years old. How accurate could their memories actually be? A child's brain is mush. A child's brain is like oatmeal, as far as I'm concerned.

So Mimi, our mother, came first. She and Stan met in school. Mom was a women's lib major, or whatever they were calling it then; Stan was an engineer. They met, they fell in love, they married, they procreated.

Whitney came along four years after Mom died. She was a botanist and worked at the Atlanta zoo. Our best guess is that Stan thought he was marrying our cure—a woman who could beat our blues: take them outside, chop them up, and be done with them for good. We also guess that his motivation was as simple as finding and marrying what essentially became a live-in babysitter. These are the excuses we've come up with, and as far as Whitney goes, excuses are necessary. She was the kind of stepmother people write bad screenplays about. She's the one who locked me out of the house overnight when my father was gone on business and I had to call the Rutherglens from a pay phone to come pick me up and let me stay over. She's the one who read our journals and wouldn't let us use the phone to call our friends. She lasted only three years—just long enough to have one successful pregnancy, which resulted in the birth of the twins,

Stan Jr. and Lily. If my math's right, they're somewhere close to twenty-five or twenty-six years old now.

So Whitney took the twins and some alimony and moved out when Elliot and Nell were teenagers; I was twelve. Stan waited till Elliot and Nell were in college before marrying again. Next came Joyce. She was old. Not just older than Stan, but actually *old*. Dough-skin old, hate-your-neck old, plastic-surgery old. Stan sold the high-rise condo we'd been living in, and he and I moved in with her for a few years. They stayed married for seven total, but only actually lived together for four. When I went to college, Stan moved out. I'll never know what Joyce's appeal was; maybe it was just that she was rich. What I remember is that the house smelled like mothballs and liquor, and Nell and Elliot never came to visit unless they had to. By the time their divorce was finalized, Stan was already living with Louise, who was already three months pregnant. We call Louise the baby factory. She produced Lauren, Libby, and Lucy, who are probably somewhere between ten and sixteen years old now. By the time they were born, I was long gone from the state of Georgia and the only times I went back were when Nell and Elliot were going back, too. At first it was once every two years. Then it was once every three years. Then we all just stopped going south. Ever.

Sasha came on the scene six years ago. Stan was sixty-two when they met. She was a big-boned tennis pro at the local country club. Somehow he wooed her. It hadn't even occurred to me—to any of us—that he had another baby in him. Sasha was twenty-seven when they married. She was pregnant within weeks. We didn't go to the wedding. We didn't visit when Mindy was born. By then it just seemed like a bad joke. I remember one conversation with Elliot after we found out about Mindy. Pigpie had just been born and we were marveling at the fact that his youngest daughter would have an aunt who was roughly the same age.

"I used to think we were from a good family," Elliot said. In Atlanta, *good family* was a term you heard often, and somehow, you just knew what it meant. It meant money, yes. But it meant taste, too. Or if not taste, then discrimination. "But now," he said, "I don't know."

"Elliot," I said. "We're from a lousy family. We didn't even have a mother."

"We had a mother," he said.

"She had cancer," I said. "You can't have a cancer mom and be from a good family. Not in that town."

"It's not our fault she got sick."

"Okay," I said. "But our father's been married five times. He has more children than we can count. We stopped being from a good family decades ago."

"Jesus," he said. "I wonder what our friends' parents thought of us."

"Are you kidding?" I said. "We were the black sheep of Atlanta."

"I'm so glad we got out."

"You and me both, mister."

BUT NOW WE'RE HERE, back in Atlanta, stretching and flexing, huffing and puffing, and gearing up to mourn this man, this relative stranger, this hoarder and baby maker and consummate ass, and I'm the only one who sees how shallow it all is. I'm the only one who objects to the performance. Where is Matt Damon when I need him? Where is my star when I'm seeing black and all the world is shouting, "WHITE!"?

22

—◦—

Billy calls

I'm in the living room, helping Elliot set the table for dinner. I still haven't figured out how Sasha affords this place. Nell's said that she comes from money, but the three of us arguably *come from money*, and look at me. There's no way I could afford a condo on my own, much less a whole house. In Druid Hills. On a quiet, quirky street. With enormous sidewalks. And poplars keeping watch over every home. And, more, it's like she's lived here for years. She and her antique dining room table and her legitimate Oriental rugs. They've all been here for years is what it feels like. Except just six months ago she was living in an attached condo off Pharr Road with my father, the ancient sperm donor. Which begs the question: Why? If this house is possible now, why wasn't it possible then? Who *is* this woman, and what was she doing with our father?

Right now she's in the kitchen with Nell and Mindy. Paul Simon is blasting from the stereo; he's been working on a rewrite. Elliot keeps handing me pieces of silverware, which I keep dropping. I'm moderately to substantially drunk. My sobriety seems to change depending on what I'm leaning against—the table (not so drunk), a chair (slightly drunker), a napkin (drunk). I'm about to throw in the towel on this entire day—just sit down right here, put my arms on the table and my head in my arms and pass out—when my phone starts buzzing in my back pocket.

Elliot looks around.

"It's mine," I say.

He nods.

"I'll take it upstairs," I say, trying not to sound overly enthusiastic.

He nods again, but I can see he couldn't care less. He's so ensconced in his own personal meltdown that he can't see I'm in the middle of my own. Fine by me, man. Fine by me.

I take the stairs as calmly as possible, my heart getting noisier with each step. *This is it*, I think. This is Peter. He's ready to talk. To talk to me. His wife. He's ready to map out a course for our relationship, to find a way for us to get back on track. He'll make demands. I'll give in to all of them—not immediately, not so quickly he thinks I'm not even listening. No, I'll show him I care. I'll show him every word he says is getting through. I'm not just *hearing*. I'm *listening*, too. Sure, just yesterday, almost twenty-four hours ago now, I told him to have a nice life, but I didn't mean it. He knows I didn't mean it. My constant text messages have *shown* him I didn't mean it. *This is it*, I think. This is it.

I close Mindy's bedroom door behind me, pull out my phone without even looking at the caller ID, and answer.

"Hey," I say.

"Hey," says a voice that is definitely not Peter's.

Momentarily, I'm flummoxed.

Just for a second, I truly have no idea who's on the other end of the line. It could be a member of the Republican National Committee for all I know—that's how confused I am by the voice not being Peter's. I was sure, I was so sure this was it.

"Kate," says the voice. "Kate?" And that's when it hits me. That's when I recognize the timbre, the pitch, the clipped midwestern accent.

"Oh God," I say.

"I just want to talk," he says.

"Billy," I say. "I told you never. Never. Never call me."

I hiccup into the phone. I think I might barf.

"Are you drunk?"

"I'm in Atlanta," I say. "My father is dead."

"What?"

My father is dead. What a pitiful sentence to mutter into a phone.

"He shot himself," I say. "In the head." I hiccup again.

"When are you coming back?" he says.

"Did you hear me?" I say. "Did you hear what I said?" If ever there were a Get Out of Jail Free card, if ever there were an excuse to get away with anything I ever wanted, this is it. But Billy's not playing along.

"When are you coming back?"

"Never," I say, and hang up the phone. Then, like a kid, I stash it under the pillow on the top bunk. As if changing the past and all the things I've done is as simple as that. Wish you hadn't cheated? Regret that vasectomy? Marriage falling apart? Have no idea how you'll pay the bills if your husband actually divorces you? No problem! Just put your mistakes under a pillow and they'll all go away.

If only.

At the foot of the stairs, Elliot calls dinnertime. I go to leave the bedroom and the pillow starts vibrating. I take one last look, to make sure I've fully suffocated the thing, then shut the door and head downstairs. Maybe I can't make my mistakes disappear, but I can certainly ignore them a little while longer.

Okay, so listen, dinner smells and looks amazing. And it's not just that I'm drunk—or who knows? Maybe at this point I'm actually a little bit hungover. People think of hangovers as being a morning thing. But that's a myth. Take it from me. Total propaganda.

Anyway, it's not just that I'm drunk or hungover or whatever, it's that Nell and Mindy and Sasha actually whipped together something that looks undeniably delicious. I take a seat between Elliot and Nell.

"Was that Peter?" says Elliot.

"He says hi," I say.

Nell gives me this look like she knows I'm lying. And, yeah, maybe she suspects it, but there's no way she could know it for sure. Not unless she was a fly on the wall upstairs in that bedroom when I was talking to Billy. She might even have her suspicions that someone like Billy exists, but like I said, there's no way she could know for sure.

Mindy says, "Who's Peter?"

I say, "My husband."

Mindy says, "Gross."

I say, "Well, yeah, sometimes."

Mindy giggles and suddenly I realize I'd like nothing more than to win over this little gray gargoyle. It's a sickness, this need to compete with the people around me, even if they're people I love, but I can't help it. Suddenly, it's like—I don't know—I want to win.

Mindy says, "What is God?"

There is silence. I look at Elliot, but he's staring at his pasta like it's a foreign substance. He's a zombie over there. Totally worthless. I open my mouth to speak, but Mindy beats me with an answer to her own question.

"God is all around us," she says. She spreads her arms in front of her slowly and solemnly.

"Like fairies?" I say.

She shoots me a look. "Not like fairies," she says, and folds her hands in front of her all dainty-like. "Like angels."

I shoot her back a look that says, essentially, *I'm onto you, bucko*. And, honestly, I think I am. This little kid is sharper than she looks. She doesn't buy this God crap for a minute, but she likes that her mother thinks she does. This kid is all manipulation. A total con artist if I've ever seen one, and trust me, I have.

"Speaking of angels," says Sasha slowly and stretches out her hand to rest on her daughter's knee. "We need to talk to you about your father."

Mindy looks up, suddenly and woefully doe-eyed. "Daddy?" she says.

"Daddy," says Sasha.

"Is he with angels?" says Mindy, and I swear to God, this is the doe that knows the car is coming, doesn't care, and can't wait until the driver swerves and does a face-plant into the nearest tree.

Sasha swallows and her eyes make this pinched-with-pain expression. "Yes, baby," she says. "He is." Then, after a pause, she says, "How did you know that?"

Now the little kid is misty-eyed, glassy-eyed, and it's wrong of me, but I'm actually impressed with her abilities. I'm actually moved by her chameleon ways. She gives a little sniff from her colorless prepubescent nose and says, "Kate said so."

This gets even Elliot's attention. Nell has put down her napkin, like an angry parent.

Sasha looks genuinely hurt. "Kate," she says, "I thought we talked about this."

I'm shaking my head. At first I don't understand how Mindy knows to pick on me. But then I get it. She was upstairs, outside the bedroom, listening while I was talking to Billy. I'm trying to figure out the quickest, easiest lie, but nothing comes to me.

"I'm sorry," I say. "I was careless. Really, I'm sorry." I say this last bit directly to Mindy, who winces. Game on, Kiddo Jr. Game on.

Mindy's clearly reading my mind, because she looks up at her mother, all tender, all heartache, and says, "Mommy, what does 'shot himself in the head' mean?"

Sasha drops her fork and looks right at me.

"Seriously?" she says, which is funny, because that's exactly what I'm thinking.

23

showering after dinner

After dinner, I go upstairs to shower in the guest bathroom and give the real grown-ups a chance to talk about me behind my back. It's becoming clearer and clearer that I've got some issues that need sorting out.

I check my phone. Two more calls from Billy, no messages, nothing from Peter. Against my better judgment, perhaps against any judgment at all, I send a new text to Peter. *I'll do anything.* Which is funny, because right after I send it, my very first thought is *Well, actually, no I won't.* Then, a minute later—as if to test a theory—I write, *Please take me back. PLEASE.* And it's like the theory might be valid, because my first thought after this text is *But I'll be okay if you don't.* I'm tempted to try one more, to nip this entire thing in the bud once and for all. But something stops me. It's as though I don't want to see what's right in front of me. Not yet.

I take my phone with me to the bathroom—the game is afoot with Mindy and I know for a fact that my belongings (and more so, my privacy) are no longer safe—and I take, like, an hour-long shower. I turn on only the hot water, step under, and stand there. My skin gets pink and blotchy. I start itching. I don't even care. At some point, I get tired of standing and I let myself sink to the floor of the tub. Bad things live in bathtubs. Take a look sometime. Take a look at the little crevices between the tiles, the ones that once upon a time used to be white. There are entire families of germs living in those crevices, whole planets, entire solar systems. I don't doubt it for a second.

Here is what I'm thinking: I'm thinking that at some point soon I'm going to have to stop moping about and walking around feeling sorry for myself and make a decision about what to do next. At some point, much sooner perhaps than I'd like, I'm going to have to shake this wallowing off. There's a very good chance that my marriage is over for good; there's even a chance I'm happier about that than I'm letting on. What's certain is that it's beyond my control, which is probably what's making me try so hard. I don't want Peter to get the deciding vote. That just seems wrong. What's also certain is that my debt isn't going away, but my paychecks are, at least for the summer. A natural extension of that fact, then, is that I need money. Now. Eighteen thousand dollars. Marcy has made me an offer—an unbelievable offer—but it's one I can't consider.

What all this amounts to is going back to Chicago when the funeral nonsense is over, packing my things, renting a place, finding a summer job, and moving out. I'll sign whatever Peter puts in front of me. It'll be that simple and that messy. If Billy keeps calling, I'll change my number. Classes will start and I'll teach them. Days will begin and I'll wake up and live them. Nights will fall and I'll put my pajamas on. Life will continue, and at some point, enough time will have passed that it won't matter as much. I'll read more. Give up cable. To hell with Internet. Heat? Only when the pipes might freeze. A/C? That's why God made ceiling fans and coffee shops. When I finally meet someone new, I'll be a completely different person. I'll be better. I'll be a real grown-up. And perhaps I'll even be out of debt. This is the plan. That simple, that messy.

I reach up and turn the water off and then just sit there and watch while my skin evens out and the blotches disappear. There's nothing like a bathtub to remind me of how oversized my body is. I'm two inches too long in every direction. But as with my marriage, there's nothing I can do about that.

I check my phone. There's still no word from Peter, which I'm increasingly okay with. I should come clean to Nell and Elliot tonight. I should tell them the marriage is over. If they want reasons—well, if they want reasons I can always just come out and say it. It's not like I cheated on them.

I can hear Sasha murmuring in the bedroom down the hall. She's murmuring to Mindy, no doubt, telling her to forget about the big bad woman in the bathroom, to forget about the terrible things she heard me say. Nell and Elliot are downstairs on the back porch. If I wanted—if I were feeling desperately paranoid—I could open the bathroom window ever so slightly and hear what they're saying. I could prepare myself for whatever bombs will be dropped on me when I finally go down. But the whole point of this shower was to give them an opportunity to get on the same page, to give them an opportunity to bitch and kvetch and kind of start to feel guilty about how much they've bitched and kvetched so that by the time I go down, there's even the chance that no bombs will be dropped at all. All things are possible through prayer, right?

I do a cursory search in the drawers and behind the medicine cabinet for the bottle of whatever pills Sasha's been crunching but find nothing. It's the guest bathroom, after all, so I'm not surprised. I power off my phone for the night, slip past the master bedroom with the door cracked open and the murmuring voices, and go downstairs to my brother and sister. In cases like this, it is best to expect the worst. It is best to expect disappointment and anger and all that good stuff. That way you're prepared for anything. That way, if it's bad, you've known it would be bad and you're ready for it. If it's not bad, if it's better than you thought, you feel suddenly light. You feel like a burden's been lifted. You feel like a goddamned cloud.

So I walk onto the back porch with my hair in a towel, fully expecting to be excoriated for ten or fifteen minutes. What I don't expect is to find Elliot with his head in his hands, sobbing, and Nell with her arm around him, telling him it's going to be okay.

"Oh my God," I say. I kneel down in front of them. "Ell. Hey." I put my hand on his knee, and he sobs even harder. I look up at Nell, who gives me the saddest of all smiles and shakes her head. But it's not like she's disappointed in me. It's not even like there's anything I'll be held accountable for later when this is over. She mouths the words *tomato plants* and I find I am filled with relief and even, oh God, joy. This is not about me. This is not about me at all. This is about Elliot and his own crumbling world. Lucretius was right. There is nothing like another person's pain to put your own life into perspective. My brother is in tears and all I can think is *Thank God, thank God, thank God.*

a proposal

Elliot goes upstairs to wash his face or whatever it is men do after they've cried, and I make up the downstairs couch for him to sleep on. Nell watches me while I tuck sheets around the cushions and put fresh pillowcases on the pillows Sasha brought me. It's strange being in this house that I don't know, being with these people who are at once as familiar as familiar gets but also foreign. I can't say I like the feeling.

"Peculiar night," says Nell.

"Yes," I say, picking up a pillow and fluffing it like I'm some sort of chambermaid.

I'm dying to ask Nell for specifics about Elliot's breakdown—there's no way he didn't fill her in—but Nell, attuned as she is to the ether—*my* ether—says, out of nowhere, "Rita is on the fence."

"On the fence?" I whisper the words and sit down on Elliot's couch. "What does that even mean?"

"She's not sure she wants to be married."

Wait a minute. Maybe somebody *is* reading my mind. Maybe it's Rita. If I believed in the supernatural, I might even think she's gotten tangled in my brain waves, forever cursed to a life of unhappiness, a life of looking around and thinking, *Maybe the grass over* there *is a little bit greener?*

"She's approximately three kids too late for that," I say.

I think of Peter. I think of the adoption business. Then I think of this boy I once dated in college. We moved in together senior year to save on rent. A few months went by. He suggested we get a dog. I moved out the next day. He didn't mean anything to me, and so, when he asked for a reason, it felt safe to be 100 percent honest. What I said was, "The dog. I knew when you talked about the dog. My first thought wasn't 'How cute.' My first thought was 'But then I'll get attached to the dog and it'll be so hard to leave that I'll never leave.' That's when I knew."

Nell says, "Yeah, well." She sits down next to me, ruining the fluffiness of the pillows.

"The grad student?" I say.

Nell nods. "But nothing's happened," she says. "Supposedly."

"Oh God," I say. "It would be so much better if something *had* happened."

Nell owls her neck in my direction. "Excuse me?"

"Easy, killer," I say.

"Tell me what you mean."

I bite my teeth together a few times, as if I'm searching for words. Finally, I say, "If something had happened, then she'd get over it." Obviously, I am thinking of me. I am thinking of Billy. I am thinking of the shared wavelength Rita and I are currently riding. "But if it's all just fantasy," I say, "if it's all just spiritual connection, then Elliot's fucked. You can't compete with the fantasy of a better life."

What I've said is completely at odds with the family's stance on adultery. But before Nell's mouth is able to drop open any farther, Elliot appears in the doorway. Normally Elliot is like this substance you want to be in a room with. Even while he's pissing you off, you find that you're kind of craving it. Here's the thing, though. These last twenty-four hours, it's been like his addictive quality is missing. I can't quite put my finger on it.

"I'm beat," he says. He looks at the now-rumpled couch. "Thanks for making up my bed."

"Sorry," I say, and scoot Nell off so that I can reassemble the sheets.

"It's fine," he says. "It's a place to sleep and I'm totally beat."

The story is, when I was a baby and was brought home for the very first time, Elliot punched Nell in the face. They'd been fighting over whose room I'd get to sleep in. Elliot wanted me in his. Nell wanted me in hers. A blow to the nose sorted everything out.

Nell sucks in her cheeks in a way that both Elliot and I have come to know means she has something to say, which can only be to repeat my sacrilegious remarks from a moment ago. I'm tempted to call her a rat. I'm tempted to say, "You don't know what you're talking about." But then I figure, *Fine, let's just get this over with.* Now's as good a time as any. Shoot. Go for it. Knock it out of the park. Action.

She says, not looking at me, but looking at our brother,

who is standing next to me, "You said something last night about getting high?"

"Yeah?" says Elliot.

"Sasha gave me this." She holds up a small green medicine bottle. Not at all what I was expecting.

"I don't like pills," says Elliot. "But thanks."

"Hit me," I say, and hold out my hand.

Nell hands me the bottle without making eye contact—a sure sign that we aren't through with the previous conversation—and says, "It's not pills."

I open the top and find two perfectly rolled joints.

"Stan's wives get more and more difficult to pin down," I say. I take a sniff. "Dear Lord," I say. "It smells like a forest of weed in here."

"Better," says Nell, whispering now. "They get better."

"You just like her because she's our age," I say.

Nell doesn't respond to this, but Elliot takes one of the joints and inspects it.

"Anybody have a lighter?"

"Back porch," says Sasha, who has materialized out of the blue in the doorway between the living room and dining room. She's wearing a kimono that used to belong to Joyce, Stan's most ancient wife. "Let's get high," she says, then flips off the light and heads outside.

25

a memory!

You are fourteen years old. He is forty-nine. You know this because there are already plans in the works for his fiftieth at Benihana. You're living—just the two of you—in the horrible high-rise near the duck pond. This is just after Nell has left for college and a couple of months before you and your father move into Joyce's tattered stone manor on Woodhaven Road. Already, even that young—even before bills and rent and adultery—you don't sleep well. You remember missing Stan Jr. and Lily, who were only toddlers when your father divorced their mother. You remember feeling guilty and weird about missing them, since you hadn't shown much interest in either of them when they were living under the same roof. You remember thinking that emotions were unstable entities—not as they were happening, but as you recalled them in time. They were malleable things. Constantly changing each time you remembered them. They were not to be trusted. You remember trying to explain this to Stan. You have no recollection of his response.

The memory you're thinking of now, though, is very small. A speck. A smidgeon. But you think it merits inclusion. It's Sunday morning. Your father is sitting at the kitchen table, reading the paper and listening to jazz. The condo smells like bacon, which makes sense because there are three pieces left on the counter. You eat them, then wipe your fingers on a dish towel.

You say to your father, "I'm going for a bike ride."

He says, "Be safe," but he doesn't look up.

You take the elevator down to the lobby and get your bike from the storage room. But then you have a thought. It's partly out of laziness. (You remember thinking, *But I'll have to go to the trouble of putting it back.*) But partly it's something else. Partly you are entertaining the idea of a psych experiment. You only half comprehend the hypothesis—but it's there, knocking about in your brain.

You leave the bike where it is and walk outside. You cross the street and count the stories of the high-rise from the bottom up. You stop at eighteen, which is your floor. You see a person leaning over the edge of the balcony's railings. This is impossible. The only person in your condo is your father, and your father does not go onto the balcony. You think it's a fear of heights, but you've never asked and he's never said. It occurs to you that you are living with a stranger. You perform the count one more time. The person is still there. This time, the person raises its hand. Again, this is impossible.

You take off running down the hill, toward the duck pond. As you get closer to the pond, you ease into a jog. You run around the pond four, maybe five times. Then you run back up the hill and pause at exactly the same spot where you were standing fifteen minutes earlier. You perform the count one final time. The balcony is now empty.

You cross the street and take the elevator to the eighteenth floor. Your father is sitting in the same position as when you left him. He puts the paper down and looks at you. You're sweaty. It's Atlanta. You look at him.

He says, "You went for a run."

You say, "A bike ride. I told you."

The two of you look at each other for an impressive amount of time. You feel the psych experiment—whatever it is—has gone in your favor. You feel that a hypothesis has been proven.

"Okay," he says.

You think, *My god.* You think, *That was easy.*

Peter says addicts begin to recover when they pinpoint the birth of their addiction. Well, as best I can tell, this is mine.

———

the back porch before bed

Can I just say," I'm saying, while someone is lighting up the second joint, "that I'm sorry about earlier."

"She's high," says Nell. "You can tell. See, watch; see how she's tapping her teeth?"

"I'm not high," I say. "I'm just checking to make sure I can still feel them." I tap a few more times. "And I can. So, ta-da, I'm not high."

"You're high," says Elliot. "We can tell because you've now apologized a dozen times."

"Seriously?" I say. "I didn't know anyone could hear me."

We're all outside, sitting in the dark, trying to remember to whisper so as not to wake up Mindy, who's asleep in the bedroom above us.

Sasha says, "I know, I know. Mindy explained everything. She said she was eavesdropping. It's a habit she picked up last year. We're working on it."

I nod and try to remember that I've already apologized and

not to do it again. Then, just as quickly, I forget what I'm trying to hold on to. I should become a pot smoker. I should
smoke pot before bed instead of considering drugs like Paxil.
List making? On pot? Impossible. I could wake up at three in
the morning and not know what year it is, much less what's
troubling me in my real life.

Year. *Last* year. What Sasha means is it's a habit Mindy
picked up when they were both still living with our father.
Our father. My father and Mindy's. And Nell's and Elliot's.
Nelliot's father. The man lying on that lonely slab in a funeral
home thirty minutes away with his head under construction.
Tomorrow the ex-wives arrive, and their horde of children.
The day after that, we'll drive to the home and look at his
body. The day after that—who knows?

Actually, I'd make a terrible regular pot smoker. I get
twitchy, like I'm getting right now. And I get paranoid—not like
I think people are talking about me, but like I think I sound
stupid. I hate sounding stupid. I hate not being able to control
the words that are coming out of my mouth. Like, for instance,
right now, sitting cross-legged on the concrete porch, looking
up at Nell and Sasha, who are rocking back and forth on the
swing and who are saying something very serious to Elliot, who
is sitting cross-legged across from me, I am trying very hard to
pay attention to the topic of conversation and trying very hard
not to blurt out something irrelevant like, "What about Stan?
When are we going to talk about Stan?" But apparently I'm
doing a piss-poor job of following along and staying quiet, because now Sasha and Nell, up on high, are looking down at
me, not at Elliot, and I realize I've asked my questions aloud,
even as I specifically was telling myself *not* to.

Elliot reaches over and takes a joint from my hand. A joint that I didn't realize I was holding.

"Kiddo," he says. "We *are* talking about Dad. We've been talking about Dad for the last hour."

It's not fair: a funeral. The star of the show isn't even able to defend himself. Stan doesn't want all his wives in the same room, gabbing. He probably doesn't even want *us* in the same room. On the same porch.

"Oh," I say, still looking down at my fingers, trying to remember which muscle is responsible for making them move. "I'm sorry."

"We know," says Elliot. "You're very sorry."

"And very stoned," says Nell.

I look up.

"Where did you come from?" I say.

Nell gives me this *You're adorable* smile that lets me know I'm behaving every bit as idiotically as I fear.

"I need to go to bed," I say. I grab at my forehead. "Can I sleep here? Is this a bed?"

Elliot says, "Take the couch. I don't think you'll make it upstairs."

It must be the weed, but right now, my brother is the light of my life. He is everything that is decent and good in the world. All I want is for him to be happy. All I want is for Rita and him and those three gorgeous girls to be happy. I'd give up everything for the guarantee. I'd give up all my toes. And, I don't know, I'm looking up at Sasha and it occurs to me that she's the most generous, loving hostess in the world.

"What a mother!" I say, perhaps assuming they are following my thoughts.

"To bed," Elliot says. "Get."

"I love you guys," I say.

"Same here," he says. He pushes at me with his foot. "Get some sleep."

I'm trying to stand up, trying to keep myself from saying anything else, trying to get inside the screen door and onto the couch before I do anything else adorable (read: embarrassing). But it's too late; even while I'm telling myself not to, I'm already saying it: "What if I wet the bed?" And then, just like that, waterworks.

"Oh brother," I hear Nell saying. "I've got this one."

I feel an arm around me and then I feel the air-conditioning of the inside and it feels like we are floating across the wood floor. I feel a cushion under my thighs and then under my shoulders and then under my head.

I'm crying now, but I've already forgotten why. I'm afraid I've been left alone in a dark room in a strange city, and I'm about to call out when I feel a cold washcloth on my forehead.

"You're okay," says Nell, her hand on my cheek, the washcloth on my forehead. "It's okay. Don't talk."

"I do," I say.

"Shhh."

"I really do," I say. "I really do love you."

"Of course you do," she says.

"You're my best friend," I say. I am falling back, melting back into the pillow. My brain weighs fifty pounds, but the weight feels good because it's resting so perfectly on this perfect pillow.

"Get some sleep," she says.

"Am I yours?" I say.

"Get some sleep," she says again. "Shhh."

And I do get some sleep. I get the sleep of my lifetime. I get the first full night's sleep I can remember in years. The sleep itself is wonderful. The sleep itself is this transformative experience, like swimming in a cold bath of liquid rejuvenation. It's the dreams I don't like. Matt Damon is nowhere to be found. Instead, a telephone call. Crying. A limb being removed. My brother circling but not talking. Sasha and Mindy weeping, whispering. And Nell, Nell at the center, standing in front of me, a phone in her hand. "We can be together," she's saying. "Now we can be together. You and me." I'm shaking my head. I'm trying to talk; I'm trying to tell her no, no, that's not what I meant. She's pleading with me. She's screaming now: "You said you loved me." I'm shaking my head still and I'm trying to make her understand, but my mouth is gone. My lips are still there. The hole to my mouth is still there, but it's just a giant cavern, it's just a hole leading nowhere and to nothing. There is no tongue, no larynx, no voice box. All I can do is shake my head.

I wake up to what sounds like a gunshot. I sit up in bed. Sasha is sitting in the chair next to the couch. It's sunny and I realize I've slept later than I wanted. It's the fear of all youngest children, to be the last to wake and therefore the only one to miss the thing you don't even know you're missing.

"Did you hear that?" I say.

Sasha puts down the newspaper.

"Hear what?"

I rub my eyes and stretch my arms out in front of me. My body is not yet prepared to be awake.

"Like a gunshot?" I say. I'm groggy, but at least I'm not high anymore.

She smiles and looks back at her newspaper.

"Your father had that," she says.

"Had what?"

"Exploding head syndrome."

Maybe I *am* still high, because I'm pretty sure Sasha's just made the most tasteless joke in the world.

She looks up suddenly.

"Oh my God," she says. "That's not what I meant. I didn't—"

I must be giving her a hateful look, because suddenly she's sitting next to me, holding my hand.

"Your father had a syndrome. He saw a doctor for it," she says. "I haven't thought about it since..." She trails off, then shakes her head and takes her hand away. "You must think I'm a monster."

My mouth tastes like a burned-down forest. "Are you saying there's actually a thing called exploding head syndrome?"

"Yes," she says, nodding but not looking at me.

"And it sounds like a gun going off?" I say.

"Yes," she says. "It woke him up almost every night." I've embarrassed her, which is not how I wanted to start the day. I wanted to start the day a better person, but now I'll have to put it off until tomorrow.

"They should really come up with a better name," I say.

This world gets more and more perplexing. Fact: the longer I live, the less I understand.

———

morning, kitchen, eggs

Elliot goes for a jog and Nell goes upstairs to take a shower. Sasha is tidying up the living room, getting ready for the day's guests. I am in the kitchen, drinking coffee and nursing a mild hangover. There are two new text messages from Marcy. There is no word from Peter.

A carton of eggs is on the counter in front of me. I don't know what the menu is, but I'm assuming it's something brunchy and inoffensive. My money's on quiche or strata. I open the carton of eggs and look at them. They're the brown type. Organic. Big, with little mole-like flecks. I've always liked the look of an egg. Joyce kept a basket of hollowed-out ostrich eggs as a dining room centerpiece.

I pick up one of Sasha's eggs and close my fist around it. I'm tempted to disprove the myth—that an egg squeezed in a palm won't crack—but I don't. Instead, I put the egg back, close the cardboard cover, and then, very slowly, use my finger to push the carton across the counter until it falls to the floor. The sound is stunning.

"Shit," I say.

I wait, but nothing happens. Sasha must not have heard me.

"Shit," I say again. This time louder.

She appears at the entryway to the kitchen.

"I'm so sorry." I bend down and start picking up the eggs. "I think they're all broken." The mess isn't too bad. Only a little goop has escaped. But all twelve eggs are, in fact, broken.

Sasha gets a roll of paper towels and bends down next to me.

"No problem," she says. "I have to go to the store anyway. I forgot the pasta salad."

I look up. Of course! It's what I wanted all along.

"I'll go," I say. "It's the least I can do."

Sasha grabs a bottle from under the sink and sprays the floor. Then she puts down a wad of towels and uses her foot to finish the job. I've always liked people who use their feet for chores usually reserved for hands. It reminds me that we came from monkeys. Or apes. Whatever. It reminds me that we all came from the same place.

"Take my car," she says. "Keys are on the front seat."

"Make me a list," I say. "Anything you need."

She ducks into the pantry and I try not to think about how easy it would have been just to say, "Hey, I need to get away for a few minutes. I'm panicking about the arrival of the ex-wives. I'm panicking about the idea of the half siblings. Do you mind if I take your car and get some air?" Is there a chance in hell that she would have said no? No. There's not. And so why couldn't I have been direct? Why couldn't I say what I wanted? At least I didn't hide the eggs. At least I didn't take them upstairs and stash them under the bunk beds to be found, no doubt, by Mindy at some inopportune time.

Sasha reappears with a list.

"You know how to get there, right?"

"I remember," I say.

"They have about a hundred different pasta salads. Pick one with lots of colors," she says. "Your choice."

She hands me the piece of paper and I put it in my pocket, which is when I rediscover the two five-dollar bills, which is when I remember I am without funds.

What I think is: *At least I know when it's raining*.

What I say is: "This is embarrassing."

I make an exaggerated face.

"Can I borrow some cash?"

"Sure," she says. "Of course. But, you know, they take cards."

Of course they do.

"I lost it at the airport." A lie. "I canceled it, but it'll be a few days and they're sending it to Chicago."

"Of course," she says.

I am lying to a saint.

She opens a cabinet above the stove and takes down a tin of coffee. "Take what you need."

She pushes the tin across to me. I open the lid. There's a few hundred dollars in there. Maybe more. I am being tested.

"You do it," I say. I push the tin back to her. "I'm already so embarrassed."

She counts out five twenties and hands them to me.

"Kate," she says. "For real, don't be embarrassed. I lose my entire wallet every six months. I'm not kidding. I've been to the DMV three times this year. No joke."

I fold the twenties up with the list and put them in my back pocket.

"And now you know where the money is," she says. "Take whatever you need whenever you need it."

I am definitely being tested.

She puts the tin back above the stove.

"Hey," I say. "Would Mindy like to come with me?"

It's the guilt talking. Bill Cunningham would be so disappointed in me.

Sasha cocks her hip and looks at me. "Are you sure?" she says.

No. No, I'm not. I take it back.

"Absolutely," I say.

"She'd love it," says Sasha. "You're sweet to offer."

grocery shopping with Mindy

Sweet? I don't think so. But whatever I am—unsteady, un-safe, unstable—it's how I ended up here, with Mindy, at the fanciest, cleanest, coldest grocery store in Druid Hills, pick-ing out stinky cheeses and multicolored pasta salads.

Mindy is acting timid and clingy. Whenever I turn an aisle, she grabs onto my shirt and looks up at me, as though to make sure it's still me. I feel culpable. Nobody ever asks kids what they want to do. Decisions are always being made on their behalves. Probably Mindy wanted to stay and hang out with her cool half sister Nell. Probably she wanted to bake and churn and stir and taste and greet the guests as they arrived. Instead, she's helping push a cart down a too-cold grocery store with Big Scary Kate.

"You and your mom seem super tight," I say.

I look down at her. She's nodding, scanning the shelf in front of her.

"Does she have lots of friends?"

We're moving slowly through canned goods now, which we don't need, but it's a way for us to talk—walking side by side, pushing the cart in front of us—without having to look directly at each other. I'm trying hard not to shock her into complete silence.

I look down at her again. Now she's shaking her head.

"Your mom doesn't have lots of friends."

She shakes her head harder, but doesn't look up.

"She's so pretty, though," I say.

Still the shaking.

No words.

"I would think she'd be popular," I say.

Mindy stops in front of a display of soups. I stop too. She tilts her chin up toward me. Her face is bright red, her eyes completely bloodshot.

"Mindy," I say, and squat down so we're eye to eye. "Oh, kiddo." I pull her into me. "What's wrong?"

She lets me hug her, which surprises me, and I almost think I've fallen for some trick—like she's maybe twisted the skin on the inside of her wrist so hard that she's made herself cry (something I've thought about doing with Peter)—when she starts full-on hyperventilating and spits out the words "I miss him." The phrase comes out wet and I feel moisture seeping through the shoulder of my shirt from where she's crying into it.

I pull her off me gently, just so I can look at her and reassure her.

"Who?" I say in a near-whisper, wiping under her eyes with my thumbs.

"Dad," she says, and clutches me all over again.

Of course. Dad. They probably came to this grocery store together. The seventy-year-old and the seven-year-old. They probably had a blast going up and down the aisles.

Tentatively, because there's every chance in the world this could go very badly, I hold my hands up, palms facing Mindy. Her eyes widen.

"Do you know this game?" I say.

She bites on her upper lip and nods. My heart flutters. It's nearly imperceptible, but the butterfly wings are there, behind the rib cage, just inside the right ventricle, flapping.

"Will it make you feel better?"

There are people in the aisle with us, other women, probably women who are mothers. If they're watching, then they're judging, but we don't care.

Mindy nods again.

"Okay then," I say.

I kneel so that I am directly across from her, my hands parallel with her shoulders.

"Hit me," I say softly.

She gives my right palm a little punch.

"Again," I say.

She punches me again.

"Ouch," I say. It doesn't hurt, but she cracks a little smile and that smile makes the wings flutter faster.

"One more?" she asks.

"Go for it."

She lands a perfect little *thunk* in the middle of my palm.

"You're strong," I say.

She nods. "Dad said so."

"He was right," I say. I want to cry. He never told me I was strong. But this isn't about me. "Want some ice cream?"

Her eyes go buggy.

"Don't tell your mom, though, okay?"

"Okay."

AND SO NOW we're in the car in the grocery store parking lot, the A/C on full blast, and I'm watching Mindy eat an ice cream cone in the passenger seat up front. There's forty dollars and some change in my back pocket. I didn't touch the two fives.

"Is it good?" I say.

She nods. Her eyes are still a little bloodshot, but the snot at least has abated and the tears have dried up. I reach over and tuck a piece of hair behind her ear. She looks at me out of the corner of her eye and smiles. I should be having some sort of breakthrough right now. I should be thinking something about me and motherhood. Something terrifying and big, like, *Oh fuck, it's not that I don't want children—mine or some poor stranger's—it's that I don't want children with Peter.* But that's a breakthrough I don't want to make. That's a breakthrough for another day, if at all. Sure, I'm able to see the timeliness of the thought, but nope, I'm not yet willing to lock it into place in any meaningful or long-lasting way.

"I'm sorry," she says, a pause between licks.

"*You're* sorry?" I say, and give her a big, friendly, dopey smile, actually thinking the words *big, friendly,* and *dopey* to try to make my face behave the way I want it to. "What are *you* sorry for?"

"Getting you in trouble."

"You mean last night?"

She nods and eats her ice cream.

"I'm just really sorry you found out like that."

Stan must have thought about Mindy. He must have considered how she'd get the news. A walk at dusk, just Sasha and his youngest. The girl's little hand cupped around a few of the mother's fingers. Something gentle and strangely sweet. Something to bring the two of them—his last wife and his last daughter—even closer than they already are. He didn't have to worry about Sasha saying anything about suicide. Not her speed. But me. Stan probably hadn't considered me. He probably didn't imagine what I might do. He couldn't have known that his thirty-four-year-old would drunkenly spill the beans while on the phone with her ex-lover.

"I told Mom," she says.

"What did you tell your mom?"

"That I was spying," she says.

I wipe a bit of ice cream from the seat.

"I did a bit of snooping when I was a kid," I say.

"You did?"

I nod. "They called me meddlesome."

"Who did?"

"Joyce," I say.

"What's meddlesome?" she says.

"Snooping," I say. "Paying attention when you're not supposed to." Which, now that I think of it, probably isn't the best way of saying it, because honestly, paying attention when you're not supposed to doesn't sound all that bad. Unless, of course, it's a kid who's doing it. Then it sounds bad. Or if not bad, tricky.

"Meddlesome," she says back to me, nodding gravely, like she's got the weight of the world on her shoulders.

This kid. This little gray-skinned, gangly kid. I can't believe that just last night, I was thinking of her as some sort of mastermind, some sort of long-awaited opponent. She's just a girl. Just my weirdo little half sister who, according to my brother, anyway, looks just like me.

"You ready to get home?" I say.

She holds out the last of her ice cream cone.

"You don't want it?" I say.

"Last bite is best bite," she says, which is something my father used to say, and for a minute, I think I get it. I think I understand what all the fuss is about. For the briefest of seconds—a second split into nanoseconds—I think, *I miss him too*.

"Are you okay?" she says.

"Yeah, why?"

She nods at my chest. I look down. I'm clutching at my breast like some sort of lunatic, and I realize my heart feels too big for its cavity.

"I'm fine," I say, which is a lie. But I manage to take the piece of cone she's still holding in my direction and pop it in my mouth.

———

29

Nell figures things out, sort of

Nell is standing in the driveway when we get back from the grocery store. There are two other cars—cars I don't recognize but that must belong either to some of our grown half siblings or to their mothers. My chest is still expanding, trying to escape from its cage.

Mindy hops out first and runs to Nell.

"Hey, kiddo," Nell says. "Have fun?"

"Yulp," she says. "Double yulp."

"Is that ice cream on your chin?"

"Yulp," she says. So much for secrets.

"Don't tell your mom," says Nell. "She'll be M-A-D."

Mindy holds out her hand like I taught her before things went south at the store. South, but only momentarily. We seem at this juncture to be on a northerly swing.

"Give me five," she says.

Nell slaps her hand and looks at me.

"Up high," says Mindy, raising her hand higher. Nell slaps it.

"Down low," says Mindy. She lowers her hand, but moves it away too slowly and Nell has to deliberately miss. "Too slow," says Mindy.

"Yeah, yeah," says Nell. "Inside." She shoos her away.

And now it is just me and Nell in the driveway. Her arms are crossed. She's got that pissy look working on her face that always makes her appear older than she is.

"What's up?" I say, shutting the driver's-side door and going to the trunk for the groceries.

"You were gone three hours," she says.

"Was I?" I disappear behind the open trunk. I could write this scene in my sleep.

"You were," she says.

I root around in the trunk longer than I need to. Sadly, there's really nowhere to go. Nowhere to hide. The trunk offers very limited procrastination.

"Did you borrow money from Sasha?"

"Are you asking me a question or are you telling me that you know I borrowed money from Sasha?"

She doesn't say anything.

"I lost my card," I say.

Still nothing.

"I can write her a check."

"Peter called," she says.

I stand up, knocking my head against the roof of the hatch. I did not see *that* bit of dialogue coming.

"Shit," I say.

"Thought that would get your attention."

I shut the hatch and rub my head with my free hand.

"You're bleeding," she says.

I look at my fingers. "I am?"

"Christ," she says, coming over to me. She takes the groceries and sets them on the gravel. "You're a mess."

She removes a damp paper towel from her back pocket and wipes my forehead with it in a not-exactly-delicate way.

"What did he say?"

She pulls down on my chin to get a better view of the cut. "What do you think he said?"

I twist my mouth off to the side. "That he's trying to get in touch with me?"

"No," she says, and then steadies my face so that we're looking squarely at each other. She's so maternal sometimes. I have no idea where she's learned all these mannerisms I equate so thoroughly with the mannerisms of a mother. It's essentially gentle manhandling, and I kind of like it. "He wants you to stop calling."

I nod. "Okay."

"And texting."

"That makes sense," I say.

"See," she says, and gives my forehead a final hard dab, "but it doesn't make sense. Not to me, anyway."

"Right."

"Because last time I checked, he was your husband."

"Right."

The back door opens, and Elliot sticks his head out. "You guys coming in?"

"In a minute," says Nell, without turning to look at him.

"Who's here?" I say to Elliot, hoping that Nell will let me go.

"The twins and Joyce."

"What about the twins' mom?" I say.

Elliot takes a step toward us and stage-whispers: "We have not yet been blessed with the arrival of Whitney Somerworth, botanist extraordinaire."

"Ah," I say. "Too bad."

Nell turns and looks at Elliot. "Can we get a minute?" she says. "For real?"

"Fine, fine," he says. "Do what you want. Do what you want." My ally disappears inside.

Nell looks at me. "Give me something," she says. "Anything."

"He wants a divorce," I say.

"Yes," she says. "He told me that much. He said I should ask *you* for the reasons."

Somewhere deep down I feel like crying. Somewhere in this corpus of mine there are real emotions at work. I know it. I can feel them. I can feel the springs moving, the gears turning, the wrenches churning. Somewhere.

I take a deep breath and just say it. "I was unfaithful."

"Unfaithful," she says, but not like a question.

"Yes."

She pushes me away from the house and toward the garage. "And is that why—" She's hissing quietly in this spit-laden, overly dramatic way that makes me want to slap her. "Is that why you said Rita should just get it over with? That's why you think adultery is such a good idea all of a sudden?"

So listen. Things are getting overly polarized out here on this driveway, overly histrionic, overly black-and-white. But that's not something I can point out to Nell. Not when she's like this and not when she's *technically* in the right. I say *tech-*

nically because she's not the one I cheated on and she's not the one I kept a secret from. But I also say *technically* and leave it at that because it's also *technically* none of her business and *technically* not my job to fill her in on every aspect of my life immediately, as it goes down. All this to explain why I am willing, at least at this specific juncture, to give her overly simplified question an overly simplified answer.

"Yes," I say.

"Because suddenly adultery is okay in your book."

"No," I say.

"What about Dad?" she says.

How did Stan do it? How did he keep so many secrets and tell so many lies? Maybe he had a notebook. He probably kept it in his back pocket. Every time there was something new, he'd just pop open the book and record it beneath the last entry. I wrote myself an email once. It said, "Thai, Himalayan, Giovanni's." It was a list. A list of the three places I'd eaten that month with Billy. It was a reminder not to look at Peter one day and say, accidentally, "But we just had Thai last week."

Nell again: "You didn't learn anything from his bad habits?"

I did! What I learned was this: It's easy. It's so unbelievably easy. It's disgusting how easy it is. Until it isn't. Until you need a notepad or an email just to keep the lies organized.

What I say is this: "You two are the ones who want to be here for this. You two are the hypocrites."

"Me?"

"Yes."

"Elliot?"

"Yes," I say. "It's all for show. This is"—I search my brain for the word Elliot used so many years ago—"horseshit."

She shakes her head. "So your excuse for cheating is what?"

"I think—" God, I want to get this right. "I think a certain type of person can learn something from it."

"Ha," she says. "Double ha." She jabs me in the clavicle and I slap her hand away.

"And what," she says, "did *you* learn from it?"

The truth is, I hoped it would be like in the movies—where the man steps out just once and, in stepping out, realizes that everything he already has at home is all he wants, all he needs. I wanted the affair to make me feel so lousy with guilt that my love for my husband would suddenly and magically be renewed. I wanted to believe that he was right, that our lives were empty before and a baby would change everything. Instead, it appears I've learned that our marriage has an expiration date that we're rapidly approaching. It appears that while I followed Bill Cunningham's advice and didn't take Stan's money (and, yes, yes, I know, it wasn't actually offered), I did take Peter's money and help, which obligated me to him in a way that was not immediately clear to me. It further appears that there's a very good chance that maybe I do want children, just not with Peter, but that maybe it's now out of my hands. Maybe the choice is no longer mine. Maybe I'm on the same sad trajectory as Nell. But all this strikes me as too mean and too complicated for Nell's black-and-white world. It strikes me as too difficult a thing to go into right now, and so I keep my mouth shut.

"For how long?" she says when she sees I'm not going to answer. "How long did it last?"

It's a good question, actually. It's a question I wish Peter had asked.

"Long enough for me to have learned a lesson that I didn't learn in time."

She's shaking her head in this *I am so very burdened by the knowledge I have been given* kind of way.

"Pithy," she says. "Real pithy. Good for you. You should write that down. You should use that."

"I'm not trying to be pithy," I say. And I'm not. I'm trying to be honest. More and more, I see that honesty is the only way out, but just because you make the realization doesn't mean that it all of a sudden becomes an easy thing to do. Just because you trace the source of the addiction doesn't mean the addiction magically vanishes.

I've lost her. It's too late. She doesn't care anymore. In a matter of moments, I have transformed myself from sister to stranger.

She picks up the grocery bags.

"I'm sorry," I say.

"Whatever," she says.

She gets halfway to the porch and turns around. "Do what you want," she says. "You already have."

Now *that*, I think, is pithy.

30

———

the party begins

Here's what we're dealing with inside the house: The twins, Lily and Stan Jr., who—I was right—look to be firmly in their twenties, are in the kitchen with Sasha, Mindy, Joyce—more ancient than ever—and Elliot. Lily, who looks kind of like me in that she is tall and big-nosed and big-chinned, is playing patty-cake with Mindy, who's sitting on the counter over by the refrigerator. Stan Jr. and Elliot are standing on the other side of the refrigerator doing their manly man catch-up. They're each holding a glass of red wine, and I understand immediately that Elliot is attempting to school Stan Jr. on this particular vintage or whatever but Stan Jr. isn't having it. He's holding his own. It's gross—being in this kitchen with all these people who grew up with money and somehow retained it. I feel like a total phony.

Joyce, who is—at this exact moment—the first to officially notice and acknowledge me (hug, hug; kiss, kiss; oh my goodness her skin is saggy and cold and loosey-goosey), pulls me to her side and escorts me to the stove, where she's been watching Sasha cook. Nell is nowhere in sight.

"Look at this one," Joyce says, fawning all over Sasha while holding tightly onto my elbow. "Look at this beauty your father got his hands on. Can you believe he was ever married to me?"

Joyce has a point. There's a forty-year age difference between the two of them. It's pure lunacy that one man would have had both these women. Pure lunacy that the man who pulled it off wasn't a Hollywood exec but was Stan Pulaski, late-in-life hoarder and breeder of babies. Stan Pulaski, adulterer. Stan Pulaski, suicidalist. Stan Pulaski, my father. What must it have been like in that brain of his?

I take a slice of carrot from Sasha, who gives me this conspiratorial look that kind of melts my heart and wins me over all at once. She's lucky. She gets to hang out with Mindy whenever she wants.

"Wine?" says Sasha.

"Yes," I say. "Please."

I suspect, from the camaraderie Sasha is showing me, that Nell has not yet told her about my marital shortcomings. Although, who knows? Maybe she'll come down all hip and forward-thinking on my side. After all, she married Stan. Elliot, judging from his goofiness in the driveway a few minutes ago, doesn't know either.

Lily pries herself away from Mindy long enough to give me a hug, and it's hard not to wonder if other people are as freaked out hugging me as I am hugging Lily. It's off-putting when women are our height. It's hard to know where to put your head. You always end up doing a kind of chest-to-cheek-to-chest press. It's ugly.

I start to walk over to Elliot and Stan Jr. to do the right thing, to say hello to the only other male in the litter and, as far as I'm concerned, the haughtiest of all the half siblings, when he—Stan Jr.—holds up his hand and gives me the *just a minute* signal, and I think, *You know what? Forget you.* And maybe I'd even have said it aloud—or worse—but Sasha saves me by putting a glass in my hand and giving me a wink.

"You and I," she says, "need to talk later."

"Do we?" I say.

She nods and winks again. "Oh yeah," she says. "We do."

"Did Nell say something to you?"

She cocks her head and puts a hand on her hip. "Did she say something to *you*?"

"Wait," I say. "I'm confused." Maybe they really are lesbians! Maybe they're about to make my day! Why have I not been taking notes already?

Sasha bites her lip and scratches her head, which is something I thought only monkeys in cartoons did when they were confused. I'm not being catty. I'm not comparing Sasha to a monkey. I'm just genuinely surprised to see a cliché used sincerely. It's charming, actually. It's sweet, unexpected.

Joyce sidles up next to me again. She grips my wrist with her knobby hand.

"We'll talk later," Sasha says, and gives me a toothy grin. If it weren't for the grin, I'd say she somehow knew I didn't lose my credit card. But she's being all loopy and goopy, which is not the way to behave when you're about to introduce the discovery of a lie. No way, no how. What on earth could this woman want to tell me? The meaning of life? The secret to happiness? I'd take it. I'd gladly take advice from anyone just now.

"I missed you," says Joyce.

Sasha slinks away from us.

"Come sit with me," says the second woman to call herself my stepmother. "Tell me about yourself. Tell me about being young."

She's a skeleton, this one is, but she's got a grip, and she pulls me with uncanny ease to the kitchen table to sit.

"Golly, you're young," she says. "And so tall."

"Yes," I say.

"I missed you," she says again.

It makes sense—that Joyce would latch onto me. Nell and Elliot never lived with her. She never got to know them like she knew me. And now she's here without children. She's come by herself to remember my father, her onetime husband. It's touching in some ways. But also a little wacky. It makes me think she must be very lonely, which makes me think that being very lonely must be very sad and, if possible, avoided.

"You did not," I say. "You couldn't stand me."

She slaps her thigh and cackles.

"Battle-ax," she says. "That's what I always called you."

No, I think. *That's not what you called me, but fine.* I was a lousy daughter and my father was a lousy dad. But maybe there's still time to be a decent stepdaughter.

"Want some booze?" I say.

"You read my mind," she hisses, and grips my arm like she means it.

31

Dad's favorite

By three p.m., the entire gang is here. The ex-wives: Whitney, Joyce, and Louise. The widow: Sasha. The half siblings: Lily, Stan Jr., Lauren, Libby, Lucy, and Mindy. And us, the originals: Elliot, Nell, and me. It's a bit of a madhouse in here. Nobody wants to leave the kitchen. All parties are like this. The living room, the den—it doesn't matter how nice the house is or how nice the rooms are, people get nervous when they venture too far from the food and booze. Out there, with the sofas and couches and side tables, there's too much opportunity to get lost. Or worse, to be cornered by a former stepmother. The half siblings, with the exception of Stan Jr., who is and always will be a monumental Republican pain in my side, aren't really that big a deal. You can tell they want to be here even less than we do. They're even more frightened of the living room and den, even more frightened than we are of being caught away from the others, being caught away from their fellow young.

Lucy, the ten-year-old, is getting to be a pest. She and Mindy are just outside the kitchen, sitting on the bottom step of the stairway that leads up to the bedrooms. I'm trying really hard to maintain a conversation with Lily, who's been telling me about her one terrible season in the WNBA a few years back. But I keep overhearing Lucy's high-pitched voice behind me. She's picking on Mindy—"There's so much space on your face" and "Why does your hair look like that?" and "You have warts on your toes" and "This house smells bad"—and I keep trying not to notice. Mindy is not my responsibility. She has an advocate here—her mother, whose house this is. It's not my job to look out for her, but this Lucy chick is eating away at my nerves. I'm trying really hard to stay out of it—and trying also to make reasonably intelligent observations about the WNBA—but when I hear Lucy say to Mindy, "I was Dad's favorite. He didn't like you at all," I realize I've had enough.

"Whoa, whoa, whoa," I say, excusing myself from the conversation with Lily and going over to the staircase, where the girls are still perched.

"Lucy," I say. "That's totally uncool."

Lucy is petite and blond and tan. She's wearing fold-over socks with lace around the edges. Her hair is in two perfect braids. She is everything I hate about Atlanta.

Mindy, who for the party has changed into lederhosen and a bow tie that I know for a fact belonged to my mother's father, is close to tears, but she's hanging in there. The little champ.

"Un*cool*," says Lucy. "Un*cool*, un*cool*."

"Are you taunting me?" I say, understanding that slapping a ten-year-old won't go over well with this crowd.

"Are you *taunting* me?" she says.

Mindy reaches over and holds my hand. She gives me this baby-bird look of appreciation, as if to thank me for the masticated worm I've just offered her simply in being present. I pick Mindy up and look down at Lucy.

"You're a brat," I say.

"*You're* a brat," she says.

"And you weren't Dad's favorite," I say. "Not by a long shot." There's a chance I've gone too far. There's no rule that says an adult can't make two children cry in one day. Though I'm sure there are rules that say you shouldn't. I won't be surprised at all if this one breaks down in tears too, or if she rats me out to mass-producing Louise. But I'm not sticking around long enough to find out. I turn and with Mindy on my hip—Mindy, my six-year-old half sister who is fast becoming my favorite person in the world—I make a beeline for the back porch, where we find Elliot and Nell.

"Beer?" says Elliot as we open the screen door. He holds up a bottle.

"No," I say. I set Mindy down and she clambers over to Nell and sits in her lap. Little monkey. She's like a little monkey the way she does that—scoots from adult to adult like she's going from tree to tree.

Nell's being icy, but with Mindy out here, she won't say anything nasty. Note to self: six-year-olds come in handy when you're looking to avoid confrontation.

I take a seat on the swing next to Elliot.

"This strikes me as fairly antisocial out here," I say.

Elliot shrugs. "What's the scene in there?"

"Lucy was beating up on Kiddo here," I say, and stretch

out my foot so that I can wiggle my toes in Mindy's face. She scrunches up her nose and laughs.

Nell turns Mindy toward her. "Really?" she says. "Are you okay?"

Mindy nods. She seems unprepared or flat-out unwilling to tell on Lucy. Maybe it's something about the proximity in age. Maybe a ten-year-old who's closer in height is more threatening than a thirty-year-old who might as well be living up in the trees—that's how foreign the perspective is.

"Lucy was just saying how she was Dad's favorite and how Mindy wasn't even on the radar," I say.

"Man," says Elliot. "Rough."

"It's not true," says Nell, holding Mindy close. "Anyway, you're *my* favorite."

It's probably a sign of shallowness that I like Mindy less when there are other adults around.

Elliot says, "Doesn't matter what Lucy says. I was Dad's favorite." I can't tell whether or not he's joking, but it strikes me as a potentially inappropriate comment to make in front of Mindy regardless.

"You were," says Nell. "Totally."

"He was?" I say. "Really?" Probably in other families, families more nuclear than ours, this is a conversation that siblings have early and often. But I can honestly say that before this moment, it never occurred to me that our father had a favorite. It never occurred to me because I never cared.

"Oh, for sure," says Nell, momentarily, it seems, forgetting that we are not on perfect terms. "Firstborn, golden child and all that? Nobody else stood a chance."

Mindy is hanging on every word, but she's smart enough

not to speak. She knows speaking will remind the others—
the grown-ups—of her presence and could therefore potentially stop the conversation. Eavesdropper, indeed.

"What about Mom?" I say. "Who was Mom's favorite?"

"Nell," says Elliot.

Nell nods. "It's true. I was. I really was," she says. "I'm so
glad you knew that." She kicks Elliot's foot with her own.

"It was obvious," he said. "She was addicted to you."

What's obvious is that Nell and Elliot have considered
this before. Just like Lucy had considered it, so have Nell and
Elliot. It makes me feel left out—like someone forgot to give
me the booklet on how to be someone's child.

"Whose favorite was I?" I say. I hate the sound of my
voice.

"No one's," says Nell, shaking her head.

"That's right," says Elliot. "You weren't anybody's favorite."

I can't tell if they're pulling my leg or if they've suddenly
become the most callous siblings in the world. If they
planned this as some sort of joke, it's not funny.

I look to Mindy for some relief from this pig-piling. My
face says, *Just give me something, kid. Anything. Even a lie.
Tell me I'm your favorite. Tell me I'm the best. You don't even
have to mean it.*

But she says nothing. She's too mesmerized by the discus-
sion of adults to dare speak out of turn.

Peter. I used to be Peter's favorite. But I've put an end to
that.

32

talking to Rita

In the middle of the insanity that is my father's wake, here's a lesson I'm trying to teach myself: scan, process, react. It's how Elliot, when I was fifteen, taught me to drive. *Scan* the current environment, *process* what you've detected, and then *react* accordingly.

Obviously, though, I'm not talking about driving.

I'm talking about life. I'm talking about evaluating *before* acting.

What I'm saying is this: even before sneaking outside and dialing Rita's number, I weigh the pros and cons—and, yes, the cons are many, including but not limited to a) the three healthily poured glasses of white wine I've already had this afternoon, b) the fact that Nell and Elliot seem to be ganging up on me more than usual and in front of all my stepmothers, and c) I'm feeling slightly fatalistic given the state of my marriage and the state of my bank account and the state of my father's skull, which has put me in a perhaps unstable state of mind—and I decide regardless in the phone call's favor.

When Rita answers, I say, "Do it." That's it. That's all I say, no greeting, no nothing.

"Do what?" she says.

"Have sex with that kid."

I'm standing behind the garage, watching the back porch, making sure nobody is within earshot.

There's a muffling on the other end of the phone, something like the rearrangement of a device from one ear to the other. I hear a door open, footsteps, then another door close.

"Hello?" I say. "Are you there?"

Crouching in hiding, whatever the circumstances, always gets me a little manic, a little excited. My heartbeat starts to speed up and I think, *Life, life, life*.

There's more silence—enough silence for me to think again, *Life, life, life*—then Rita says, in a whisper, "What are you talking about?"

"Where are you?"

"I'm out," she says. "I'm in public."

"Are the girls with you?"

"No," she says. "I dropped them off at camp this morning."

Of course. The girls are at camp, and Rita is all alone.

"Have sex with him," I say. "Tomato-plant guy. Get it over with."

"Are you drunk?" she says.

"Holy aphid," I say, crunching ice into the receiver. "Aren't people getting tired of asking me that?"

"Do you really want an answer to that question?" she says.

"Touché," I say. "Are you with him right now?"

"No," she says.

"Are you telling the truth?"

"No," she says.

I nod like I'm some kind of guru, which I'm not and I know I'm not. "What you'll realize," I say, and now I'm headed off the map, now I'm headed full speed and without warning into uncharted territory, the words coming even before the thoughts are fully formed, which is exactly the kind of behavior I'm trying to avoid, "is that all men are giant babies." Am I thinking of Elliot? Am I thinking of my father? Am I thinking of Peter or Billy? The answer: I am thinking of you all. I am thinking of every single one of you and, at least at this very minute, I mean every word I'm saying. "You think there's something special about him, about this kid who knows that tomatoes grow better in coffee cans than in planters. You think you don't love Elliot anymore. You're wrong."

Again there is silence.

"Rita," I say, and now, heading back to charted territory, having weighed this, having taken this in my palm and measured its texture and worth, I say very carefully, "this is something I know about."

"Wait," she says, also slow, also steady. "Firsthand?"

"Yes."

"Peter cheated?"

I cough and crouch lower. "No."

It's taking her a minute to process what I've said. It's nobody's first guess that the woman is the one who's stepped out—even another woman who is currently contemplating such a move for herself.

"Oh," she says after a minute. Then: "*Oh.*"

"You get it," I say.

"When?"

"This year," I say. "End of last year, beginning of this year."

"And?"

"And Peter found out."

"When?"

"Last month."

"And?"

"And what?"

"How are things now?"

"He wants a divorce," I say.

Now there is dead silence on the other end. Not just regular silence, but bone-dead, big-eared, long-fingernailed silence.

"Wait," she says. "You and Peter?"

"We're splitting up."

"Does Elliot know?"

"No," I say. "I don't know. Only if Nell's told him."

"You told Nell but not Elliot?"

"It's not really a time to be concerned with etiquette," I say. "But no. I didn't tell Nell. Peter did."

"Kate," she says. "You have to tell Elliot."

"Yes," I say. "I know. But we're dealing with other things at the moment."

"Of course," she says. And of course I feel guilty because of course, yes, we *are* dealing with other things, but no, they aren't really that dire. Stan's dead. Nothing is changing that fact. My impending divorce, Rita's potential infidelity—none of these things changes the state of Stan's cranium, which, hopefully, is being rebuilt as Rita and I speak, since the viewing is T minus twenty hours and counting.

"But what you're advocating for me..." she says.

"Listen," I say. "You're talking about leaving Elliot. You're talking about walking away from a beautiful, stable home where three kids—and two parents who happen to adore those kids, even if they don't adore each other at the moment—live. All I'm suggesting is—if you think you're going to leave him anyway—why not test the goods of the guy you think is all that first? Test the waters, and if you still want to leave, then leave. Just don't be all high and mighty about it. Things are going to get dirty in a divorce. They might as well get dirty now. Especially if there's a chance the dirt might save everything."

"And you think Elliot would be okay with that?"

"No!" I say, spitting out a little wine accidentally and then wiping it from my chin. "Of course not. He's going to hate it. You can tell him or not tell him. But what I know is, he wants you. And he'll forgive you if it means you'll stay. Kids change everything."

"Have you talked to him about this?"

"No, Rita, I haven't." I'm shaking my head as if she can see me, as if she were right in front of me, which, now that I'm thinking of it, I wish were the case. I wish she were here to hug me, to hold me. Whatever kind of hug Nell was talking about—a hug just to say *Here I am. Here I am. Here I am.* But she's not here. She's nowhere close to here. "No," I say again. "And I'm not going to. I'm just throwing it out there. I just thought I'd weigh in on your life as a way to get a minute's respite from mine."

I remember like it was yesterday: Peter said, "Just answer the question." I said, "But first you have to know that—" He said, "Answer the question." I said, "It's not that simple." He said, "Yes or no?" I said, "Peter, please; there was so much pressure; you weren't listening to me." He said, "Yes or no?" I said, "Please, don't; I felt so lonely." He said, "Yes or no?" Finally I looked at the floor and said, "Yes." He said, "Billy? His name is Billy?" And on and on it went.

"Oh, Kate," says Rita.

"Yeah," I say, still crouching outside the garage, still watching the house like a thief. "I know. I know. I'm a mess."

---

a partial list of the secrets I keep track of while I lie awake in bed most nights

I wish more people liked me.

I wish people liked me more.

Sometimes I steal gum at the grocery store.

Sometimes at Starbucks I take someone else's order, even though I've paid for my own.

Sometimes in the middle of the day I go to the bathroom and undress completely and just stare at myself in the mirror. I always look different from the way I think I should. I am always 10 percent too tall, 10 percent too large, 10 percent not as good-looking as I want to be.

When I was fifteen and it was winter and I had sleeves to cover the evidence, I hit my thighs and my upper arms until there were bruises. I did this every day for two months straight. I was too wimpy to try cutting. Hitting was easier and cleaner. There isn't a person in the world I've ever told about this.

Sometimes, after the adoption business and after Peter had fallen asleep, I'd masturbate in bed next to him. I did it quietly. Sometimes I wanted him to catch me. He never did.

In the middle of the night, sometimes I wake up and I can't breathe just thinking of all the things Peter and I have accumulated. A whole moving truck's worth of stuff. Not just a box or a station wagon or a van, but a moving truck's worth of stuff. And I feel so empty and sad and weighed down by the emptiness. That home. That idea of home. Of a household. It's suffocating sometimes. Before I agreed to marry him, before I told him about my debt and he helped me find a credit counselor and a debt-management service and promised to pay for everything while I paid off what I owed, before all that, it was the numbers that kept me awake—the numbers on the statement and the numbers on the calendar and the way the due dates seemed to come faster and the balance wouldn't stop growing.

There was a year, maybe one entire year after we were first married, that I slept through the night. But then my brain turned back on and started looking around, looking at all the crap we'd acquired, and I stopped sleeping again. When we were talking about adopting, it was the baby that I would think about at night. Some stranger's baby. Living in our home. One more thing that we'd gotten our hands on. One more reason I'd be stuck forever. Those nights, I'd have to get out of bed and go to the bathroom and sit on the toilet with the lid down and struggle for breath. If I ever accidentally woke Peter, I'd just say, "It's nothing. A nightmare." And he'd fall back asleep and I'd think, *I'm not lying at least.* Because, really, it was a nightmare.

* * *

AND THEN THERE IS THE SECRET that is Billy. The secret that was. The secret that is no longer a secret. He was a way to pretend all those household belongings didn't matter, didn't *belong* to me—me, the woman who, when confronted with her sister's outdoor furniture, understands what it is to covet. The human heart is nothing if not confusing and confused.

I found Billy online, on a message board. It wasn't slutty. Or who knows, maybe it was. My judgment isn't what it could be. He didn't know I was married. The first time we met it was just for coffee. He brought his dog. That was probably what sealed the deal. I've never owned a dog. I've never owned a pet, unless you count the series of elephant fish that I had during Whitney's reign. She'd always liked fish, so her one moment of support was in encouraging my father to let me have a small aquarium in my bedroom and one elephant fish. It died after two days. The next one lasted a little longer. The third one died the same day it came home. I buried them all in the backyard. Nell and Elliot didn't make fun of me, but they didn't help me bury them, either. I kept the aquarium filled with water but empty of fish for a year. At night, I'd lie awake and just watch the little treasure lid bubble open and closed. I must have kept it around so long because I liked the light, liked having a night-light that wasn't technically a night-light. But then Whitney had the twins and everything old was thrown out. Anything that could carry germs. And I was moved into Nell's room and the twins were given my bedroom as a nursery. By then I didn't care about the aquarium. By then I didn't need the night-light because I had Nell just an arm's reach away.

But Billy's dog. It was this white fluffball of a thing. It wasn't a breed I would ever have chosen voluntarily. It was small and girly and ugly. But it had a personality! And on that very first day, it slept on my feet, just right there under the table, and I had this feeling like I was looking through a window at a different life, at a different version of my life. Who was this woman with this man and this silly white dog? What kind of place did they go home to? What kind of bills awaited them there? What kind of furniture? Did they rent, or did they own? Was there a mortgage? Were they debt free? This woman looked simpler to me, smaller, more easygoing, more carefree. She owned less than I did because she'd bought less than I had. This woman slept soundly through the night. I was sure of it. And if she didn't, she at least had a dog to check in on.

Obviously, if these were my feelings, I should have gotten a dog. I should have put my foot down with Peter and said, *Listen, guy. We're getting a dog, okay? A baby is too much for me. But I'm unhappy. And I see that I need something that needs me. And I see that you do, too. We're missing something— don't get any ideas, guy, I'm not talking about a baby, okay?— but I think a dog will help. And if a dog doesn't help, then maybe therapy—not with you leading the sessions, okay? You could refer me to someone, though. And if therapy alone doesn't help, then maybe some of those drugs you're always talking about. And if not drugs, then we'll think of something.* But of course, it was more than just the dog. I wanted the whole package. I wanted the whole fantasy. I wanted Billy and I wanted whatever feeling it was that the simple crude act of infidelity caused in me. It was the same feeling as taking someone's drink at Starbucks, but better. Bigger. It lasted longer. Not that long, but longer. A week instead of an hour. And it infected my whole body—my fingertips, my toes. I liked it. That's the thing. I liked it.

There is maybe even the chance—somewhere way deep down in the darkness—that I wanted to do what my father had done. It was in my DNA. The way certain babies are born with alcohol in their systems. It's there. Everyone knows it's there. The little baby grows up and gets married and his wife looks at him every day and every day she's thinking, *Is today the day that he becomes his father? Is today the day?* I didn't become my father. I did what he had done to prove I could, to prove it meant nothing, to prove that we weren't the same. And you know? Now that I'm thinking of it, I might even have done it to prove I was different from Nell and Elliot, too.

Billy himself—Billy devoid of his body—I wasn't as obsessed with as I was with the feeling of wrongness. The personality belonged mostly to his dog. Of course, I am saying this now. I am saying this *after the fact*. If you'd asked me then, if you'd asked me midthroe, I probably would have said he was a dish. Or something equally icky and sticky.

When I got bored, which took only a handful of months, I finally told him I was married. He didn't believe me. He thought I was lying. Did I mention he was younger? He was. He was in his late twenties, which, for a single man, is the equivalent of being a large puppy. I laughed when he didn't believe me. I wasn't being cruel. What it was was that

I couldn't help but imagine all the girlfriends before me—girlfriends! You get married and you think, *Thank God, I never have to be one of those again.* But then the years go by, and you think, *Girlfriend! There's a thing I'd like to be again. There's a word that sounds young and unburdened and lithe*—and I imagined all these young, long-legged, tanned girls, at least one of whom had, at some point, probably claimed pregnancy as a way to keep Billy around. It was probably an ugly and hard-learned lesson for him when he found out she was lying. Now here I was claiming marriage as an excuse to break up. Of course he didn't believe me. It wasn't till I showed him the ring that he finally got it. And then he got mad. And then the dog peed on the carpet. (This wasn't a new thing. The dog was always peeing on the carpet.) And then I left. He only started calling two months ago. He left me alone through the spring. I don't know what happened. Probably it's as simple as he'd never been broken up with before. Probably he went through a few more girls after me and they were boring and he's since mistaken my being married for not being boring. But he's wrong. He is wrong. I'm as boring as they are. I'm more boring. I'm doing him a favor being cruel like this. In the long run, I'm doing him and his future wife a favor. He'll learn something from this. Exactly what, I can't say. But he'll learn something. That's the guarantee. That's what they teach you while you're growing up. What doesn't kill you makes you stronger. Fact.

the speeches begin and end

By six p.m. Sasha has somehow gotten everyone to move into the living room. The A/C is running full blast, but so many bodies are making the room thick and a little bit funky. What's funny is that for the most part, the half siblings are at the sides of their mothers, which gives the occasion a *Family Feud* feel, as though questions will begin soon and the teams will have to fight to stay in the game. We should have done this when Dad was alive.

Joyce is back at my side, smelling boozier than I am. Elliot, Nell, and Sasha are teamed up on the sofa beside mine, Mindy sitting half on one of Sasha's knees, half on one of Nell's. I have no idea what Sasha wants to talk to me about, but the anticipation feels like Christmas Eve.

"So listen," Elliot is saying, leaning forward now so his elbows are resting on his knees. "We thought it might be a nice thing to take a few minutes and let people say a few words about Dad." Lily, across from me, sniffles, and Whitney puts an arm around her. Whitney, who is wearing a leopard-print halter top and has obviously had some work done, is not about to cry over Stan Pulaski, man of the hour, but it gives me a little bit of joy seeing that her daughter might genuinely have cared for the guy.

"He didn't want a funeral, per se," says Elliot, and I'm not so sure about this. Stan Pulaski was a maudlin man. He liked speeches. He liked speechifying. But Elliot's got the floor and God knows I'm not about to push for something more intense than what's already happening. "He didn't want anything formal," Elliot's saying. "So tomorrow there won't be speeches. There won't be prayers. It will just be a time to say goodbye. Today, though, we thought he wouldn't mind if we remembered him together, casually, as a family."

Family. This word is getting bandied about in a way that's making me dizzy. It's got less meaning in this room than it does at seven p.m. on ABC, where a Chinese dude and a lovely Latina can have the world's most beautiful black baby with no questions asked. Is this my family? Are these women, who came in such quick succession but who divorced me as easily as they divorced my father—are they my family? And these children, this rainbow of ages and heights and features—are they my family because half their DNA says they'd make good donors if and when the time comes? If this is what family is, then count me out.

There's an awkward silence in the room. Joyce pulls my ear down to her mouth and whispers, "Will you say something?"

I look at her and shake my head. I mouth the words

No way, José, which is what she used to say to me when she caught me looking at her liquor cabinet when I was younger.

She squeezes my arm and in a boozy whisper repeats her new mantra: "I missed you, I missed you."

I squeeze her knee lightly—all bone!—and hope she'll stop talking.

"If nobody wants to go first—" says Elliot.

"I'll go," says Sasha.

Louise, Dad's wife before Sasha, purses her lips into a nasty little downturned smile. She hadn't wanted the divorce and she's always maintained that Sasha stole him away from her. She probably thinks she'd still be married to him if it weren't for Sasha. She probably thinks he'd still be alive.

Sasha scoots Mindy onto Nell's lap and stands. She brushes off her skirt in a nervous way. Her cheeks are turning crimson and she hasn't even started talking yet.

I turn around and spot an open but warm bottle of white wine on the console behind me. I pick it up delicately and, as quietly as possible, pour some into my glass and also into Joyce's glass, which still has ice and what smells like scotch at the bottom of it. She doesn't mind.

Lucy, sitting cross-legged next to the unlit fireplace, burps, and one of her older sisters laughs. Nell shushes them and Louise shoots an ugly face in my sister's direction. I wish I were drunker. Or better, I wish I had some of that pot from last night. This situation could be a whole new scene if I'd smoked some of that magic weed. I could bring myself to tears, perhaps. I could say a few things about my father. We'd all pee ourselves, then go our separate ways until tomorrow. After that, we'd never have to see one another again. A goodbye to Stan Pulaski and a goodbye to one another. For good.

"He was best at mealtime," Sasha says. She's got her face pointed at the floor, and it's funny to try to imagine this suddenly shy woman ever giving tennis lessons or commanding the court with her instructions.

"He fell in love easily and often," she says. That's certainly one way of looking at it. "It's what made me love him and what drove me crazy about him." This woman is generous to a fault.

Across from me, Louise looks bored. Whitney looks pissed. Their children—all of them but Lily—look checked out. Joyce's head is now resting on my arm and I think she might actually be asleep.

"You want it to make sense," Sasha says, and she raises her face suddenly. "You want for something like this to have some meaning." She looks at Mindy and winks. Then she looks at me. Right at me. "You get the news and the first thing you think is 'What does this mean? What's the significance?'" She's quiet for a minute, but she doesn't sit down. Lucy and Lauren start squirming. My underarms are itchy, sweaty. Joyce is officially snoring. "You want it to make sense," Sasha says again, still looking at me, and I wish she'd look away so I could look away. "But it doesn't."

Mindy makes a sniffling sound, which I use as my cue to break eye contact.

Then, with a sort of exhaustion, as if the spirit has left the medium's body, Sasha sits suddenly back down and, in an entirely different voice—the voice, in fact, of a tennis pro—she says, loudly, almost giddily, "Phew. That's it for me."

I wonder how it happened—Stan and Sasha. Did he see her at the country club and just know? Was it love at first sight? Whatever it was, it was more than what I had with Billy.

Nell glances in my direction and offers me a timid little smile, and—just like that—we are sisters again.

"Anyone else?" says Elliot.

"I would just add," says Nell, "that he'll be missed."

"Absolutely," says Elliot. "How about we raise our glasses?"

He raises his in the air.

"I just want to know—" It's Louise talking. Louise, the ultimate baby maker. "I just want to know why there isn't going to be a proper funeral."

"Like I said," says Elliot, lowering his glass. "He didn't want one."

"Says who?" Louise is sitting up straight now. She's holding her hands in the shape of a little ball in her lap, and I can see from here, from across the room, that she's gripping herself so tightly that her veins are popping up and down. And I realize she's probably been planning this tiny explosion all day. She's been holding it in and holding it in until just the right moment. She thinks she's setting an example for her girls. Showing them how to fight the godless in a morally triumphant way. She has come to defend her dead ex-husband's honor. Or something like that. God, I wish I were high.

"Dad," says Nell.

"*Dad*," says Louise. "As if you have the right to call that man *Dad*. As if any of you heathens have the right to call that man *Dad*."

Well, okay. Now we're getting somewhere. I too take issue with our use of the word. I might even agree with her. But I also take issue with the word *heathen*. I think, perhaps, I would like to hear more about this word. I'd like to hear her God-fearing evidence. I sit up a little straighter and accidentally knock Joyce to attention, which in turn knocks Joyce's glass to the floor.

"Oh dear," says Joyce, genuinely embarrassed. Sasha is kneeling in front of us almost immediately with a dish cloth in her hand. She's rubbing Joyce's knee, telling her it's nothing while simultaneously dabbing up the spilled wine-and-scotch mixture.

"It's nothing, it's nothing," she's saying.

"I'm old," says Joyce. "You can't take me anywhere."

"This is a sham," says Louise, standing up. "This is a disgrace."

Nell starts laughing, which makes Elliot start laughing, which makes Mindy start laughing.

Joyce grabs my wrist and says, "Are they laughing at me?"

This makes me start laughing and I grab onto her other hand, which is grabbing onto my knee, and say, "No, Joyce. No. They are *not* laughing at you."

Louise is gathering her girls together like a woman scorned.

Joyce says, "Who, then? Who are they laughing at?" She is like a blind woman asking to be shown the way.

Sasha is still on her knees, still collecting the little pieces of ice and doing a once-over on the Oriental.

I point at Louise so Joyce and everyone else can see me. "Her," I say. "We're laughing at *her*."

Louise and her gaggle of girls don't even bother turning around. They're out the living room door and soon out the front door, and soon after that, they are out of our lives for good.

35

after the party, doing dishes

I'm standing at the sink doing dishes with Sasha. Mindy is to my right, standing on a kitchen stool. I hand her a dish; she takes it, dries it, stacks it with the others. Nell and Elliot are sitting at the kitchen island behind us, drinking wine and watching us clean. Normally I would mind, but they did the undesirable tasks of seeing Whitney and the twins to their cars and calling Joyce a cab. I'm happy to do some manual labor if it means I'm not required to participate. I'm happy to stand at the sink and watch the suds form and dissipate. Mindy and I can eavesdrop just fine from over here.

Nell is saying, "You know what I think about? I think about that cabin we used to go to before Mom died, where we'd all play Monopoly and wait for the snow. Mom would make bread and Dad would cook some huge meal and you and I would shake cream until it turned into butter."

By *you* she must mean Elliot, because I have no memory of this cabin or these happy idyllic times, and so I break my self-imposed stupid vow of silence and say, "I don't remember this."

"Because you weren't born yet," says Elliot. "Or maybe you were just a baby."

"I remember this one time," Nell continues, "maybe the last time—it seems more romantic that way—"

Elliot groans. He's a million miles away. My beautiful brother. He is on autopilot and his life is shit.

"Listen," she says. "It was hunting season and Dad was out hunting and Mom made us stay inside all morning until the gunfire stopped. You and I"—again with the *you*, and I feel I am being made acutely and deliberately aware that this story is for Elliot, not for me, and that I am being allowed to enjoy it only as an audience member, as someone no different from Mindy or Sasha—"stood at the window looking at the snow, waiting for the quiet. We kept sneaking on our coats and every time Mom passed through the kitchen she made us take them off so we wouldn't burn up."

"I remember this," Elliot says. Perhaps he is closer than I think. Perhaps he is merely far away from me.

Mindy is as quiet as a mouse, entranced by potentially inappropriate adult material.

"There was a series of volleys," says Nell, "and you pointed and a hunter in the distance walked out of the far woods toward three little mounds."

"The hunter was Dad," says Elliot.

"Don't ruin my story," says Nell. I imagine her elbowing him in the side, but I don't turn around to see. "But, yes, the hunter is Dad. He passes the first mound and you say, 'It's a goose,' but I say no. He passes the second mound and you say again that it's a goose. He gets to the third mound, the one closest to us, and by this time I can tell that it *is* a goose, because it's moving a little bit."

I hand Mindy a dish. She is standing dead still, staring at the cabinet in front of her. She is waiting to learn the fate of the goose, and I wish I could tell Nell to stop, to remind her that a child is in the room—a child who might have nightmares about dead geese—but I can't tell her to stop, because I don't want to tell her to stop, because I want to hear what happens next. I want to hear if, at some point, I, as a little baby maybe, become part of this memory after all.

It occurs to me that Nell might finally be drunk, which would be a kind of relief to me. But who knows? Maybe she's just feeling maudlin.

"I'm watching, really watching," she says, "because I'm curious what the hunter will do."

"Dad," says Elliot.

"I'm curious what he'll do. I know I was young and naïve, but I really didn't know what to expect. I think I wouldn't have been surprised if he'd picked the thing up and hugged it."

I glance at Mindy. She's come back to life enough to take the dish from me, but I can see her focus is entirely on the story being told behind us. Little kids must love hearing stories from adults about their time as children. It must be a way to compare and contrast what they're doing right and what they're doing wrong. They're probably always listening, waiting for an adult to accidentally offer a possibility or an adventure they'd never thought possible.

"He gets to the third goose and Elliot turns away." *Elliot*, not *you*; I look over at Sasha and see that she is now facing away from the sink and listening to Nell's story, which Nell must also have observed because now she's telling it for more than just Elliot's benefit. "Elliot says, 'I can't watch,' like he knows what's coming, but I don't know what's coming, and the next thing, Dad is digging his heel into what I'm assuming is the neck of the goose. Dig, dig, dig. Elliot yells for Mom but still I keep watching. Dad goes to the middle goose, walking now toward the woods again, the one goose already in his arms, and does the same to it, and he goes to the last goose— the one closest to the woods—and repeats the motion. Heel into neck. Heel into neck, over and over. What economy he had! The way he walked past the first two birds. The way he came back, one by one, so he'd have to carry them only so long and so far."

There is a pause in the story. I turn around and see Nell take a sip of wine and I think, *Definitely, definitely she is drunk.* She says, "That's what I think about."

"You think about the economy of your father, of the hunter," says Sasha, smiling. "Dark."

"It is, isn't it?" says Nell. I've never liked when she sees her own charm, when she's aware of her own oddness. It's like watching her watch a mirror. It's disconcerting.

"Those four years," I say, and hand the last dish to Mindy, who takes it carefully and dries it lovingly, her attention now returned to her chore. "Those four years extra that you guys got because you were older, and all the living that got done before I was old enough to be aware of it—it seems like some of the greatest living Mom and Stan ever did."

"Give me a break, okay," says Nell. "I'm just telling a story."

She's taken my comment as a jab, as sarcasm, which isn't how I meant it. This is why sincerity trumps everything else. This is why a person should never turn to dissembling and lies. When you're ready to come out of it, when you're ready to stop being cynical, people don't know how to read you.

"No," I say. "I mean it. I'm jealous that you had four more years with them when they were younger and happy. I'm jealous Elliot had five more years." I look at Sasha. "I hope it's okay that I'm talking about Dad being young and happy. I'm really not trying to say anything inappropriate."

Sasha touches my forearm, gives it an itty-bitty squeeze, then says to the room, "When did everyone get so sensitive?"

The pink outside the windows has faded finally. The street has filled with cars belonging to people coming home from work. It's Saturday night. They still have half the weekend ahead of them. The streetlight at the foot of the driveway hesitates, then glows thick and steady. The ginkgo in the front yard seems all of a sudden brighter, more golden in the light. We are at the peak of summer. It is nearly three days since my father walked onto his back porch and bit down on a loaded gun. But it feels like an eternity since then. An absolute eternity.

things come to a head in the kitchen

I walk into the kitchen. It's after midnight. Mindy and Sasha went upstairs hours ago. Only the stove light is on in here, and Elliot and Nell are on opposite sides of the island, leaning toward each other, whispering. Elliot's got his cell phone in his hand.

I hear Nell say, "I don't know what to tell you. She's gone too far. I agree. But still."

I flip the overhead switch to let them know I'm there. Elliot stands up and rubs at his eyes. "What the fuck?"

I correct him. "We say 'aphid' in this family, young man." I'm trying to be playful.

"Turn the light off," says Nell.

I turn it off. Nell is still leaning over the counter, but Elliot is standing there, looking at me with his arms crossed. Neither of them makes a move to speak.

"Listen," I say.

Now or never, I'm thinking. *Now or never. Tell them.*

"Kate," says Nell.

"I have something to tell you guys."

"Not now," says Nell.

"Yes, now," I say. If not now, when? Life is now. Life is right this second, whether we like it or not. What changes later? What changes tomorrow? Nothing. Peter needs me to stop calling him. He needs me to stop texting. He needs his space and his time. But to what end? Decisions have been made. Let's get on with it already. Let's face the facts and move on.

"The funeral's tomorrow," I say. "The next day we'll all go home. This isn't a conversation I want to have over the phone." In fact, I have no idea where I'll be going the day after tomorrow. Not home. But Elliot will go home. Nell will go home. I'll go back to Chicago and begin the grave task of separating my things from Peter's, of figuring out how to pay my impossible bills.

Elliot looks like he wants to punch something. He looks, in fact, like he wants to punch me. Probably I should take Nell's advice. I should turn around and slink back upstairs. I should get into the top bunk, fall asleep, and in the morning go to the funeral with everyone else. I should call a cab from the funeral home and have it take me to the airport immediately after. I still have forty dollars and some change. I can make it stretch if I have to. So, yes, we all agree then: I *should* keep my mouth shut. But I don't. Like I said, life is being lived right now. Right this very second.

"Six months ago—" I say.

"Don't," says Nell, standing up straight suddenly.

"—I had an affair."

"Fuck," she says, and stoops over again, so that now her head is resting on her arms, which are resting on the kitchen island.

"You did what?" says Elliot.

"I had an affair."

Nell isn't even looking at me. She's exhausted.

Elliot, though, is at full attention.

I say, "Peter wouldn't stop talking about adopting. Nobody was listening to me. I had an affair."

Elliot takes a step toward me. "Is this why—?"

Nell says, "No."

"Are you going to hit me?" I say. The whole thing reeks of melodrama, like something one of my freshmen would come up with as a substitute for a real climax: the three of us standing in the dark at midnight in a near-stranger's kitchen—our father's funeral looming, me finally sharing my secrets, Elliot considering violence, Nell trying to keep the peace.

"You selfish little—"

Nell interrupts him. "Don't say anything you can't take back, Ell." She puts a hand on his shoulder.

"Ha." He says it in that gross, dull voice that I'm beginning to think all men are capable of. "'Don't say anything you can't take back?' How about 'Don't *do* anything you can't take back?'"

"Like an affair?" I say. "I get it." And I do get it; some decisions are irreversible. But like I've said, sometimes it's the irreversible ones that help a person get to know herself a little better. It's the consequences that matter. It's the fact that there are no do-overs that makes life matter at all.

"You *don't* get it," Elliot says. "You have no idea what you're talking about. That's your problem."

One night, after I'd told him I didn't want a baby—ours or anyone else's—Peter woke me up. I'd cried out in my sleep. "What is it?" he said. "What is it?" He had his hand on my chest. He was trying to comfort me. "Tell me," he said. There was nothing but me and him and the sound machine in that room, and so I told him: It was a dream. A terrible dream. And in the dream I'd awakened in a strange room, a room I'd never been in. A gang of children was crowded around me. "Where am I?" I said to the children. "You're home," they said. "You live here." I shook my head. "I don't," I said. "Tell me where I am." But the children said I was wrong. They said I belonged to them and they to me. I pushed them away. "It's a dream," I told them. I was filled with relief. "It's a dream." But they shook their heads and chased after me. "It's not a dream," they said. "It's real. You want to take care of us. It's real."

I told all this to Peter. My guard was down. I wasn't thinking.

He took his hand away from my chest. "You're trying to hurt me," he said.

"I'm not," I said.

He sat up. Our bedroom was dark. I couldn't see his face.

"Then you have no idea what you're talking about," he said. He slept on the couch that night. I started looking on message boards the next day.

The point: Peter was right then, and Elliot is right now: I have no idea what I'm talking about.

"Oh, Kate," says Nell, but she doesn't say it with any sort

of sympathy. Instead, she's looking at me like I'm some ragged kitten that can't take the hint that this isn't a no-kill shelter.

"You're vile," says Elliot.

I am. It's true. But I'm cornered, trapped. I feel I must claw my way out, and so I say, "You know what? My agent wanted me to write about this."

"Write about what?" Elliot looks bored with me. They both look painfully bored with me, with this stranger who's been masquerading all these years as their sister.

"But I told her there was nothing to write about." I can't stop myself. "I told her there wasn't a story here. I told her, my family is tedious. I told her, my family is shit."

The three of us are just standing here, no longer a single united still life. Lines have been drawn, sides have been taken, teams have been formed. It is me against them.

Elliot's right. This is boring. This late-night run-in feels forced and ultimately inconsequential. To hell with Atlanta. To hell with this funeral. To hell with these people.

"Forget it," I say.

Neither of them responds. They've won. I've lost. I know that much. But the question is, won what? Life? What would that even mean?

They've both got their arms crossed now. They're looking at me like I'm a rat drowning in its own excrement. They're giving me nothing, not even a twig to hold on to. If car keys were on the counter in front of me, I'd grab them and walk out the door. If a bottle of bourbon was on the counter in front of me, I'd grab *it* and walk out the door. But there's nothing on the counter in front of me, and so there's nothing for me to grab, and so, in a completely undramatic fashion, I turn away from them and walk empty-handed and alone out the back door.

"Wait," I hear Nell say.

"Let her go," says Elliot, which is what they both must decide on, because they do let me go.

Outside it's not exactly cool, but the humidity has dissipated and it's actually kind of pleasant. I've always liked Atlanta late at night. Wait. Let me rephrase: at night, I find the city tolerable. There are fewer people (depending on what part of town you're in, obviously). The crickets are out. The crickets *and* the cicadas. It seems almost manageable at nighttime. The streetlights soften the edges, cushion the hard lines.

I take a right out of Sasha's driveway and cross so that I'm on the lighted side of the street. There is no plan. There is no place for me to go. But a walk will clear my head. A walk will calm me down. That's the theory, anyway.

I knew Elliot would react strongly to the infidelity. I knew from the very beginning. So it's not his reaction that comes as a surprise to me. And I knew Nell would be disgusted. But Elliot had called me vile. *Vile.* I can't remember the last time I've even seen that word in print, much less heard it. You'd think I cheated on him. It was hatred I saw on Elliot's face, a look of impasse, as if this time I really have gone too far and now there's no possibility for forgiveness—short term or long.

I was hoping Elliot would take the news more like Rita had, or if not with such generosity, then that he might have reacted with disappointment, but also with pity, also with sadness, also with an air of reassurance. Some indication that *We can get through this, and we'll do it together.* As opposed to

Pack your bags. You're out of this family. Am I missing something?

I replay the scene in my head.

The kitchen. The dark. Nell saying, "Don't." Nell saying, "Not now." And what about what she said when I walked in? Did she say, "She's gone too far"? I had assumed they were talking about Rita. I had assumed they were huddled in the darkness in the kitchen to talk about Rita and Rita's choices.

But Nell said, "Don't."

Nell said, "Not now."

In Elliot's hand there was a cell phone. He must have been on the phone before I walked in. He'd been on the phone with Rita. And Rita—Rita had been on the phone with me.

Thunderbolts.

Lightning.

Clarity.

They were talking about *me*. As in, *I* had gone too far. In advising Rita to cheat, *I* had gone too far. Rita called Elliot. Of course she called Elliot. And she told him. She told him that I thought she should have an affair.

It doesn't feel good, but the revelation actually feels better than my pure lack of understanding. Elliot isn't mad about the affair—well, I'm not sure I should go that far just yet— but what's *really* eating away at him, what caused that gnarly look of hatred, is that I counseled his wife. I counseled betrayal.

Of course. Of course.

It all makes sense now. Which isn't to say I wouldn't do it again—counseling Rita, that is; I'd undo my performance in the kitchen just now in a heartbeat—which *is* to say I do think there's some unpopular sensibility to my logic. But at least I understand the offense, which means I can begin to craft an apology.

And Nell—Nell had said, "She's gone too far." And she'd added, "But still." *But still. But still.* Which means that she sees my side. She might not agree with me, but she is able to see my side; she is able to remember her role as a sister and our roles as family members. We are still a unit. A unit in crisis, perhaps—massive fucking crisis—but still a unit.

I stop under a streetlamp and look up at the muted yellow light. The electricity pulses in the air and makes a thick, buzzing hum. All around the bulb are black winged things that are also buzzing and humming and pulsing, buzzing and humming and pulsing.

And I think, *It's getting closer.* Yes, yes. The epiphany is getting closer. I can feel it. I can feel it knocking about in me, shaping itself, forming itself into something that—one day, one day soon—I will be able to hold on to.

waking up in the middle of the night

I wake up in the middle of the night. My back is moist, my hair damp. I look at my phone. It's 3:15. I'd assumed Mindy was the one who would have nightmares about those geese. But it was me, and in my dream, Nell's story came to life. Only I was Stan. I was the one killing geese. I was the hunter.

I slip off the top bunk and tiptoe downstairs. There's nothing specific that I'm after. No middle-of-the-night sip of wine or bite of ice cream. It's just that Atlanta is starting to feel small again. I'm starting to feel its suffocation. I've been away from my own world too long. I feel displaced, uneasy.

Downstairs, Elliot is fast asleep on the couch. He's thrown off the top blanket. I tiptoe toward him and place it carefully at the foot of the couch. If he wakes up and he's cold, it'll be within his reach.

There was a time—so many years ago it hurts, but there was a time—when I could have crawled into bed with Elliot and there would have been nothing out of the ordinary about it. Nobody would have raised their eyebrows or thought any-thing suspicious was going on. It would just be a brother and his little sister curled up together like two sleeping puppies.

I miss being young. I miss the lack of boundaries. I miss the easy cluelessness of it all.

I make a beeline for the kitchen before I talk myself into getting into bed with Elliot, which would be sheer madness, but there's no trusting me at all these days. And of course, as if to prove the theory, the cash tin is sitting on the kitchen island. Just sitting there. All by itself. My heart makes a thud-ding sound.

Outside the kitchen window, there is a spark of fire. A moment later, I smell cigarette smoke. This makes sense, be-cause when I open the back door, I find Sasha sitting on the swing, sitting in darkness and smoking a cigarette.

"Guilty pleasure," she says.

Thud, thud, thud.

I close the door quietly behind me and take a seat on the concrete railing across from her. "I thought weed was a guilty pleasure," I say. This is the first time the two of us have been alone since she winked at me.

"I am a woman of many vices," she says. Then, after a slow inhalation, she adds, "Do you want one?" She holds the pack toward me so the moonlight hits the plastic wrapper.

I shake my head, then say, "Actually, yes. Sure. That sounds different."

I take a cigarette. She lights a match and holds it so that I have to lean in close.

"You left your money on the counter," I say.

She nods. "I hide the cigarettes underneath."

"I can put it away." I half rise. *Thud, thud, thud.*

"No, no," she says. "Sit."

I do as instructed. "Where do you get it?"

"Get what?" she says. "The weed?"

"Your money."

She lowers her cigarette to a coffee mug next to her feet and taps the tip gently at its mouth.

"You're a nutso little thing," she says.

I clear my throat. "There's nothing little about me."

She smiles and shakes her head. To Sasha, I am both adorable and inappropriate, and for some reason—at least at this moment—she's fine with the combination. "My parents have been generous," she says.

"Family money," I say. Thought so.

"But I'm not a trust-funder or anything. I saved a lot when I was younger." She pauses, as though she's really considering the question, as though she's never had to put the answer into words before. "I wanted my twenties to be about working on my body and working on my bank account. What my friends were doing—drinking, shopping, eating—looked boring to me."

I nod. She wouldn't have liked me in my twenties.

"Your father and I found each other at an interesting time in our lives."

I nod and smoke my cigarette, which is making me instantly light-headed.

"He didn't have any real friends," she says. "At the club, there were people who glommed on to him, but he was too generous. They took what he had and moved on."

"Not you?" I realize it sounds like an accusation, which

is definitely not how I mean it, but there's no going back now.

"You know what I loved about your father?"

It's a rhetorical question—of course I don't know what she loved about Stan. I'll never know. That's the point. And yet she's certainly taking her time with the answer.

"Listen," she says. "There are people—lots of people, most people—who spend a terrible amount of time caring about what other people think. Your father wasn't one of those people."

Maybe he should have been. Maybe he should have cared more.

"I know what you're thinking," she says.

"Yes," I say. "You probably do." And it's true. I have no doubt in the world that she can guess my thoughts. They'd be the thoughts of any kid who felt given up on, abandoned.

"He had this—" She stretches her hand into the air and grabs at it. Then she catches herself and laughs. "You're going to say I sound like your father. But he had this, like, goddamn joie de vivre or something. He wanted to live. It was infectious. It was sexy. You know?"

"Until he didn't want to live." I say it matter-of-factly. Maybe I'm trying to bring her down. Maybe I'm just trying to reestablish a more appropriate mood. I don't know. But Sasha isn't having it.

"Yeah," she says, this goofy grin still smashed across her face. "Yeah, but. Wow. The man oozed charm."

She's remembering something. She's got a specific scene playing on the screen in her noggin. It's private and probably intimate and even if I could see it, I wouldn't understand. But

I do believe her. I do believe in the way he must once have made her feel.

"I don't believe in spiritual connections or telepathy," she says. "But I've been sitting out here for the last half hour willing you to wake up and come talk to me."

"Oh yeah?" I say. Please, please, please, do not let this woman make a pass at me.

"And now here you are," she says. "Maybe it's kismet."

"I had a bad dream."

"The geese?"

"Yes," I say, completely surprised.

"Me too," she says. "It was a nasty little story. Mindy's up there sleeping like a rock, but I tossed and turned just thinking about those terrible boots."

The cigarette is making me nauseous, but I don't want to be rude.

"Were you the goose or Stan?" asks Sasha, and I wonder how she knows to ask that question. Is the choice so obvious? Are there only two ways to incorporate such a story into a dream? What about the little girl? What about Nell? Is there no room to adopt her point of view?

"The hunter," I say.

"Ha," she says. "A guilty conscience."

Yes, I think, a guilty conscience. But unlike Peter, I don't put much stock in dreams unless they feature famous actors.

"You were the goose?" I ask. "Zero guilt?"

"No," she says, stubbing her cigarette into the coffee mug. "I was the little girl. I was Nell."

I feel I've been tricked, but I can't say how and so I say nothing.

"Are you working on anything lately?"

The Failed Comedian, starring Matt Damon as Matt Damon.

"No," I say.

"Maybe you'll get some material out of this visit."

I can picture it now:

```
Fade in on KATE PULASKI, a woman two
   inches too long in every direction.
   She sits next to FRANK, die-hard
   Packers fan, in the last row of an
   airplane that's just made an emer-
   gency landing in Indianapolis. Her
   phone buzzes.
```

"Help me," I say. "I hope not."

Then I think of Marcy's requested memoir. How might that number begin?

My father is dead.

Everybody's father is dead. Try again.

My marriage is over and my father died this morning.

Good God. If I were reading that book, I'd throw it across the room before I finished the first sentence. Try again.

My mother died when I was a little girl. My father died when I was a woman.

Am I trying for chick lit? Keep it simple. Be honest. Facts only.

On June 16, at roughly eight thirty in the morning, I get the phone call that my father is dead. That's not quite right, but it's better. I'd need to get the gun in immediately. *Suicide sells*, said Marcy. Now that—*that* is vile.

Sasha says, "Wait here, yeah? I have something for you."

She gets up and slides quietly inside the dark house. I sit in silence and slowly finish my cigarette. The nausea passes. In college I dated a boy who said it took exactly seven minutes to smoke a perfect cigarette. At the time, I'd thought that was just about the coolest thing in the world. I'd thought he knew something about life and love and what it all meant. I let him pee on me once. It was the last time we went out. I hadn't done it right, I think. I'd just lain there at the bottom of the tub, my knees bent awkwardly so that both he and I could fit, and watched as he took aim and peed. I hadn't held my hands up. I hadn't opened my mouth. Afterward—after I'd turned the water on and washed myself thoroughly—he'd sat on my windowsill and smoked a seven-minute cigarette. Then he said, "That's not how I fantasized it happening." If I could go back, if I could go back to that moment, I would have said something better. I would have said, "You think that's how *I* imagined it?" Or "You *fantasized* about that?" Or "What the aphid is wrong with you?" Instead, I just looked down at the pilled yellow carpet and picked at its weave.

Sasha returns with a shopping bag that she sets carefully next to her on the swing.

"What's that?" I say.

"Two things," she says. First she pulls out a large jeweler's box, which she hands to me. I'm surprised by its weight.

"What is this?"

"Open it," she says. I wonder if Sasha has been having

moments like this with Nell and Elliot, if she's been pulling them aside and bequeathing them random gifts as well.

I open the velvet clamshell. My mother's gold Rolex is inside. It's suddenly difficult to breathe. This watch is worth the equivalent of my debt.

"I don't understand," I say.

"It's yours, isn't it?"

"It's my mother's."

"But it was meant to be yours. Your father told me about it when we married. He kept it in a tiny safe in the bedroom."

I take it from the box and slip it onto my wrist. The last time I wore it I was eight, maybe nine years old, and it was far too large for me. Now, though, it fits beautifully. I imagine Stan showing it to Sasha, teaching her how to lock and unlock the safe. It wouldn't have been his style to give me the watch himself. Of course it had to go down this way, cloaked in a veil of mystery.

"I thought it was gone," I say.

She shakes her head.

"This is not what I was expecting when you said we needed to talk."

"There's more," she says, and begins to take something else from the plastic bag. "Wait," she says. "What did you think this was about? I'm curious."

"It's embarrassing," I say, and it *is* embarrassing. People are so much more interesting than my bland preconceptions allow them to be. If only I could turn off my brain's tendency to overthink.

"Tell me."

I look down at the watch. My mother must have looked off balance in such a large piece of jewelry. She was more delicate than me, more bird-boned, more petite.

"It's just—" I say. "Earlier, when you said we had to talk, I had this far-fetched theory that you were going to tell me that you're Nell's lover."

She takes out another cigarette and puts it in her mouth but doesn't light it.

"Why did you think that?" she says.

I shrug my shoulders and twist the watch back and forth.

"Who knows?" I say. "You two just seem so close. My mind goes too far sometimes." She says nothing. "It's a bad habit." Still she says nothing. "Like eavesdropping."

She strikes a match and finally lights the cigarette. She takes a long drag that feels silly and mannered. "I am not your sister's lover," she says. Then, after mulling it over, she says, in this sort of tragic way, "We're friends, Kate."

"Yes," I say. "Yes, of course."

"I really was in love with your father. Until he made it too hard. Then I left."

I nod.

"Can I ask you something?" I say.

"Why not?"

"With Mindy?" I'm struggling for the right way to ask this. I don't want her to think I'm judging her. "Did you ever think he was too old, or that it was a bad decision?"

"Are you asking me if I ever thought about not having her?"

"Yes."

"Yes," she says. "I thought about it."

We sit in silence. The A/C inside shakes on and the back porch hums.

"But?" I say.

"The pros outweighed the cons."

She yawns. Like everyone else, Sasha is growing bored with me.

"Can I ask you something else?" She could be *my* friend too, couldn't she? That's how friendship works. It's not a limited substance.

"I guess," she says. "Go for it."

"That you know of, did he cheat on you?"

Why does it matter? I don't know. But I feel the answer might bring me insight.

She shakes her head. "I knew what his habits were," she says. "The story we sold the family was that he was divorced from Louise before we got together." She takes a quick drag. "That was a lie. He cheated on Louise with me. I knew he was married."

Another adulteress. It *is* easy. I was right.

"But because of that, because I knew what he was, I made him promise."

I nod. "And you think he never did?"

She lifts her shoulders, then lets them fall back into place bit by bit. "Maybe I'm naïve, but I believed him," she says. "I never felt unloved. That's the important thing. I left when his mind went, and that's a burden I'm going to have to deal with all on my own."

I've asked her too much. I've invaded her space.

"You would have liked him," she says. "If he wasn't your father. You would have liked him."

She's probably right.

I fidget with the watch. "Thank you." I stand and stretch. "I never thought I'd see this again."

She grabs my wrist.

"Wait," she says. "You forgot. One more thing."

She hands me the shopping bag.

"What is this?"

"Also for you," she says. "Your father wanted you to have it. In his note, he asked me to give this to you."

I take the bag but don't look inside.

Wait.

"There was a note?" I say. Nell said nothing about a note. Elliot said nothing about a note. Which means either they don't know about it or they *do* know about it and have said nothing to me.

"Yes," she says. "There was a note. For me."

She stubs out the second cigarette in the same coffee mug at her feet, then rises and squeezes my shoulder.

"Bedtime," she says. "I'm beat."

And, according to Sasha anyway, this is the end of the conversation.

—·—

alone in the bathroom again

I go upstairs and get into the top bunk. Nell stirs, but she doesn't wake up. Honestly, I wish she would. I wish she'd all of a sudden kick the bottom of my mattress and say, "Are you awake," and I'd say, "Yeah, are you?" And she'd say, "Do you feel as lost and lonely and out there as I do?" And I'd say, "Yes, yes, yes." I'd tell her about the note and we'd decide *as a family* what we think about that. We'd decide whether we should demand to see it or whether we're all right with it being something personal, between husband and wife.

Outside, on the porch, I was tired. But now I am wide awake, my heart and brain racing to see which can go faster.

I climb back off the bed and just stare at Nell. I try to will her awake, attempting to summon whatever black magic Sasha summoned in order to will me awake. She doesn't budge. I could just wake her. I could just shake her until she groggily comes to, but that would seem too theatrical. That would seem like the kind of thing you do when someone is newly dead, not when he's a few days dead and all you've done is discover that he left a note.

I go to the guest bathroom and take my shopping bag with me. I lock the door before lowering the toilet lid and taking a seat.

It's a book. That's all. A copy of *The Egoist*, by George Meredith. I open the front cover and find exactly what I thought I'd find—an inscription from me to my father. *Happy 50th. Maybe you'll learn something.* I close the cover. Heat rises in my cheeks. This is what shame feels like. I remember this gift very clearly. I remember how dignified I felt, how righteous. I hadn't even read the book myself, but I thought the title would somehow disgrace him, would somehow suddenly shine a mirror in front of him. We were in the process of packing up the high-rise and moving in with Joyce by then. Nell and Elliot were off doing their own things at college. They never would have approved of such a gift. They would have said it was funny in theory only. In reality, it brought me to his level. And now here I am, sitting on a toilet, clutching it to my chest as if it's the man himself.

In a note to his wife, my father told her to return this to me. I am completely ashamed. What must Sasha think of me? No wonder she wants to keep the note to herself. I wouldn't want to share it with me, either. What kind of daughter gives a gift like this to her own father, no matter what kind of father he is? A worthless daughter. A cruel daughter.

It isn't fatigue that comes over me now. It's lethargy. It's sheer lack of energy or willpower. I could die on this toilet for all I care. I could sit through the night and let them find me tomorrow, toppled over and, if we're all lucky, magically dead from a head wound incurred in the fall. Would anyone inherit my debt?

And now I'm feeling sorry for myself, which is even worse than shame. Even worse than just owning up to how I was and maybe even how I still am. I open the book and reread the inscription. This book is my punishment. From the grave, Stan Pulaski plays a powerful final move.

I flip to the opening chapter and am surprised to find a series of pencil-scribbled notes. I rub my eyes, squint, and bend closer to the text. Though miniscule to a degree that borders on obsessive and not the way I remember it, this is my father's handwriting. I flip through a few more pages. Each one's margin is filled with penciled notes. I stop randomly somewhere in the middle and read: *They let me get my hand in the pork and beans, and it was good and it was sweet.* I flip ahead and find this: *I went and did and gratified. Go and do and gratify.* I flip to the last page, which is covered entirely with the same thing: *Ack ack ack. Ack ack ack. Ack ack ack.* I flip to the title page. Beneath *The Egoist*, he has written, *This is a story about passion. About not letting your brain die. Don't let your brain die.* The words of the last sentence are underlined. One at a time. <u>*Don't*</u> <u>*let*</u> <u>*your*</u> <u>*brain*</u> <u>*die*</u>. The only other bit of his handwriting on this page is at the bottom. It's written more carelessly than the writing beneath the title, as if it was a last-minute thought or as if he hadn't planned to add anything else to this page, but then changed his mind. It says only this: *He was best at mealtime.* It was how Sasha began her eulogy—if you can call it a eulogy—which means she's read this book. Or at least she knows what's here. I don't blame her. How could I blame her? I'd have done the same thing.

I turn the book upside down and hold it by its covers. The pages open like an accordion. I give the book a gentle shake, and a piece of paper falls into my lap. How did I know to do this? Because I am his daughter. Because I'd have hidden a note, too.

I close the novel and set it on the floor next to my feet. The paper is thin and waxy. The writing is even more delicate, even more miniature than the writing in the book. I hold it up to the light and read. *You think I don't feel anything, but that's not true. I feel everything. I feel too much. It is the same with you. You think I'm being mawkish. What I'm being is an original. What I'm being is on the fringe.*

There is a knob at the base of my throat, a fast-distending knob.

He used to hold up his hands and say, "Hit me. It will make you feel better." And do you know what? It always did make me feel better, which made me hate him even more. I was young. I didn't want a simple solution. I wanted to struggle.

It must be close to four or even four thirty by now. The viewing isn't until ten. If I get back in bed now, I might get an hour or two before the sun comes up, before someone makes their way to the kitchen to brew coffee, before Mindy heads to the TV room and turns on the morning cartoons just a little too loud.

Ack ack ack. What troubles me is that I think I know what he means.

— ···· —

39

Peter calls

Morning comes sooner than I want it to. Little baby birds chirp outside the window. Electricity in use purrs all around me. I'd insisted to Peter I wasn't depressed, but surely there is something wrong when the sound of morning birds—when the mere sight of daylight—fills your brain with sorrow and woe.

I bend over the top bunk and look below. Nell isn't there. I listen harder, ignoring the nest of hungry bobwhites outside my window. The shower is running.

It doesn't smell like anyone's started coffee yet, so if I go down, at least there will be something for me to do.

There's a buzzing beneath my pillow. I lift it and there's my phone. I must have stashed it there when I finally climbed back into bed. Dad's book is also beneath the pillow, and I have no memory of having put it there. I crack my neck, which thankfully appears to have no memory of having slept on the six-hundred-page novel.

I answer my phone. It's Peter.

"Hi," I say, sounding, no doubt, stunned.

"Hi," he says.

I've been waiting for this call. But in all that waiting, I've not planned anything significant to say.

"Is this a good time?" he says.

"Sure," I say. "Yes. Of course." I sit up in bed.

"Here's the deal," he says. He's already had coffee. Either that or he's been up all night. He sounds entirely too alert for six a.m. on a Saturday morning. But that's Peter. Entirely too alert. More alert than I've ever given him credit for.

"Listen. I'm sorry about the airport."

"Me too," I blurt out.

"Let me talk, all right?" His tone is gentle, not at all aggressive, and this—not yesterday, not the day before, not the day before the day before, but now, this very instant—is when I know for sure, 100 percent, that it is over. If we had a fighting chance, he'd be livid. But all the fight's gone out. Of him. Of me. It's what I knew was coming, and maybe even what I've wanted, but now it has arrived. I'd heard the whistle, but now the train has officially reached the station.

"All right," I say.

This is it. This is how two grown-ups end a marriage.

"Go ahead."

"I'm sorry about the airport and I'm sorry about Nell."

He pauses, but I don't dare interrupt.

"I could tell by how she sounded that you hadn't told her yet. I didn't mean to out you. I want you to believe that. I really, truly thought you'd have told her."

He pauses again. I say very quickly, "I believe you," and

I do. And it dawns on me: Peter is still the man I married. He's every bit the decent, intelligent man I chose all by myself more than a decade ago. The man I confided in about my credit card bills. The man who, without an ounce of judgment, helped me chart the slow path to recovery. Nobody had a gun to my back. Nobody forced me into a corner. It's not his fault that his biological clock started ticking. He was only being honest.

"You're dealing with things down there. Things that I'm sure are different and probably harder than you thought they'd be."

He pauses. I am not crying. Perhaps we are both disappointed. Perhaps we are relieved.

"I'm going to go away for a little while."

Another pause. Still no tears.

"I'll be gone for a week at least. At least through next Sunday."

Another pause. And while I am not exactly crying, I am aware of a swelling in my ducts. I am aware of a burning in the bridge of my nose.

"You'll have the place to yourself to pack up," he says. "This seems pretty fair to me."

And it seems pretty fair to me too, but I am unable to say anything.

"Kate?" he says. "Are you there?"

I nod, but of course he can't see me.

"Kate?"

Just then the bedroom door opens. It's Nell, in a towel. Her hair is dripping. I hold out the phone to her. She doesn't immediately understand, but something on my face—a look of panic, a look of heartbreak, a look of acceptance—clues her in enough to take the phone and answer it.

All I can do is nod, which Nell relates perfectly—as perfectly as I would have her do it—to Peter. With intermittent pauses for his words—I know better than to guess the specifics—she says, "We understand. No, of course. We think that's very fair. Yes, of course. You too, Peter. You too."

She closes the phone, and I take a deep breath. If tears were imminent a moment ago, they've passed now.

"Are you okay?"

She hands me the phone.

"Better now," I say. "That will be the worst of it." Then I tap my chest. "In here. That will be the worst of it in here. We've been headed this way for a while, I think. Even before."

She's looking up at me where I'm sitting on the top bunk, my legs hanging over the side. She puts her hand on my knee. "It's all going to be fine. You know that, right?"

I nod. "I know that."

"You have some work to do, though."

"With Elliot?"

"With everyone," she says, then moves her hand from my knee to my wrist. She turns the watch so it faces her. "It looks good on you."

"You think?"

"Yeah," she says. "You wear it well."

Of course she isn't surprised by the watch, which means she's known about it. Which means she might also know about the book and perhaps even the note. I look at Nell—Nell, whom I'd always regarded as an open book. Yet another thing I was wrong about.

"Why do you do it?" she says.

"What?"

"Lie."

I look at the ceiling, but there are no answers there, no cue cards written out.

"I don't know," I say. "I really don't."

She nods. "You should think about seeing someone."

Now I nod.

"A therapist," she says.

"But not Peter," I say.

"No," she says, and she gives me a queer little smile. "Not Peter."

"Nell?" I say.

She twists then squeezes her hair so that large droplets of water land on the rug at her feet.

"Are you still mad at me?"

"I don't think so," she says. "I'm just trying to figure you out." She fake-punches me on the shoulder and says, "Let's do this thing."

By which she means, let's go say goodbye to our dad.

the silent treatment

Nell lets me sit in the front seat on the drive to the funeral home. She doesn't admit it, but I know what she's doing. She's trying to keep a little distance between me and Elliot. It makes no difference. His contempt is palpable from the back-seat. I tried over coffee to break the ice, but he just turned around and walked out of the kitchen. He didn't say anything. He didn't give me a dramatic stare. He just turned around and walked away. To me, this means the ball's in his court. Not that he owes me an apology, but if you're going to thwart someone's attempt to right a wrong, then it's on you to let that person know when you're ready to hear offers. If Elliot wants to be left alone, I can leave him alone. At least, I can try.

On the drive over, Mindy is somber and somewhat frantic where she sits in the booster seat behind her mother. She looks grayer than she has the past few days. She wouldn't eat break-fast, and now her hair is hanging lopsided into her face. Her immediate mission is to complete a scarf she started knitting only last night. She wants to put it in the coffin with Stan. She's asked permission. None of us has a problem with it, and heaven knows those funeral directors have seen worse and weirder. Mindy has been told that she will be seeing her father for the last time. She has been told that he will look the same, but also different. She's been told that if she feels scared or sad at any time, she should simply tell Sasha, and Sasha will whisk her away. But it's unclear what Mindy actually understands. It's hard enough for *me* to understand exactly what's about to happen. Of course it's hard for a six-year-old.

Mindy's knitting needles click away in the backseat. Sasha turns up the A/C and turns down the radio.

"I talked to Louise this morning," she says.

"How'd that go?" says Nell.

"She's not coming."

"Fine by me," says Elliot.

"Whitney and Stan Jr. aren't coming either," says Sasha.

"Is there anyone you didn't talk to?"

"I didn't talk to them," she says. "Only Louise. She couldn't wait to tell me."

"That woman is a piece of work."

"I did call Lily, though," she says. "And she said she's still coming, so I asked her to pick up Joyce."

"Good," says Nell. "That was good thinking."

And it was good thinking; it was great thinking. Here's this woman, this woman who is younger than I am, my father's fifth and final wife, and she's handling all the exes and their children. What is she, a superhero? Why isn't one of us—me, Nell, or Elliot—handling this? Why is it I feel we are some-how the children in all this? Not adult children, but *children*

children. Sasha makes me feel young and incapable. Is it just that she has a kid and has to behave more maturely? Is it that simple? I'd probably be more bothered by it except that I'm just so relieved that all this organizing has been taken care of by somebody else. And it's so nice to have things taken care of! I miss having parents.

"So it will be just the seven of us," she says, "and we can stay as long or as short as you want. I promise not to get all sappy in there."

"Get as sappy as you like," I say, sort of surprising myself. "For real. Who knows what we're walking into? I mean, how can anyone prepare for this sort of thing?"

No one says anything, which makes me think they haven't understood.

"I mean an open casket," I say.

Still nothing.

"Because of, you know." I tap my head.

"Jesus," says Elliot. He punches the back of my seat. "We get it already."

Mindy knits more furiously.

"Sorry," I say.

I look out the window. I am eternally dense.

To my right is Bitsy Grant, where Stan used to play tennis on the weekends. Golf was for suckers, he said. Golf was for Republicans. He'd been a Republican when he was younger, when there was more money, before all the alimony and child support. Then he became a liberal. He became a liberal who believed in playing tennis and bulk-buying at Sam's Club. Then he became a depressive and a hoarder and, somewhere in there, suicidal.

Joyce and Lily are sitting outside the funeral home when we pull up. There's this "shade garden" that's been created in the center of the parking lot. But now, because of the garden and its three myrtles and two benches, the parking lot is a roundabout.

We park in one of the spots reserved for loved ones—that's what the sign says, FOR LOVED ONES. It's old-school Atlanta out here.

Mindy dashes across the parking-lot-slash-roundabout to the shade garden, where Joyce is already beginning the tiresome task of standing, brushing herself off, and straightening her body as best she can. Lily is holding her elbow gently, and I'm reminded all over that I oughtn't punish this young woman just for having a toad of a mother.

"They're ready for us," says Lily, as they cross toward us. "But we thought we'd wait for y'all."

Normally, at a funeral, which this certainly is not—this is a viewing, a saying-goodbye and nothing more—there is someone who is obviously the lead beloved. There is the current wife or the oldest son or the most cherished granddaughter who everyone in attendance understands has the most right to grief. But here, it is not so simple. Not so obvious. There is the current wife, who is also the estranged wife and about whom I am still feeling the tiniest bit silly for having mistaken her winks and touches as flirtations. There is the oldest wife, who is also the most removed, the most out to lunch, the closest to death. There is Lily, who—though she came after us—was probably just as neglected as we three were, if not more. Dad hated Whitney. He would have had an even easier time writing off the twins than he did us. There is

Mindy, who probably really does love him more than anyone else here, but she is the youngest and therefore the slowest and least able to comprehend. There are the three of us and we are here, we did come here, we did make this awful trip, but that certainly doesn't merit title of chief beloved.

And so, as a result, the seven of us walk toward the French doors of the funeral home as a sort of stilted blob—none of us wanting to claim the lead, none of us wanting to be left behind.

I'm right there in the middle of the blob, right there at its heart as we funnel clumsily through the doors and into the icy, achy air-conditioning of the reception area. There is a hand at my back and I turn and there is Mindy, my little confidante. My gangly angel fairy. My sister.

"Here," she says in a throaty, high-pitched whisper. She holds up the world's narrowest and least effective knit scarf. "Do you think he'll like it?" She is all sincerity, all earnestness and honesty. There is not an ounce of treachery or cynicism in her.

I take the scarf and study it. In fact, the stroke work—except where she ended and was in such a hurry—is quite skillful.

There is a whole universe at work in Mindy's brain, a whole universe of thoughts and wonders and concerns. There is an entire person in there, just waiting to get big and grow up and regret life. And suddenly, I see that the most important thing in the world isn't that I missed my own childhood, but that she not miss hers.

"He'll love it," I say. "He'll just love it."

41

goodbye

The problem with funeral homes is that there's all this formality and forced solemnity. There are *expectations*. For instance, there are the two funeral directors' expectations that Stan Pulaski's family members are—at this very moment—emotionally crippled by their sudden and wholly unexpected loss. (Perhaps we *are* emotionally crippled, but if so, it's a pre-existing condition, not one that was spurred by our father's actions and can therefore be healed by our time with him here today). And it's my belief that these expectations, more than anything, are what make people behave like emotional cripples when, really, all most of us want to do at times like this is get in and get it over with. It's what I'd like to do, anyway. I'd like to get in there, do whatever it is we're here to do, and go home. Or go back to Sasha's, at the very least.

The thing is, this makes me sound like I'm not having some reaction to all this. And I am. Since my time alone in the bathroom last night, I've been feeling—what's the word?—*moved*. It's not that his scribblings have, overnight, corrected whatever was wrong with us—with me and him—it's more that I am willing, in a way I formerly was not, to see that there were depths to him. There were sides of him I couldn't see or that he chose not to show me. All I'm saying is that there was more to the man than I suspected or allowed. And while there's still every possibility that it's entirely his fault, as a parent, for not exposing me to the other sides, the more interesting sides, the more honest sides, there is also the possibility that I backed him into a corner. That I made certain decisions about him that he didn't know how to refute or lacked the energy to disagree with and so he simply assumed the role I believed him already to be fulfilling. "Giraffe," he'd said once, and I'd watched as his hands bent and molded themselves into the head of that great animal. "Rooster," he'd said. And I couldn't take my eyes away.

The air smells like formaldehyde, and I feel a little light-headed. It's possible the A/C's laced with laughing gas. If I were a funeral director, I'd lace the air with laughing gas. It would be my first order of business on my first day on the job. I'd say, *Get these mourners drugs, and do it STAT.*

We are now in the room with the coffin, and he is there, just over there, on the other side of the thin coffin wall. There is no procession. There is no line. There are two couches and we are huddled around them and periodically one or two of us stand, stretch, pretend to consider coffee, and then make their way slowly over to the man. To Stan. Where he has ostensibly been reconstructed.

Those of us who are still sitting, who have not yet wandered over—we are respectful of the quietude of the ones who have. We pretend not to see them as they approach the coffin. We pretend, when they return to our small gathering at the sofas, that we do not notice that the blood has drained slightly from their cheeks. We pretend they have gone to get coffee, nothing more. It is coffee and coffee alone that explains their absence. This is what we pretend. Ah, family!

It is only me now who has not ambled awkwardly over to the coffin. Sasha took Mindy, holding her hand, and we all pretended to look the other way. She picked up her daughter and rested her on her hip so the lanky thing could look down and see him, see what was there, what was left of him and how he looked in her freshly knitted scarf. And now they are done; they are among us once again, and it is down to me. We sit a little while longer and I can feel that there is a push for me to go. There is a tacit agreement that now it is my turn and my burden and I must go. Go and do and gratify. The sooner I have performed my duty, the sooner we can leave.

I stand. My knees feel gummy, my vision rubbery. Perhaps this is visible to the others, because now Sasha is at my side, her hand is beneath my elbow, and she is walking me, pushing me, moving me noiselessly like a Ouija planchette toward the correct answer.

"Why are you doting on me?" I say out of nowhere, not even knowing that I'd been thinking it. "Why are you making me feel special?" No one can hear us. We are too far from the sofas now and the A/C is too noisy.

"Because you seem like you need it," she says.

We are approaching the coffin; we are approaching the edge of it.

"Need what?"

"Attention," she says.

"That's it?" I say.

"That's it," she says, and gives my elbow the slightest squeeze to let me know that we are here, that we have arrived. Finally. At long last.

There he is. Shiny. Strange. His large face with its large features. His hands, folded together, a million different animals hiding in those fingers. Oh, Stan. Oh, Dad. Sasha thinks we would have been friends, if only I hadn't been your daughter. But that's not exactly right, is it? We would have been friends if I'd *been* your daughter and you'd actually *been* my father. If there hadn't existed eleven different versions of me in your life. If you could have picked me. Decided on me. Then, maybe, we would have been friends.

"Okay," I say.

I feel sick.

"I'm good," I say.

I start to pull away.

"Wait," she says.

From her back pocket she removes a small piece of paper. She takes a deep breath and hands it to me.

"What's this?"

"It was wicked of me to mention it and then not offer," she says.

I start to unfold it.

"Wait," she says, her hand on mine, the paper in my palm, still unopened. "If you have to read it, I understand. But what I wanted was for you to give it back to him."

"I don't understand."

"It's not something I want to be burdened with," she says.

"I think it's unhealthy, keeping something like this around to put on a pedestal, like it actually has answers."

The note. Of course. How did it take me so long to understand? Between *The Egoist* and Peter's phone call, I'd forgotten all about the note. The note from my father. To Sasha. Not to me. Not to Nell. Not to Elliot. But to Sasha.

"All this?" I say. "Just to give it back?"

"And for Mindy," she says.

I want to turn and look at Mindy, to find her in that small crowd of family behind us, but I'm afraid I'll catch them all watching. It's just as important that they too go unnoticed. There is a spell at work. A funeral home spell of gravity.

"Why me?" I say. Sasha's hand is gone from mine now. It is returned to her own person. The note is mine. It is in my palm and I know that I will never open it and I know it does not matter.

"Like you said. I want you to feel special."

I am overcome with gratitude.

"One question," I say. I'm looking at Stan, but I'm talking to Sasha.

"Anything," she says.

"To write a letter. To ask you to give me that book. He must have been lucid, right?"

She puts her hand around my waist and leans into me. "No clue," she says. Her breath is warm. She smells like the South. Like Chanel and old women and daffodils. "Not a clue in the world."

I move the paper to my right hand, then lower it slowly to his breast pocket.

"Here?" I ask.

"Good," she says. "All done. How's your heart?" She looks at my chest. I follow her gaze and look down too, at my hand, my telltale hand, clutching yet again.

"My heart is fine," I say.

Very fine. Thanks for asking. Finer than it's been in years.

—·—

cooking dinner

Mindy," I say. "What's your take on life? Where do you come down on things?"

We've pulled up stools to the kitchen island in order to watch Nell and Sasha slice and dice and prep for dinner. Mindy is in control of a package of M&Ms, which she's strategically emptied onto the counter in front of her and is now arranging into tidy rows.

She raises an eyebrow and scrunches up her nose. I want to gobble her up.

"I like bread," she says, and continues with her M&M organization.

"I like bread too."

"But I *really* like bread," she says, and she seems suddenly sad about it. As if, yet again, the weight of the world is on her shoulders. As if her feeling for bread is so strong it's unmanageable and therefore a little frightening. She has a bit of our father about her. A bit of that all-or-nothing mentality. I see it peeking out at me.

"Know who else likes bread?" says Sasha, wiping her knife on her apron. "This one here." She jabs Nell in the side with her knuckles.

Nell turns from the stove and winks at Mindy. "I do. I like bread and I like butter. In fact, I *love* butter."

I look at Mindy; she is unimpressed with these two. As am I. I'm much more interested in my half sister and her M&Ms right now. The casual cooking banter is too kooky. It really is like they're flirting, but maybe this is simply what friendship looks like these days. Maybe this is intimacy. It's been a while since I've experienced it firsthand.

"Seriously though." I undo a row of Mindy's M&Ms. She corrects them and flits my hand away. "What are your plans for life? Do you have a career in mind?"

"Cashier," she says quickly, not taking her eyes off the candy.

"A cashier?"

She nods. She's embarrassed, I can tell. This cashier business must previously have been a secret. But she also seems privately pleased to have finally told someone.

"What kind of cashier?"

She says nothing.

"At the grocery store?"

"Yes."

"Why?"

"Is it bad?" She slides two M&Ms in my direction. I pick them up and pop them in my mouth. She giggles.

"No." In fact, cashier is something I might consider this summer. Sasha's done a good job of teaching Mindy about being open-minded. When I was a girl, if I'd told Stan I wanted to be a cashier, he'd have said, "Try again."

"It's great," I add, play-knocking my shoulder into Mindy's. "I just want to know more about you."

Sasha turns and smiles at me, but I can see she's dubious about my line of questioning.

"They're so nice," Mindy says. "And I like the buttons."

"On the register?"

"They're popular."

"The buttons?"

"The cashiers!"

"Oh," I say. "The cashiers are popular."

"Yes."

She is again very serious.

"And *you* want to be popular?"

"Yes."

I nod. I wish I'd been this honest when I was young. I wish I'd known it was all right to admit to wanting friends, to wanting many friends. But I was always so ashamed. Self-reliance seemed to be what was valued in our family. Popularity was for the common man. We were individuals. We needed only one another and our minds and a few solid birthday parties at Benihana.

"Popularity isn't everything, though, right?" says Sasha, looking at her daughter.

Mindy looks down at the M&Ms and blushes. They are now divided into rows of two. She pops a pair into her mouth and I imagine Noah's animals. There they go, two by two. It seems a fair and gentle way to kill an M&M, with a friend at its side.

"But it's not awful either, is it?" I address this to Sasha. "I mean, is it? I wish I'd been more comfortable with popularity when I was in school. I wish I'd been less embarrassed."

"You had friends," says Nell.

I think about last night, sitting on the back porch, Sasha insisting my father had no real friends.

"I didn't," I say. "I'm not looking for sympathy. But I really didn't. I had boyfriends."

"Oh," says Sasha. "She had *boy*friends. 'Look at me, I'm Kate and I have *boy*friends.'" She does this playfully and with a singsong quality to her voice.

Mindy giggles and two more M&Ms bite the dust.

I laugh to show I'm not offended and because laughter is expected at this moment, the way solemnity was expected earlier at the funeral home. "That's not how I meant it."

"Yeah, yeah," says Sasha.

"I just mean, I think I was pretty lonely for a child, especially after Nell and Elliot left."

"I would have been nice to you," says Sasha.

And, you know, I believe her. Even if she hadn't liked me, she would have been kind to me. I bet she was the kind of girl who defended the kid at the back of the class who got caught picking his nose. She probably picked her own just to make him feel comfortable and to shame her classmates for being brutes. She probably ate the booger just to drive the point home.

Mindy polishes off the M&Ms. Noah's ark is closed for business. The boat is officially at sea, bobbing about in the furious waves, waiting patiently, if not fretfully, for the promised dry land.

Elliot's on the phone in the living room. He hasn't said anything to me since the drive to the funeral home. After the viewing, he looked peaked. And I couldn't tell whether it had to do with me or with Rita or with Dad. There's a connection between fathers and sons—even ones who aren't close— that must be beyond a daughter's understanding. Seeing our father lying there must have been, to Elliot, a little bit like seeing himself lying there, like seeing into the future to his own death, either timely or untimely. Or maybe I'm making too much of the situation. Maybe I'm imposing significance where there isn't any.

"What's for dinner?" says Mindy, hopping off her stool and going around to Nell and Sasha. She is bored with me now that her M&Ms are gone.

"Indian," says Nell, who has once again stripped down to a tank top, boxers, and an apron.

"We're going to eat an Indian?" I say.

The three of them turn and look at me.

"Inappropriate," says Nell.

"But funny," I say.

Mindy bites her bottom lip and smiles. What could be better to a child than to see an adult being disciplined?

"Yum, yum, yum," I say, ignoring Nell and Sasha and rubbing my stomach for show. "That Indian better stay in my belly."

"Totally messed up," says Nell, shaking her head and turning back to her pots. She's not really annoyed. She's just trying to set an example. We play this game all the time with

Elliot's girls. Good aunt, bad aunt; crazy aunt, sweet aunt; et cetera, et cetera.

Sasha nudges Mindy with her spatula. "It's the Indian's fault," she says. "For being so tasty." She looks at me and winks, as if to say, *You're cool. It's all cool.* And I think, *This family is fine. Perfectly fine, if you ask me.*

43

movie time

After dinner, Nell and I sit outside while Elliot and Sasha do the dishes. Mindy's upstairs taking a bath. She's been promised she can stay up late tonight, since it's our last night in town, but only if she's in pajamas and ready for bed.

"I don't have a return flight," I say.

Nell and Elliot are both scheduled to leave midmorning.

"Sasha will let you borrow her computer," Nell says.

I push us back in the swing and wait. The crickets are quiet tonight.

"Could you buy the ticket for me?"

What I expect is a barrage of questions. What I expect is a complete lack of sympathy.

Instead Nell says, "You didn't really lose your credit card, did you?"

"No."

"Didn't think so." She takes out her wallet and hands it to me. And it's this, this complete willingness to be generous without further explanation, that does it, that gets the honesty flowing.

"I'm in debt," I say. Just like that. As plain as plain can be.

I explain the first thousand. The way it doubled, tripled, then grew and grew and grew. More than anything, she seems curious and a little floored by the idea.

"Forty-eight *thou*sand?" she says.

"There was interest."

"And Peter?"

"Peter saved my life," I say. "I mean that."

"But it's not gone completely—the debt?"

"Ten or eleven more months," I say. "Twenty-something more installments. Every two weeks. But the thing is—"

She cuts me off. "You were only able to make the payments because of Peter."

I nod.

She touches my wrist.

I look down at the watch, the only thing left of our mother.

"You could sell it," she says. She twists it so that the gold glows in the final bit of sun.

I shake my head. "Not an option."

To be honest, I've thought more than once since last night about selling the Rolex. It isn't until this moment that I realize I can never part with it.

"Were you serious about the memoir? Does your agent really want you to write one?"

I shrug. "The problem is I'd have to include me," I say. "And I'd want to leave me out."

"Maybe there's a movie in it?"

But I'm done as a screenwriter, and Nell knows it.

"What's the plan, then?"

"I can still wait tables," I say, and I can. The truth is, I just didn't want to. The truth is, I've been lazy. I teach three days a week when school is in session. There's no reason I can't waitress every weekend. I'll have the time. My apartment will have to be cheap. And I won't be able to furnish it the way I want—the way I was raised. But plenty of people have less. Millions. Millions have less than me. What was it Trump famously said to his finance chief after the bankruptcy? Didn't he point to a bum and say, "That man's at zero, which puts him millions ahead of me"? Or something like that, anyway.

"I can help a little." She says this after some time has passed. After we've both taken another turn or two pushing the swing with our toes.

"If you don't take money, they can't tell you what to do, kid." I lower my voice and say it with a sort of bad New York accent.

"What is that? You're always saying that."

I explain Bill Cunningham. She seems unimpressed.

"Yeah, but—" She waves her hand in front of us. I look out at the yard. "I'm never going to tell you what to do."

Again we sit in silence. Again I wait for the crickets, the cicadas, but tonight they are minding their own business.

After a while Nell says, quietly so they can't hear us in the kitchen, "He'll forgive you. He just needs time."

"I know," I say. "I just wish I could explain it better to him. I hate it when he's mad at me."

"We all hate it when he's mad," she says. "It's the worst

feeling in the world." It's true. It *is* the worst feeling in the world.

"So did Rita do it?" I say. "Did he tell you?"

"He told me she's thinking about it. And in the meantime, she's talking to Elliot about it."

"Weird," I say.

"Maybe," she says, surprising me yet again with her tolerance. "Or maybe more people should be this open."

"Should I text her?" I say.

"You should stay out of it."

We sit in silence for a little bit more. It's getting darker. The streetlamps will turn on soon.

What I understand is that Elliot is conflating me with Rita. Not like he thinks I'm his wife, but he's taking my infidelity more personally than he should because of Rita. He's thinking, *If Kate can do it, then Rita can do it*. He's thinking, *The women in my life are shit*. I'm not saying his logic is flawless, but I am saying that I get it. He's human. We're both human. Too human. If this is my big epiphany it's a pretty quiet one. There's a really good chance that the message that's been waiting inside me to finally take shape is simply "Life is hard." Which makes me not much better than that three-foot talking Barbie from the eighties who opined, when you pulled a string on her back, that math is hard. Well, you know what? Math *is* hard. So is life. Maybe a simple message isn't the worst thing in the world right now.

"Did you think this was how Dad would go out?" Nell asks. She isn't looking at me, just staring out at the middle distance, at the buzzing and pulsing and humming of the streetlights now coming to life. "I'm not trying to get all sentimental on you or anything. But, you know, when you got the call, what did you think?"

I shake my head. "I don't know." But I do know. I felt hoodwinked. I felt duped. I felt like someone had played a joke on me that wasn't funny. I felt left out and made a fool of.

"I don't know," I say again.

Inside, pots and pans are clinking together and the A/C is whirring. Outside it's just me and Nell, and I feel very nearly at peace with the world.

"You know what you were saying before?" says Nell.

"Irmus," I say.

She pinches me. I zip my mouth shut.

"About not having friends when you were little?"

"Yeah?"

"That's my life now," she says. "In San Francisco."

"You have a million friends," I say. We talk on the phone all the time, and Nell's always telling me about some bar or some restaurant or some joke that someone told.

"I have colleagues. I have acquaintances," she says.

I want to disagree with her, because I want her to be wrong. I don't want to think about her in terms of Dad, of being friendless, of the possible implications.

"Kate," she says. "I hate my life. Do you know how many spinach quesadillas I eat for dinner alone in my kitchen each week?"

I open my mouth.

"I'm like a character from one of your screenplays," she says. "That's how two-dimensional I am."

She doesn't mean it as an insult, so I don't pretend to take it as one. I put my hand on her knee. She rests her head on my shoulder. Together we push back in the swing with our bare feet.

"I didn't know you were so unhappy," I say.

"I'm not unhappy," she says. "I just hate my life." Then, out of nowhere, she laughs.

"What?" I say. And really, I'm curious. I'd like to know what's making her laugh like that. Because *I'd* like to laugh like that. It looks fun. It looks like it *feels* good.

"I just realized," she says. "We're orphans."

"Oh, Nell," I say. "We've been orphans for years."

"We have lots of stepmothers," she says. "There's that."

"Including Sasha."

"I wouldn't really call her a stepmother."

I tap her knee so that she lifts her head from my shoulder and looks at me. "I was kind of hoping that you two were gay."

"God," she says, sitting up straight and cracking her back. "I wish. That would solve everything." Then she knocks my head with her knuckle. "It's a busy place up there, huh?"

"Yeah," I say. *Ack ack ack.* "Very busy."

The screen door opens.

Here is Mindy, arms akimbo, decked out in ladybug PJs. I can't remember what it was like when I found out our mother was dead. I was a year younger than Mindy. I must have cried, because it was expected and because I saw other people crying, but there's no way I could have understood it. The way Mindy struggles with *tonight* and *tomorrow* and maybe with time in general just like Pigpie, I'm sure I must have struggled with the idea of *dead* and *gone for good* and *no longer around*. But the specifics of the event are missing, and

I think maybe that's not a bad thing, and I hope, for Mindy, it will be the same. I hope that as she gets older she misses her father, but I hope the pain isn't there. What's there is just a missing piece. A little empty space and a pleasant memory of a man who was around until he wasn't. A puzzle very nearly, but not completely, finished.

"Mom says we can watch a movie," says Mindy.

Sasha appears in the doorway behind her daughter. "Elliot said we should get started without him."

"Is he on the phone?" says Nell.

She nods. "Upstairs." She covers Mindy's ears and Mindy tilts her head back in order to read her mother's lips. "Lots of F-bombs being dropped," says Sasha. "Lots and lots."

Nell pats my leg. "It's not all your fault," she says. "Just remember that." She stands and then offers me her hands. "Up we go," she says. "Movie time."

"Do I really have to go home tomorrow?" I take her hands and rise from the swing.

"You need to be getting on with your life," says Nell, pushing me in the direction of the back door and toward Mindy and Sasha.

"What's 'getting on with your life'?" says Mindy. She leads the way inside.

"That's what I'm trying to figure out, kiddo. When I do, I'll let you know. Deal?"

"Deal," she says, and hops away from us toward the living room. She's already forgotten all about me. All about our deal.

I wish my brain were young again. I wish hopping from one room to the next were enough of an activity to clear away whatever trouble had been plaguing me mere seconds earlier. Peter has cautioned me against such thoughts. "Wishes are for children," he's told me before. "Don't *wish*. Do." Wishes *are* for children, it's true, but that doesn't stop adults from trying. It's a human instinct. To wish we were shorter, prettier, more popular. It's impossible not to entertain the notion, no matter how aggressively we caution ourselves against it. I wish. I wish. I wish. I wish. But Peter does have a point. The word is magic when you're young. When you're older, it's just plain sad.

44

⸺

a minor revelation

In the middle of the movie, with Elliot and Mindy passed out on either side of me—Elliot still not having acknowledged me—I get up to see what's taking Nell and Sasha so long with the popcorn. They're sitting side by side at the kitchen island, their backs to me. Sasha's laptop is open in front of them.

"What are you guys looking at?" I say.

They don't seem startled, exactly, but they perform this curious back-and-forth conversation with their eyes that drives me just a little bit crazy.

"Tell her," says Sasha.

Nell swivels halfway around on her stool so that we're only partially facing each other. She twists her mouth off to the side.

"Tell her," Sasha says again, this time shoving her elbow into Nell's ribs. Maybe they are gay? But they wanted to tell me together? "She can handle it," says Sasha. "I promise."

"I canceled my ticket," says Nell, shutting the laptop and turning fully toward me.

"To go home?" I say.

"Yes."

"Why?" What I'm thinking isn't actually *Why?* What I'm thinking is *How come I have to go home if you don't have to go home?*

"There's still Dad's condo," she says. "We need to figure that out."

The condo. That dreaded place with its dreadful boxes and stacks of *things*. It was only three nights ago that we stayed there. It was only three nights ago that I wet the bed and that Nell threw away the evidence and that we slept holding hands in a room filled with Mindy's glowing stars. It seems a world away, that night. Time does pass. Things do change. But Mindy is right to be confused.

"Okay," I say.

Sasha makes an arc with her hand as if presenting an invisible platter. She's inviting Nell to say more.

"And I might stay on here," says Nell. "For a while. Even once the condo is sorted."

If there is a lightbulb in my head, it is not at this moment flickering to life. I feel 100 percent unable to follow along.

"I don't get it," I say.

"I told you already," she says. "I hate San Francisco."

"Come to Chicago," I say. My voice sounds plaintive.

Nell stands and comes toward me. Why does it feel like I'm being broken up with? Again.

"I miss Atlanta," she says.

"You don't really know anyone here anymore," I say.

"I know Sasha. And Mindy."

And that's when it hits me. "You're going to move back," I say.

She puts her hands on my shoulders like we're about to slow dance or something. "I want friends," she says. "I want a life. I want a chance to meet a man."

"What about your job?" I say. "What about money?"

The thought of my sister, nearing forty, giving up her out-rageous salary and moving halfway across the country scares the shit out of me. Maybe I'm thinking about her offer to loan me money—my ability to take her up on it even though I've already turned her down. If she doesn't have that job, does the offer still stand? But if it's what she wants, who am I to try to stop her?

"I'll come visit you," she says. "I promise. This doesn't mean I can't come to Chicago for a visit."

I let out a sigh and sit down at Nell's abandoned stool. "So what's the plan?" I say.

Sasha says, "She can stay with us as long as she wants. We'll take care of her."

In the movie version of this night, I'd be inexplicably an-gry. I'd storm out of the kitchen and cry my eyes out about feeling excluded. In the movie version, I'd call Nell a terrible sister. I'd say, "You have a sister already. What do you need *her* for? I'm your friend too, you know? I'm supposed to be your best friend." But this isn't the movies, this is real life, and the thing is, my sister is excited about this change. It's all over her face. And it makes me happy to think she has someone to hug good night for a while, even if it's only this weirdo tennis pro who's just a really good friend.

"In the movie version of all this," I say. "I wouldn't be nearly as understanding."

"In the movie version," says Sasha, "I'd be Uma Thurman."

"And I'd be Angelina Jolie," says Nell.

"I'd just be shorter," I say.

45

—— ·—— ——

in bed

In the movie version—the screenplay that is my life—the shot would end here, with me on the top bunk, my hands behind my head. The camera would pull up and away. It would break through the invisible ceiling, pull up and out, show the roof of the house, the neighborhood, the trees. We'd see a sweeping overhead of Atlanta, at night, when it's prettiest. We'd continue up—up and up and up—until Atlanta wasn't even a city, it would just be a map, just a piece of the state, a piece of the globe, a piece of the world.

The director would call "Cut" and I'd roll out of bed and thank the crew. I'd thank Matt Damon, my costar, my best friend, my right-hand man. I'd take off my costume and put on my own clothes and go back to my other life, my real life, and I'd speak my own words, not someone's lines, and everything would be easy-peasy. But this isn't the movies. This is my life. And sometimes life is easier than the movies and sometimes it's harder. Right now, though, it's just longer and slower. No one's there on the other side of a camera, waiting to edit out the boring parts.

I look up at the ceiling, which is so close I could touch it if I wanted, and I realize there are no glow stars here. Mindy hasn't put any up yet. Maybe she's forgotten. And maybe she won't remember. Maybe six months will turn into a year. She'll go from six to seven to eight years old. By the time she remembers, it'll be too late. She'll think she's too old for glow stars and so she'll never sleep under them again. Which strikes me as just about the worst thing in the world.

My first stop once I'm back in Chicago will be the toy store. I won't even go home. I'll get the taxi to take me straight there, so I don't forget. And I'll buy as many as forty-five dollars can get me. But they won't be for me. They'll be for Mindy. If I send them, she'll have to put them up. Because when you're given a gift, there are expectations. Even if she already thinks she's outgrown them, she'll have to put them up. Her mother will make her. If Nell is still here, I'll have Nell make her. It seems absolutely essential that I— that *we*—keep her young as long as we can; that she see life through the eyes of a little girl for as many more days as possible. Growing up is inevitable. What's the point in rushing it?

I close my eyes and imagine the camera panning away. I close my eyes and wait for sleep, thinking, *This is the night. This is the night I will finally sleep all the way through without a single dream or thought to disturb me. This is the night.*

the end

It's five in the morning and Elliot's in the kitchen eating a bowl of cereal over the sink. Only the stove light is on, so I plug in a string of tiny lights that circle the ceiling. The room fills with a milk-yellow half-glow. The lights must be left over from Christmas. It's sentimental—maybe even mawkish—but it's hard not to imagine Sasha hanging them by herself six months ago, her first Christmas alone in this house, our father still alive, still at the condo, just then by himself.

"Coffee," I say to my brother. The only neutral greeting I can think of. "Thank God."

He turns, unsurprised, and nods at me.

I wheel my bag toward the back door and park it there. When I turn back, Elliot's got an empty mug in his hand and is holding it toward me.

"Thanks." I walk over to the counter and go through the boxes of cereal that Sasha left out for us before she went to bed. Mindy is lucky. Sasha is a good mom. They're going to be okay.

I pour myself a cup of coffee and a bowl of cereal and hop up on the counter near the fridge. Elliot is washing his dishes in what appears to be a deliberately slow manner. I have misinterpreted so many actions this past week. I have misread so many signs. But I feel confident just now that his thoughtful gestures at the sink are a silent invitation for me to speak, and so I do. Carefully. Quietly.

"At some point," I say, watching the flakes in my bowl expand as they absorb the milk. "At some point, you're going to have to talk to me again."

He nods at the suds in his hands. "Yes," he says. He does not turn to look at me.

"At some point," I say, venturing further, "you're going to have to forgive me."

"Yes," he says. Still he does not look at me.

I don't want to speak out of turn; I don't want to push him away, but I feel he needs to hear it, and so I say, "And you might have to forgive Rita, too. At some point."

"I know," he says.

"Okay."

"But it's not going to be right this second."

"Okay."

"You were out of line."

"Yes."

It's an odd time to have the realization, but whatever mojo my brother was missing when we got here has found its way back. This isn't a spiritual discovery I'm making. This is a fact. He's mad at me and I know he's mad at me and he'll be mad at me for a good long while, but even knowing this, I'd still rather be in a room with him in it than a room with him not in it. It's as simple as that.

"You didn't have to get up," I say. His flight is five hours later than mine. "But I'm glad you did."

Nell coughs from the kitchen door. "Good morning," she says. She's got her hair in a pile on top of her head again. It feels like a million years have passed since she knocked on the bathroom door at Dad's place, my wet sheets bundled in her arms. But it's only been three days, and I have no idea when I'll see her again.

Elliot, in this jokey kind of way, says, "What? You again?" and then pushes the cereal boxes toward her.

Peter says he's never understood the way we interact. He says it's not normal. Whenever Nell or Elliot calls, I answer by saying, "What do you want?" And Peter always leaves the room, kind of disgusted, muttering, "What kind of greeting is that?"

I tried explaining it to him once. I told him that it's how we say *I love you*. He told me most people just use their words. I told him that words don't always mean what you think they mean. He said maybe that's why my screenplays never work out. He should have known then. We both should have known.

"Elliot is tolerating my company," I say, feeling it's all right to goad him a little. To remind him we are all fallible. "He doesn't talk much, though. He's a taciturn thing."

Nell looks at Elliot. "You haven't told her?"

"No," says Elliot. He pours himself another cup of coffee.

"Tell me what?" I say.

What I'd like is for my brain to turn off, to give up on guessing, to stop trying to see into the future, into someone else's soul. It's so noisy in my brain. Will he tell me he's dying? Will he tell me he doesn't love me anymore? The questions are jockeying for position when all I want is for them to stand still already.

"We can talk on the plane," says Elliot at last.

"What plane?"

I'm slow. So slow. I must be the slowest person on the planet.

Nell pushes me off the counter and takes my spot. I hand her my dirty bowl and my dirty spoon, and she fills them anew with cereal and milk. "Elliot's going with you," she says through a mouthful of food. "We switched his ticket."

I look at Elliot. He shrugs and says, "Someone has to help you move out."

There are a million things I could think to say—there are a million things I *want* to say—but I choose the easiest and simplest one.

"Thanks," I say. And to anyone else listening—our invisible audience—it would seem so insufficient a response. But to Elliot and to Nell—these two people who have been there, for better or worse, since the beginning, who know me best of all even as they are continuing to get to know new sides of me and I of them—it is enough. It is plenty. It borders on too much.

"I can't pay you back," I say. "Not anytime soon."

He nods—which means he knows, Nell has told him everything—and leans back against the island and studies his cup of coffee. "It's funny," he says.

"What's funny?" says Nell, again through a mouthful of cereal, and I can't help it, but my heart swells with what must be the feeling of happiness at just being in a room with these people and at just knowing they are mine and I am theirs.

"Do you ever feel like you're still sixteen?" he says.

Yes.

"Because I feel like I'm still sixteen."

Yes.

"And you're fifteen."

Yes.

"And you're eleven."

With knees like a giraffe.

"The only thing that's changed is how we look."

Yes, yes, yes.

"And now you have a family," says Nell. She puts her spoon down on the counter. She's ready to get serious if she needs to, ready to defend Rita, to defend the sanctity of family and forgiveness, et cetera, et cetera.

"Now I have a family, sure, but even that doesn't change things." He pauses, shakes his head, says, "I can tell you this. I can tell you that if, twenty years ago, someone would have suggested that I'd be the first one to have kids—the *only* one to have kids—I would've laughed."

He brings the coffee cup to his mouth but doesn't take a sip.

"This isn't my life," he says, as if there's nothing more to add to the matter.

"But it *is*," I say, and I feel suddenly and wonderfully sure about this.

It is.

ACKNOWLEDGMENTS

I first encountered the word *irmus* after reading Ann Beattie's article "Me and Mrs. Nixon," which can and should be found in the *New York Times*.

The story Kate is thinking of on page 116 is by Patrick Somerville and is part of his lovely collection *The Universe in Miniature in Miniature*.

Thanks to Helen Atsma for giving this book a home; Maria Massie for finding it; Ben Warner, Anna Shearer, Greta Pittard, and Stacy Stinchfield for being early and enthusiastic readers; MacDowell Colony for giving me time and space to write; bookstores and booksellers everywhere for persisting; my family—you know who you are—for existing in the first place; and, finally, Andrew Ewell, my husband and my most encouraging critic, for being the only person I consistently want to be in a room with.

ABOUT THE AUTHOR

Hannah Pittard is the recipient of the 2006 Amanda Davis Highwire Fiction Award, a MacDowell Colony Fellowship, and a Henry Hoyns Fellowship from the University of Virginia. Her first novel, *The Fates Will Find Their Way*, was a semifinalist for the VCU Cabell First Novelist Award. Her stories have appeared in *McSweeney's*, *American Scholar*, *Oxford American*, and many other publications. She teaches fiction at the University of Kentucky's MFA Program in Creative Writing.

READING GROUP GUIDE
Questions for Discussion

1. Do Kate's descriptions of her childhood sound appealing to you? What about her descriptions of Nell and Elliott's upbringing? Did your interpretation of whether their childhood was a happy one change at all over the course of the novel?

2. What is the significance of setting in REUNION? Does it tell you anything about the characters that Kate lives in Chicago, Elliott in Colorado Springs, and Nell in San Francisco?

3. Every character in REUNION is touched by marital infidelity in some way—Kate and Elliott in particular. Was Kate right to encourage Rita to make her emotional affair physical? How did her experiences with her father's adulterous behavior and with her own affair drive her decision? How did Elliott's experiences color his reactions to Rita's admissions?

4. Why doesn't Kate tell her siblings about her debt? Do you think she was right to keep her financial sit-

uation from her siblings, or do you think she should have told them earlier?

5. What is the significance of the condo porches, which Kate says are "for the mailman and only the mailman"? What about the glow stars that Kate resolves to buy for Mindy? Are there any other recurring images or memories in the story that may indicate themes of the book?

6. Kate often claims to be the only one in a situation who is seeing things the way they truly are. Do you think that's true? Or did you ever find yourself identifying more with one of the other characters? Which character did you identify with the most?

7. Throughout REUNION, Kate contemplates—at her agent's urging—whether to write the very story she's experiencing. She even contemplates various opening sentences, including the sentence the book does, in fact, start with. How does that narrative device change the story for you? How would you describe Kate, as a narrator? Is she reliable? Is she a protagonist or an antagonist?

8. We learn right away that Mindy resembles Kate physically, but they seem to have more than appearances in common. In what ways are they similar? Is Mindy ever a foil to Kate? What other similarities do you notice among the family members?

9. Do you believe divorce is the only solution for Kate

and Peter? Is Peter's desire to have children irreparably incompatible with Kate's commitment to remaining childless? Is Kate's adultery unforgiveable? Do you think Peter and Kate are being fair to each other about their differences and shortcomings?

10. At the funeral home, Kate observes "This has happened before. All these things have happened to other people before us. The world has thought of everything." Do you find this comforting? Does Kate?

11. How would you describe the Pulaski family? Does your description differ from the way the characters describe it themselves? Who is a member of the family? Are they close? Dysfunctional? How does the author indoctrinate the reader into the inside jokes and rituals of the Pulaskis? How has the family changed by the end of the book?

A Conversation with Hannah Pittard

How did you come to write REUNION? Is any of the story drawn from personal experience, or are the Pulaskis purely fiction?

This is a tricky question. REUNION is fiction and the characters are fabrications. At the same time, the story is drawn loosely from my own life. In the summer of 2011, my paternal grandfather killed himself. As Kate isn't close to her father, I wasn't—for various reasons I won't go into here—close to my grandfather. But my father asked me to go to his funeral, and I did. So did my brother and sister. So did my mother, who'd been divorced from my father for more than two decades. We showed up because he needed us. I knew it was something I'd write about eventually.

Although the characters in REUNION have chosen to live all over the country, the majority of the story takes place in Atlanta. Why did you choose that as a setting for the novel?

I was born in Atlanta. I've always wanted to write about it. I like being from the south. I also like being away from it.

As I write this, I live and teach in Chicago. But in just a few months, I'll be moving to Kentucky. I'm both nervous and excited by the prospect of the move. My husband—to whom I am happily married, by the way—and I are ready for a change. I think Kentucky will be a nice gateway state. It's the south, yes, but it's also not the south. Let's see whether or not I even agree with what I've written once I live there. At any rate, Atlanta is where my grandfather lived and died. I suppose there were certain details surrounding his death from which, for whatever reason, I never thought to deviate.

Your first novel, *The Fates Will Find Their Way*, employs an omniscient second-person narrator, which is very different than the perspective you're writing from in REUNION. Was one style of writing more natural for you?

Honestly, both voices came to me very naturally. The struggle, if anything, was to write from a woman's point of view. For whatever reason, that perspective came less easily. But after *Fates*, it was important to me to write something completely different. REUNION is as far from *Fates* as I could get: It's first-person singular, present tense, and takes place over four days instead of forty years.

REUNION addresses many issues in the news—debt, suicide, hoarding. How do you think the book plays into the broader national conversation on these issues?

Money is everywhere. I'm not talking about actual dollar bills; I'm talking about its presence in our thoughts, conversations, dreams. And yet, it's this thing that still makes us uneasy. We feel uneasy when we have it; we feel uneasy when we don't. I'm aware of which friends have more than I do and which friends have less, and I hate that awareness. Any time I start being aware of "awareness" that I'd like not to have, I know there's something worth writing about. It'll just nag at me until I do; a little dollar bill sign tugging at my sweater, saying, "Here I am. Here I am. What about me?" I have a very close relationship with early-twenties credit card debt. I suppose I felt, in some ways, that I had a responsibility to write about it. Also, I thought the little dollar bill might not shut up if I didn't.

Did other novels or authors influence the writing of REUNION? If so, which ones?

The epigraph comes from an amazingly precise John Cheever story that I adore, and I do think of my novel as being in a conversation with that story.

Even more directly, though, I might say that Jess Walter's *The Financial Lives of Poets* and Francine Prose's *My New American Life* influenced REUNION. I read those books back to back. They're both heartbreaking and hilarious. They filled me with an intense energy, which was useful, as I knew I wanted to write something funny, fast, and fiscally oriented.